WHEN SHE RUNS...

A HALLIE MILLER NOVEL

JEN MURPHY

For Lily and Kathleen, my forever loves . . .

PROLOGUE

Hallie had never smelled a dead body. Not really anyway, at least not before now. At her father's funeral, she had been intrigued by how little odor there was, not that anything could compete with the overwhelming, saccharine smell of the lilies lining the dank room and covering the bottom half of the casket like a Laura Ashley quilt. She had also encountered the stench of what she later learned was the decaying body of a squirrel who had unwittingly trapped himself in the living room wall of her hundred-year-old bungalow. But this was different, incomparably revolting, as if the stench infected her soul as much as it did her sense of smell. The putrid odor stung the inside of her nostrils and infused the beads of sweat that were accumulating just above her upper lip. Unlike her father's placid shell and the decomposing remains of the unfortunate critter in her wall, it seemed this body had been subjected to Florida's swampy, sweltering late-August heat for more than a day.

No breeze. No oxygen, it seemed. Just stillness. And, God, the heat. But suddenly waves of violence within, as Hallie's entire being worked to extrude itself from her body, to escape from the vessel that was now being assaulted by this infernal smell that could only hint at the rancor of the crime. Her mouth filled with saliva while she looked toward her neighbor, Mrs. Butler's, home, convinced that was the source of her discomfort. She pulled her sweat-stained silk blouse away from her body, but relief was futile.

She willed herself not to throw up, as she focused all her energies on swallowing. It was too late. She was too close. The sour smell of decaying garbage drowning in cat piss and human excrement announced itself, clinging to her, causing her to reflexively gag. It entered her nose, her pores, her mouth, mooring itself to her tongue like unwanted barnacles on one of the old barges docked at the Port of Tampa Bay.

"Oh shit . . . please, don't puke," Hallie mumbled as she ran towards the giant live oak in her front yard, holding onto the sturdy trunk with one hand while furiously sweeping her shoulder-length blonde hair into a haphazard ponytail on the top of her head with the other.

Hallie expelled the bitter remnants of her breakfast – two hardboiled eggs and a banana – onto the ground before frantically searching her pockets for a napkin or tissue to blow her nose and wipe away any evidence of her upheaval. Finding a wadded-up paper towel with what appeared to be old coffee stains in her back pocket, she appreciated for the first time her habit of stuffing them in pockets or carelessly discarding them nearby: on her nightstand, in her car, on her desk, in a suit jacket pocket, or stuffed in the pockets of her favorite jeans that rarely got washed, as was the case today. She tore the paper towel in half, using one half to wipe her mouth and the other to hold over her nose in a desperate attempt to keep the stench from entering her again.

"*Please* . . ." she implored to no one but herself as she held onto the sturdy tree and rested her forehead against the cool, earthy bark, silently begging the old girl to hold her steady. She closed her eyes, trying to focus on her breathing, when she heard the muffled yet unmistakably desperate cries from underneath the wooden planks of Mrs. Butler's front porch.

CHAPTER ONE

She lay there on the sand, listening to the waves crash and tumble onto the shore around her. The grits of sand were thick on her tongue, grinding between her upper and bottom teeth like tiny, shards of glass. She could taste the salt. And the blood. Her eyes stung as she fought to open them. Of all the times he had beaten her, this was the one she thought would kill her. She let her eyes close, yielding to the darkness, perhaps, forever. Yet the image of the moon rising over the ocean remained intact in her mind.

How had she gotten here? Was he out there looking for her? Sitting on the sand right behind her, listening to her ragged breath? Would he be on her again, the moment she picked up her head? Did he know she was still alive? Would he punish her again and again and again, as he had promised? Or was she already dead? She just couldn't be sure.

As her thoughts collected themselves from the haze of her concussion, they arranged themselves into one overriding emotion: *disbelief.* All she had wanted was to meet someone nice, get married one day, maybe have a few kids. And he was nice . . . at first . . . or so he had seemed. Heather McLean had been just twenty-two when she first met him; she was twenty-six now and had felt like a prisoner, his prisoner, for the last two years.

The waves rolled in, crashing in rhythm to the soft breeze that wrapped around her like a warm blanket. The coolness of the water touched her hand, then her lips, gently untangling her honey-brown hair as it ebbed back out to sea. She opened her eyes again. The moon was no longer where she had left it. She could still taste the salt and iron on her swollen lips, but her tangled hair was sticky and dry. How long had she been there? The darkness was beginning to yield to the orange glow rising above the edge of the world, spreading its fingers over the Atlantic, reaching for her, as the moon faded further out of sight.

As she struggled to survey the vacant beach, her head impossibly heavy now, her neck rigid with whiplash, a fishing vessel appeared in the distance, chasing the horizon as the seagulls danced around it. She longed to be on that boat, going anywhere, or nowhere at all, as long as he wasn't there. The incoming waves pounded and broke against the sand, ever closer to her, as if in response to her longing, offering to pull her out to sea. The seagulls, too, seemed to beckon her to fly away with them, to join them in their salty revelry. But she knew that the bottom of the sea was cruel. *No.* She knew she had to get up, to get away from him, forever. If he was still out there, looking for her, he would be able to see her as soon as the sun made its way up a little higher, illuminating the beach. But, with any luck, he wasn't on the beach, waiting for her, watching her. With any luck, he was back at the cottage, passed out as he often was after one of his drunken tirades. There was only one way to find out. And this time, she promised herself, she would get away forever or die trying.

CHAPTER TWO

David wasn't sure what to wear. He hadn't seen Lila Martinez in at least four years, not since she was a student at Hillsborough High School where he was now the principal. He picked out a black, vintage Queen t-shirt that his wife had given him for his birthday with a pair of Lucky jeans that he had bought from the women's section. He'd become so wiry from the keto diet and exercise program he had been on for the past year that men's jeans just didn't fit him right anymore. They were always too baggy or too long or too tight where they shouldn't be — women's jeans just fit him better, and he didn't give a fuck. He liked to think that he could pass for one of the young students he passed in the hallways, relishing those moments when he would catch a female student admiring him as he passed by. He sprayed his knock-off Dolce & Gabanna cologne on his shirt and neck, smoothed his dark brown hair, gargled a swig of mouthwash, and did one final assessment in the hall mirror of his Hyde Park bungalow that he shared with his wife and stepdaughter.

"Not bad for 51," he thought, admiring himself in the foyer mirror and replaying for the umpteenth time his conversation with Lila when she called him out of the blue a few days before. He wondered if she had maintained her cute figure since he last saw, hoping her breasts were as ample and perky as they had been when she was his student.

"Heading out, Hal," David called out, as he grabbed his phone and keys off the antique table in the foyer and headed for the door

"Seriously? Are you freakin' kidding me?" Hallie said aloud, reading the latest email from opposing counsel, while her dog, Juno, looked up, wagging her tail, oblivious to her frustration and rising anger.

"Um, no, I'm not kidding. What's wrong with you?" David asked, somewhat taken aback at his wife's unprovoked response.

"Sorry, babe, not you -- this jackass opposing counsel. He's such an asshole. Anyway, where are you going?" Hallie asked, briefly looking up from her computer screen towards the foyer.

"I told you this morning, parent-teacher conferences tonight."

"Oh yeah, I forgot. Okay, well, Katie is meeting her friends at the movies, and I have to work a little more, so I'm not cooking tonight. Can you grab something while you're out?"

"Yeah, sure, I planned on grabbing something anyway. A few of us might go for a beer after the conferences so I'm not sure what time I'll be home. Don't worry about me."

"Wait, shouldn't you be in a suit?"

"Thankfully, no. VP Michelson is on tonight, front and center. I'm just going to be in my office catching up on paperwork in case anyone needs me, but I have no intention of interacting with the students or their parents."

"Ah, lucky you. I'll be having a liquid dinner if I get one more email from this jerk."

"I have no doubt you will put him in his place, and he'll be the one needing a liquid dinner," David offered supportively.

"Thanks, babe. Power of the pen, right?"

"That's what I've heard," he said, winking at her. "Go for a run, it always helps you," David said as he walked out the door.

As soon as David left, she quickly tapped out a response to the email that set her off: short, to the point, professional, but unequivocally conveying that her client would not accept the insulting settlement offer that was presented. She also corrected his version of the facts and the legal precedent that was not in his client's favor. She concluded the email informing him she looked forward to seeing him and his client at trial where she would crush him. Technically, she didn't include the crushing him part but, of course, that was implied. And she would under most circumstances. But Mark Harrison, opposing counsel, did not play by the same rules as most lawyers and was not above presenting bullshit evidence to confuse the issues or the jury. God, he got under her skin. David was right; she needed to go for a run. She was too stressed, had too much on her mind, and it wasn't just her cases.

She laced up her running shoes, connected her Bose headphones via Bluetooth to her phone, selected her latest running playlist on Spotify, and ran out the front door. As she ran, she thought of everything she had to get done in the next few days: finish the purchase agreement for the cigar factory deal; call Sarah Wilt in the breach of contract case to discuss a possible settlement; help Katie narrow down her college choices and force her to start her applications before the application deadline in January; make Juno's vet appointment; and get David to clean up the dog shit and mow the lawn to get the backyard ready for their annual, Labor Day barbeque.

She hit the one-mile mark just as Pink's voice was exploding in her ears. Pink's gritty vocals and heartfelt lyrics energized her. She ran along the Tampa Bay, on Bayshore Boulevard, dodging the walkers and avoiding the roller-bladers as she strived to maintain her nine-minute pace. She was never going to be a record-breaker, but her goal since she turned forty-eight was to break twenty-seven minutes on her 5K. She looked out at the water, hoping to catch a glimpse of a dolphin, as she concentrated on her breathing – one breath in, two breaths out, one breath in, two breaths out, all to the rhythm of the sound of her running shoes hitting the pavement and Pink singing in her ears.   Running was the only time Hallie could truly disconnect from her law practice, her family, her responsibilities . . . everything. No emails, no phone calls, no pressures – just her breathing, her feet maintaining the rhythm of the song in her headphones, subconsciously aware of the beating of her heart.

"Damn, 29:23," she whispered, gazing at the time registering on the stopwatch on her phone, as she inhaled deeply and tried to catch her breath. "It's gotta be all that wine last night," she thought, privately admonishing herself for her disappointing time. She felt the muscles in her calves contract and spasm, and her thighs felt like she had lead weights strapped to each one, as she walked back towards her home, passing the mansions on Bayshore Boulevard and the picturesque, refurbished bungalows that got smaller the farther away she got from Bayshore. Just as she was catching her breath, her phone vibrated, signifying she had received a new notification. As she opened her email on her phone, she saw the all too familiar notification on her personal Gmail account: "Linda Dennis tagged you in a post on Facebook." Cringing, Hallie opened her Facebook icon on her phone to see what this latest post from her high school acquaintance would be – would it be another wine reference (how original!), or perhaps an inspirational meme? Perhaps a political rant about the shortcomings of the latest democratic nominee? Hallie knew she would "hide" or delete whatever post Linda shared to her timeline, but she would leave it up just long enough so as not to offend her.

"Just block that bitch -- you barely even knew her in high school!" her best friend, Bridget, would command. "Why do you worry about what she or any other loser we went to high school with thinks? She's always posting weird shit to your page. It's creepy, like single white female creepy."

Bridget, her best friend since the fifth grade when Bridget saved her life by getting the wasp out of her hair as Hallie stood paralyzed with fear, always said what she thought – no filters. One of her favorite and least favorite qualities about her best friend.

She pulled up Linda's post and was relieved to see it was nothing controversial – just a link to a Huffington Post article about the latest stance on whether to vaccinate or not vaccinate your child as polio outbreaks were making a resurgence throughout the U.S. and some deadly new virus was making its way through China. Considering Linda didn't have any children and Hallie's daughter was well beyond vaccination age, Hallie wanted to object to the post on her page based on relevance. But there was no sport in that since that, too, would be lost on poor Linda.

Hallie fumbled in her running shorts waistband to find her key as she approached her house, glimpsing a movement out of the corner of her eye as it retreated from the side of her front porch, and catching a whiff of something that smelled like rotting meat or garbage mixed with urine. As she looked again, she saw one of the neighborhood cats running across her cinch bug-ridden lawn towards her neighbor's house. Mrs. Butler was always feeding the cats in the neighborhood, which is why on any given day they would be around her yard. No matter how many times she asked Mrs. Butler to stop feeding them and warned her about the diseases feral cats could bring, Mrs. Butler continued to feed them. Complaining about it didn't do any good, as Mrs. Butler was oblivious to it. Instead, she managed to make a deal with one of her clients who was a vet in the area: free spaying/neutering in exchange for free legal services. Whenever a new cat appeared in the neighborhood, Hallie would set up one of the traps and the vet would take care of the rest. At least the population wasn't growing, and they kept the rats at bay, despite the fruit trees that were ever present in the neighborhood.

As she started to put the key into the lock, she was startled to feel the door give way and swing open into her house, which was immediately followed by a rush of cool air hitting her face. Where was Juno? Maybe she hadn't shut the door all the way, she wondered, trying to remember whether she locked the door when she left earlier to go on her run. David had left before her; Katie had too. David's truck wasn't in the driveway, so he wasn't home, and neither was Katie's secondhand blue Nissan Hallie had obtained from a client who owed her $5,000 in legal fees. The thoughts rushed through her head as she looked around, trying to assess if everything was in order.

As she walked into the foyer, she instantly noticed her black Coach purse on the front table where she always left it. Next, she scanned the living room and confirmed that anything of any value was just where it should be. As she looked into her office, she breathed a sigh of relief as Juno, her yellow lab, barely lifted her head to look up at Hallie from her memory foam, orthopedic bed that was situated next to her desk – the old girl's customary position since her hips no longer allowed her to get up onto the couch. Hallie went to the kitchen, drank a large glass of ice water, and checked the back door, reassured to find it locked. She took one more look around before concluding that she must have forgotten to lock the front door when she went for her run. She went upstairs to take a quick shower after securely locking the front door and admonishing herself for her carelessness.

Unfortunately, she hadn't noticed that her desk lamp was on despite having turned it off earlier or that her monitor screen was awake despite that it was set for sleep mode after being idle for five minutes.

CHAPTER THREE

David pulled into the school's faculty parking lot and into the space closest to the entrance, smiling at the "Reserved for Principal Miller" sign marking the spot. There were only two other cars in the parking lot: one he recognized as Robert Johnson's car but the other one he had no clue. Robert was one of the science teachers, chemistry to be exact, and fit the stereotypical creepy, science geek to a tee. David figured he was there, as he often was during his off hours, working up some experiment in his lab. When Robert joined Hillsborough High School's faculty during the final season of the Breaking Bad series, a rumor had started that the Walter White character was loosely based on him, which, of course, was completely untrue, but briefly elevated his status among the students to his delight. David remembered Robert telling him in the faculty lounge how excited he was his students were paying attention in his chemistry labs, with both pride and a little sadness in his eyes, painfully self-aware that it would be short lived. David didn't know much more about him, other than from his personnel file and conversations with him here and there over the years, but he was divorced, had to return to the area after his mother died, and his life was chemistry and whatever he could create in the lab. Outside of that, he didn't seem to have much of a life.

David didn't care what Robert did in his off hours. He stuck to himself, didn't cause any trouble, and overall was a good faculty member. Most importantly, he minded his own business. If David happened to run into him while he was at the school after hours on this Wednesday night, Robert not only wouldn't ask or wonder why David was there, but would probably not even think it was strange, as Robert practically lived at the school.

David checked his phone to see if he had any more messages from Lila. Nothing. He still had over an hour to kill before he met her, but he was too pent up to stay at home. He knew Hallie could easily figure out there were no parent-teacher conferences tonight, but thankfully, Hallie was so engrossed in her own work and her daughter, Katie, that she was never interested or cared enough in what was going on in his career to check, he was sure. Of course, she tried to act like she was interested and supportive, but David knew she was just placating him. His "job" as a teacher was not as important as hers as a lawyer. Even when he made principal, he thought that would impress her, but it just fell flat compared to her accomplishments that week. That same week he was promoted, she settled a huge case the night before the trial was set to start and the client paid her the equivalent of two times his annual salary. His 10% raise was a joke compared to that. He knew Hallie loved him, but she certainly didn't need him. Luckily, his students and most of his faculty appreciated him, at least he thought they did. Or at least respected him. Well, at least his pet students liked him, that he was sure of.

As he navigated his way down the dark, main hallway, usually filled with teenagers with varying shades of blue, purple and pink hair, and varying degrees of dress code violations – not that he ever actually minded that, but used it as an excuse to call more than one freshman or sophomore into his office for their skirt being too short or their crop top being too cropped, mainly so he could get a closer look – he thought about the first time he saw Lila in this hallway. She was a transfer student, midway through her junior year. So pretty. Those big brown eyes. And terrified. At first, he really did just want to help her adjust. She had come from a small, predominantly Hispanic school in Homestead, Florida, and here she was, thrust into a school with about 3,000 students, from every race and socio-economic class. Hillsborough High was somewhat unique in that it was home to the inner-city neighborhood kids of West Tampa, the kids from nearby eclectic and gentrifying Seminole Heights, and the smartest of the kids throughout the County who were admitted into the International Baccalaureate program the school offered. To transfer into that type of school mid-semester was more than a little daunting, even for the most confident of kids.

How pleased he was to see Lila show up later that day in his AP History class that he taught. Despite her shyness and apparent innocence, her developed, curvy body told a different story and would not go unnoticed, not by David and certainly not by the overly hormonal high school boys who would line up to take advantage of her. David felt it was his job, as her teacher, to protect her. That's at least how he rationalized it when he asked her to come by after school a few weeks after she had transferred in.

It started out so innocent. He told her he just wanted to see how she was doing and adjusting. She broke down, confiding in him that she hadn't made any friends and felt like such an outsider. She missed her friends from Homestead and just couldn't seem to fit in anywhere. He told her about his experience when his family moved from New York to Tampa just before his freshman year. He assured her it would get better, and she would make friends. But until she did, he told her she could stop by his classroom after school whenever she felt lonely or insecure and he would try to help her. It wasn't long before she was stopping by his classroom so frequently that he designated her as his student assistant. And it wasn't long before they both became too comfortable with each other, sharing inside jokes, talking about everything that filled their days, laughing, him sharing exciting stories about all the places he had traveled when he was younger, all leading up to the day their after-school relationship continued into the evening. Sixteen was his favorite age on a young girl: young enough to be impressed by him but old enough to have their own hormones raging, eager to be taught things to please him. Lila wasn't his first student relationship, but she was definitely one of his favorites. They had a nice thing going until her family moved away abruptly during her senior year. He hadn't heard from Lila since she moved away until she contacted him a few days ago.

His tight pants got a little tighter as he looked at the big clock on the wall of his office, reminiscing about the time Lila had sucked his cock from underneath his desk in his classroom while he pretended to grade papers. It was so reckless and exhilarating, he recalled. Glancing up at the big clock again, he was excited it was finally time to make the ten-minute drive to Ybor. He locked his office door and headed towards the faculty parking lot when he ran into Robert, also heading for the faculty parking lot.

"Hey Robert, late night experiments in the lab?"

"Yeah, just trying something out to make sure it works before I have the students do the exercise. You're here late yourself, Mr. Principal, late night principal duties?" Robert teased.

"Living the dream, Robert, living the dream," David replied as they both chuckled and headed towards their respective cars.

David left the school parking lot, heading towards Ybor City. They had agreed to meet at 10:00 p.m. at Rock

Brothers Brewing, a local craft microbrewery popular with the college kids. David liked it because it was not on 7th Avenue, the main strip in Ybor, and was just a few blocks from Centro Ybor Garage. Because it was more of a college hang out, he thought he was less likely to run into someone who knew him or Hallie there. He also didn't want Lila walking through the dark streets of Ybor by herself, so he thought going someplace near the garage and the movie theater was probably the safest place to meet. He pulled into the mostly vacant garage at about 9:45 and backed his big black truck into a spot towards the back of the first floor where he could watch the incoming cars.

He checked his reflection in the vanity mirror, smiling to make sure nothing was in his teeth and looking up to make sure he didn't have any dry, stray stragglers up his nose. Confident that he still looked pretty good, he shut the truck off and was about to get out when a silver Subaru WRX pulled into the garage. It parked in one of the first spaces closest to the entrance of the garage. Was that Lila, he wondered? He waited to see who got out of the car. As the stocky man got out of the car, David realized he knew him.

"Holy shit, that's Jay Campbell," he said aloud to himself, instinctively ducking down in his seat even though it was unlikely he would be able to see him through the dark, tinted windows of his truck parked at the back of the garage. Man, he was glad he hadn't gotten out yet.

Jay was married to Hallie's best friend, Bridget, and he would definitely recognize him. David wondered what he was doing in Ybor at that time of night by himself. He realized that Jay would wonder the same thing about him. He couldn't take the chance of being seen. He waited until Jay walked out of the garage, then started the truck and slowly drove away, looking all around as he exited onto 5th Avenue.

He headed down a dark, side street, lined with the historic casitas, row houses built over a century ago for the cigar factory workers. Many were abandoned and dilapidated while some were in various stages of reformation. He turned his lights off so he could figure out what to do. He thought about texting her and telling her he couldn't make it, but he really didn't like to leave a text trail. So far, they had only spoken on the phone, not texted. Although he was pretty careful about deleting his texts and he had saved Lila's number in his contacts under the name "Larry," it was still too risky because texts never really went away. He wanted to see Lila, but if he got caught cheating, Hallie would leave him. There was no way he was going back to living off of a teacher's salary and tending bar as a side hustle to make ends meet. No fucking way. But he was way too excited to just go home.

CHAPTER FOUR

She checked her phone for what seemed like the thousandth time. Still no text, no missed calls. 10:37 p.m. She had been sitting there by herself for over thirty minutes.

"I can't believe he didn't show," she said, looking down at her phone again, and muttering "asshole" under her breath.

She wasn't sure if she was referring to herself or to her no-show date, if you could even call him that. Lila slammed back the remnants of her beer, mostly sour backwash, slipped off the bar stool, threw a ten-dollar bill on the counter and crammed her cellphone barely halfway into the front pocket of her purse.

"What was I thinking," she admonished herself as she crossed over the threshold and out onto the deserted sidewalk, the rising warmth in her face having nothing to do with the stagnant Florida night.

Shadows danced across the graffiti covered buildings as she headed towards the parking garage and her eyes strained to adjust to the darkness outside of the bar. She had to look away to avoid the judgmental gaze of the Cuban woman, La Mujer Trabajador, painted on the side of the old warehouse, obviously aware of all of Lila's secrets, including why she had come to Ybor tonight. Next to La Mujer was a bus-sized image of a cigar, its Santaella Cigar Factory label bleached and faded by time and too many summers in the relentless Florida sun, a sad reminder that the cigar-making days for which the city had become famous were a thing of the past. Soon the cigar would be painted over, another symbol of revitalization and gentrification being promoted by the current Mayor, similar to all the others erupting almost daily on the historic buildings throughout the city.

Lila navigated across the half brick, half paved road, careful not to get her heel stuck in the grooves. The vibrant colors adorning the buildings on this side of the street – the blues, the reds, the yellows, the symbols of life and vitality and the Cuban and historic Tampa culture – contrasted sharply with her own feelings of loneliness and insignificance. She always forgot how deserted this section of Ybor City could be at night, unless the city was celebrating Gasparilla, Tampa's rather aggressive pirate-themed answer to Mardi Gras, or some obscenely overpriced movie happened to be letting out at Centro Ybor, the epicenter of the old city's revitalization. No such luck tonight.

A slight breeze rustled the trees lining the old brick street as a discarded McDonald's bag skidded along the sidewalk. The 88-degree afternoon heat had dropped about ten degrees in the last few hours and, with the winds coming in off the Gulf, she could almost taste the salt in the air. Despite the warm evening, she zipped her hoodie a little higher, hugged her arms into her ample chest a little tighter, and held her keys ready as she neared the front of the garage. Something darted across the long-abandoned railroad tracks that ran adjacent to the garage, causing her to catch her breath and stop for a moment.

"Jesus Christ," she mumbled, shaking her head, watching the wild roosters zig zag across the tracks, pecking periodically into the overgrown weeds sprouting up between the rusty rails. "Get a grip," she thought, as her fear yielded to her aggravation. When the night began, she never thought she would be heading to her car alone at almost 11 o'clock at night yet here she was, walking by herself in 4-inch heels and a short denim mini skirt. "Great, just great," she said to herself, unconsciously pulling down at the hem of her skirt and looking back over her shoulder, suddenly aware of the quiet hum emanating from the fluorescent lights hanging overhead and the click of her increasingly erratic heels echoing off the empty concrete floor. Her relief at reaching her car was short-lived as the headlights from a passing car picked up a glimmer of silver in the darkness and the silhouette of a man just on the other side of her car, instantly filling her with dread and trepidation.

"Hello, Lila," was all she heard before he slammed her head into the driver's side window of her car as she struggled to open the door.

* * *

The night was dark and still as she drifted in and out of consciousness, motionless except for the constant, barely audible sound of the thousands of mosquitos ever present on a hot, humid night and the hum of that damn fluorescent light from the nearby garage. She desperately, willfully fought the recurring urge to swat at the army that were voraciously exploring and devouring her exposed skin, so as not to give up her hiding spot. The blood under her hand seemed to be thickening and no longer pouring down her neck – maybe she was just running out, she couldn't know for sure. But her breathing seemed to be getting better too. What only moments before had consisted of frantic, fretful gulps for air had now become slight, controlled, whispered gasps, barely audible, just deep enough to satiate her lungs but hopefully not loud enough for him to hear her. Each excruciating minute that passed seemed like an eternity, yet time stood still. She was terrified that he would hear the sound of her pounding heart outside of her battered body, like the old man under the floorboards of Edgar Allen Poe's *The Tell Tale Heart*. She contorted her body into the slightest position possible, praying that the bushes that had become her refuge would shield her now just as they had when she was a child playing an innocent game of hide and seek on those many warm and sunny carefree afternoons.

CHAPTER FIVE

That Tuesday morning, before the body was found, had started out as any other ordinary morning. Hallie was sitting at her desk in her home office, struggling to focus on the work before her, while absentmindedly staring out the front window directly into Mrs. Butler's yard. She and David had converted the downstairs bedroom into an office for Hallie so she could work from home when she wanted or needed to. In this digital age, most of her work could be done remotely without ever meeting face to face with clients or opposing counsel. Even multi-million dollar deals could be closed via email and Federal Express these days. She tapped her pen on her mahogany desk that she had picked up for $150 at an estate sale a few months before. Best money she ever spent, she thought, admiring the dark, rich wood. It offered a large workspace, deep drawers, and everyone who saw it said it was very "lawyerly."

As she looked out the window, she watched a fat, gray tabby stalking a squirrel, oblivious to his impending fate, nervously gathering acorns at the bottom of the giant Oak in Hallie's front yard. Watching the gray cat triggered a flashback to her childhood cat, Persia. Her father had found the gray tiger-striped kitten outside of his downtown office after working late one night. As he walked down Madison Avenue from his office towards the dirt parking lot where he parked the family's only car, he noticed the little cat following him. He thought she would run away if he tried to pick her up, but surprisingly, she did not. She instantly started purring and meowing and that was that. He brought her home and gave her to Hallie who was only seven at the time. As soon as Hallie held her, she purred even louder, which prompted Hallie to name her Persia. She loved that cat and adored her father for rescuing the sweet kitten. She smiled as she remembered her mother insisting they could not keep her, realizing only now that her mother protested so that her father could be the hero in his daughter's eyes when he overruled that decision. She wished her father was still alive today.

Her smile faded as quickly as her sweet memory when she spotted the trash cans on the curb, the only ones still left on the street, and silently cursed David for not bringing them up last night when he got in from work.

"Jesus, one of his few fucking jobs around here," she muttered, as she slipped her socked feet into Katie's pink slides haphazardly discarded by the front door.

As Hallie picked up the recycle bin, she was hit with the same rotting stench she smelled the day before, only now it enveloped her, causing her eyes to water and bile to rise in the back of her throat. She thought again of her father, only this time the image was not of a cute kitten following him home but of his body, sprawled face down on the sidewalk, blood soaking the back of his standard navy-blue suit. Hallie shook her head. Why did that jump into her head, she wondered while trying to suppress the urge to throw up.

The putrid odor saturated the sweltering, humid air and clung to her while her consciousness simultaneously became aware of its vileness. As she looked towards her neighbor's house, the disgusting stench affronted her unapologetically. She tried to remember when she had last spoken to Mrs. Butler or saw her on her front porch where she liked to sit on most afternoons, despite the heat, sipping lemonade or iced tea, likely spiked with vodka. Was it last week? No, it had to be the week before, she thought. Hallie dropped the bin onto the curb, covered her nose with her blouse and retreated into the house to call David. No answer.

"Typical," she thought, instinctively rolling her eyes. She quickly tapped out a text to him:

"Have you seen Mrs. B. this week?"

Aggravated, she waited, seeing the little dots on her message's app, signifying that he was at least typing a reply.

"Can't talk now, haven't seen her"

"How long has it been?"

"idk maybe week or 2"

"Something smells horrible outside, really bad, like something is dead. I think it's worse near her house. And we haven't seen her. What if she's dead?"

"omg Hallie, have you been binge watching Bosch again? It's prob a dead rat or maybe one of those damn cats"

"No, it's too strong. Seriously, I thought I was going to puke. Maybe I should call the police to at least do a welfare check?"

"whatever you think, babe, but I gotta go"

Hallie walked back out onto her front porch, the odor enveloping her, stronger than before, she thought. Or was it because she was now aware of it? She headed towards Mrs. Butler's house, planning to knock on her door to see if she answered but as she got closer, the smell of decomposing flesh overwhelmed her. She fought the urge to throw up as chills ran up her spine. There was no way this was a dead cat or other animal, she thought to herself. She turned away from Mrs. Butler's house, retrieving her cell phone from her back pocket as she walked.

"9-1-1, what's your emergency?"

"This is Hallie Miller, I would like to request a welfare check on my neighbor, Imogene Butler."

"Has there been an accident?"

"I'm not sure but she's really old and, well, I haven't seen her in a few days, maybe a week or two, and there's a horrible smell coming from her house . . . something is definitely dead, but it may just be an animal. I don't know – it's awfully pungent."

"Okay, Ms. Miller, what is your address?"

"737 Sunset Drive. Mrs. Butler's house is number 739"

"Please stay on the line for a moment while I dispatch an officer and fire-rescue."

After a minute, the operator returned, "Okay, Ms. Miller, they are on their way and should be there in a few minutes."

As Hallie waited, she could no longer fight the nausea and uncontrollable urge to throw up. Hallie ran towards the giant Oak in her front yard, holding onto the sturdy trunk with one hand with the other holding her hair back off her face and vomited up her breakfast. She felt dizzy and consumed by the revolting smell. She closed her eyes and tried to focus on her breathing when she heard the muffled yet desperate sounds of what sounded like someone crying from underneath the wooden planks of Mrs. Butler's front porch, at the same time as she heard sirens in the distance making their way closer.

Within moments they were on her street, coming to a stop in front of Mrs. Butler's house. As the officers and paramedics scrambled out of their vehicles and headed towards Mrs. Butler's front porch, her front door opened and there stood Mrs. Butler, adorned in her blue paisley house dress, very much alive and very much confused about all the commotion taking place on her front lawn.

Unfortunately, the same could not be said for the young woman whose naked and decomposing body was discovered underneath the hydrangea bushes on the side of Mrs. Butler's bungalow.

* * *

Over the next few hours, Hallie answered so many questions and recounted her story to the homicide detectives, beginning from the time she first smelled the body after her run the day before until the time the paramedics found the decomposing body that morning. Poor Mrs. Butler was so distraught, she was taken to the hospital after complaining of heart palpitations. The strange crying sound that Hallie heard from under Mrs. Butler's porch turned out to be the fat tabby and her new litter of kittens, who happened to look like little replicas of her beloved Persia. They were quickly gathered up, including the momma cat, and taken away by one of the officers who assured Hallie they would go to good homes after they were old enough.

"Do you remember hearing or seeing anything unusual over the last few days," the detective asked her.

"No, nothing that I can think of," Hallie said.

The questions were redundant, as if asking the same question in a different way would illicit a different response. No, Hallie didn't remember seeing any strange cars or people in the neighborhood. No, she didn't see or hear anything unusual over the last few days or even weeks. No, neither her daughter nor her husband mentioned seeing anyone or anything out of the ordinary to her. And then she remembered finding her front door unlocked when she came back from her run. Should she mention that? Was that just a coincidence or something else? The body was already there when she came back from her run, she reminded herself, so it had to be a coincidence. She was exhausted and was tired of answering questions. She decided not to mention it.

"Was there something else, Mrs. Miller? Do you remember something?" the detective was asking her.

"No, I'm sorry, nothing else. I'm just really drained from all of this," Hallie answered.

"Okay," he said, as he handed Hallie his card. "If you remember anything that you think might be helpful, or if you see or hear anything, please call me."

Hallie glanced down and read the name on the card, Detective Marcelo Garcia, before slipping the card into the back pocket of her jeans.

CHAPTER SIX

The next few days were a blur, but no matter what she did, she couldn't stop thinking about the young woman found under Mrs. Butler's bushes. Hallie had since learned from her best friend, Bridget, who was married to a Tampa police detective, that her name was Lauren White, and she was a twenty-two-year-old University of Tampa student who had been reported missing by her roommates just a few days before her body was found. She had gone out with a group of her friends that Saturday night, hitting the bars on Howard Avenue, which ran perpendicular to and was in walking distance to Hallie's street. She was last seen at MacDinton's around 1:30 a.m. that night when she told her roommates she wasn't feeling well and was going to Uber home. No one actually saw her leave and she never connected with her Uber driver. Her cellphone records confirmed she called an Uber at 1:31 a.m., but the Uber driver said she wasn't at the designated pick up spot outside the bar when he arrived at 1:37 a.m. MacDinton's and a few other bars in the area had created a designated Uber pick up and drop off spot in one of the parking lots to keep traffic moving and to alleviate the congestion and safety issues that had naturally occurred when Uber and Lyft first arrived on the scene. After waiting for ten minutes and not receiving any responses to his texts, he cancelled the ride and picked up another fare who wanted to go all the way to Carrollwood, which was about thirty minutes north and on the way to the driver's home in Lutz. Both the Carrollwood rider, the driver's wife, and his cell phone records corroborated his story and timeline. Lauren appeared to have just vanished.

Hallie stepped outside onto her front porch with a fresh cup of coffee, happy the stench had finally dissipated. Last night's downpour surely must have helped. It was only eight o'clock in the morning, the sun already scorching, and the only remnant of the previous week's events was the yellow crime scene tape stuck to one of Mrs. Butler's porch railings, billowing in the occasional breeze that blew through. Lost in her thoughts, she quickly came out of them by the sound of her daughter's voice.

"Hi, Mom. What are you doing out here?"

"Just having my coffee, hon. Have time to join me?"

"Um, sure, I don't have to be at school until 10:30 today because the sophomores and juniors are taking the PSATs. Let me grab my tea. Oh my God, it's still so hot out here! Tell me again why we live in Florida? I'm telling you right now, I'm not going to college in Florida. I'm pretty sure everyone in Florida ends up with skin cancer, too, by the way."

"First of all, that's why God invented sunscreen, and second of all, it's too early for this Katie; please just go get your tea if you want to join me on this lovely morning."

"I told you to stop calling me Katie – I'm not twelve, Mom," *Kate* exclaimed as she huffed and went back inside to get her cup of tea.

Her conversation with her daughter amused her. A week ago, it would have annoyed her. But Hallie realized that not being able to have these conversations with her daughter would break her, and all she could think about was whether Lauren White had these conversations with her mother? Did Lauren White think her mother was "extra" and not evolved in the slightest as *Kate* mostly accused Hallie of being? The thought of her daughter being in Lauren White's place, ultimately ending up beaten, stabbed, and naked under some hydrangea bushes, caused Hallie to gasp, inhaling her hot coffee down the wrong tube, which caused a coughing fit just as Kate came out, tea in hand, triggering another eye roll followed by annoyed concern.

Being a mother was one of Hallie's greatest joys while simultaneously being her greatest source of insecurity. Since Katie was born, Hallie found herself always questioning and second guessing her skills as a mother: was she nurturing enough; did she challenge her daughter enough; was she too smothering; not smothering enough; was she too tough on her; not tough enough; was she doing enough to prepare her daughter for life? These were the questions she constantly asked herself. Also, as women tend to do, she was always comparing herself to other mothers and often seemed to come up short. She often wondered what her life, and more importantly, Katie's life, would have been like if she had stayed with Kevin. Maybe leaving him was a mistake too. She was questioning a lot of her decisions lately.

In contrast to David's complete disregard of the fact that a young college student was murdered and dumped practically in their front yard, Katie was nervous and uncharacteristically clingy since the body had been found. It was all Hallie could do to convince her to go to school and work. As she explained to her over and over, their street was a perfect dumping ground for a date gone awry on Howard Avenue – there was no reason to believe it was anything other than some type of date rape or the work of a rejected, drunk college student. Not that any of that was okay, especially for poor Lauren White, but there was no reason to believe a serial killer was on the prowl, looking for his next victim. She almost had Katie – and truth be told, herself – convinced of that when Bridget called to tell her another young woman's body had been found in Carrollwood.

Hallie had a habit, since she was a young child, of analyzing things that upset her or made her feel scared or uncomfortable. If one of her friends in the neighborhood was mean to her or suddenly stopped playing with her, she would retreat to her bedroom, once adorned with cute dog and cat posters until they were eventually replaced with the latest teen heartthrobs, where she would sit and think until she could come up with a reason or explanation that made sense to her. Her mother would try to tell her not to worry about whatever was upsetting her, that it would work itself out, but that just wasn't how Hallie was wired. She had to figure it out or at least formulate some type of logical explanation in her mind. In that way, she was more like her analytical father than her gregarious mother.

Maybe because the first body was discovered practically in her front yard, or maybe because the second body was discovered about a mile from her childhood home, or maybe because she was just morbidly curious, but for reasons she could not explain, Hallie decided to drive by the latest crime scene she learned about from Bridget.

Orange Grove Drive is a two-lane, thirty-mile-per-hour road that runs parallel to Dale Mabry Highway, one of the main thoroughfares that runs from the southernmost part of Tampa all the way north beyond its boundaries. To most residents in the neighborhoods off Orange Grove, their neighborhoods were known as "old Carrollwood" or "original Carrollwood," which, of course, nobody cared about except for the residents of "old Carrollwood." The houses were older, but, for the most part, well maintained and it remained one of Tampa's better middle-class neighborhoods in which to raise a family and one of the few neighborhoods where neighbors still knew each other, still looked out for one another. All of the lawns were freshly mowed and landscaped with perfectly sheered bushes, fragrant hibiscus plants and small palm trees. At the center of Carrollwood is Lake Carroll, its shores lined with the backyards of the most premier homes in the area and the home to many an alligator, a fact that most water skiers and swimmers either ignored or denied. Hallie's sister, Trish, who lived on Lake Carroll, swore there were no alligators in the lake, which astounded Hallie. They both grew up with the knowledge embedded in their heads by their parents that if it was fresh water, there was an alligator in it. Anyone who grew up in Florida knew that. But the soccer moms surrounding Lake Carroll, which now included Trish, refused to believe it just as they refused to believe anything existed out of their PTA meetings, country club luncheons, and, of course, Saturday soccer tournaments.

The body was found just off of Orange Grove near Stall Road, which connected old Carrollwood to Carrollwood Village on the other side of Dale Mabry. Hallie had grown up in Carrollwood Village across the street from the large Catholic church on the corner, which meant they rarely missed church, much to Hallie's chagrin. She tried to listen to the sermon but undoubtedly the time would pass, and she would have no recollection of what the priest had said and found herself constantly watching the clock, counting the minutes down until it was over. She knew the Hail

Mary, the Lord's Prayer, and the Apostles Creed by rote. She knew she didn't have long left in the mass when they passed around the collection baskets followed by the rite of peace when everyone awkwardly wished peace to their fellow churchgoers in the surrounding pews. After she moved out to go to college, she only went to church when she was home for the holidays.

After her father was murdered when Hallie was in college, her mother went through a phase when she went to church all the time, more than just Sundays, and when Hallie was home, her mother expected her to go with her. Her father, Charlie Robinson, had been a family law attorney, and they suspected he had been shot by a client's estranged husband, although they were never able to prove it and his case remained unsolved to this day. After weeks of attending regular masses with her mother, Hallie told her she just couldn't do it anymore and she asked her why she went so often. Rebecca explained, with tears welling up in her eyes and her voice cracking, "your father was always a better, kinder person than I ever was, and I'm afraid if I don't atone for my sins and seek God's forgiveness, I'll never see him again."

Hallie didn't even know how to respond at the time but seeing her strong mother, who was always in control of everything, on the verge of breaking scared her more than anything. Her mother was always full of life, outgoing, direct to a fault, and had an infectious, contagious laugh that made those around her laugh too. She adored Hallie's father who loved her for who she was and never tried to change her or stifle her. But Charlie was the opposite of Rebecca: he was quiet, preferred to be home with his family or in his den with a good book when he wasn't working, let Rebecca run the household with very little interference, and he adored his daughter as much as he did his wife. He was a good man and a great father. His death was devastating but seeing her mother falling apart was almost too much for her to bear.

At Hallie's prompting, Rebecca began counseling shortly thereafter, and the counselor suggested she try a yoga class to help her work through her grief. Eventually she was going to church less and yoga more and Hallie began to see her mother's personality slowly come back. After Katie was born, Hallie felt guilty about not going to church and wanted to give her daughter the same foundation she had, not that she entirely knew what that did for her. She believed she should get back into the church and Catholicism for Katie's sake, going so far as to having Katie baptized and enrolling her in catechism classes all the way through to her First Communion. But she never enjoyed it and felt like a hypocrite when she was there. After she and Kevin divorced and she met David, she found she was missing church more often than she was going until eventually she just stopped going altogether. And she didn't miss it at all. Seeing the large

Catholic church that she had attended every Sunday for years brought up a lot of memories for Hallie, especially of her father. She missed him terribly and regretted that she hadn't had more time with him in her life.

Hallie headed south on Dale Mabry, passing the church on her right and spotting the Countrywood apartments ahead on her left. She remembered wanting to rent an apartment in Countrywood when she started college, but it was too expensive at the time for her to live there alone. During orientation, she had met an outgoing, bubbly blonde named Amanda Browning, and despite Hallie's more reserved personality, they hit it off instantly. It turned out Amanda was looking for a roommate too, so they exchanged numbers and ultimately became roommates and inseparable friends throughout college. Unfortunately, Amanda thought Countrywood was too far away from the "action," whatever that was, so they found a place closer to U.S.F., the cheaper rent no doubt attributable to the perpetual smell of old beer and stale cigarettes rising up from the worn, industrial carpet, not to mention the occasional shooting in the parking lot. But it was college, and it was no different than any other affordable, off-campus apartment complex near a large, urban university. Living with Amanda, she soon learned what the "action" was: perpetual parties, boyfriends who didn't seem to last more than a week or two, occasional hookups with frat boys, and sun-filled days tanning by the complex pool. As carefree and outgoing as Amanda was, Hallie was serious and shy, more like her father, preferring to spend her Friday nights studying in the library. Honestly, Hallie couldn't figure out how Amanda passed any of her classes, but she always somehow pulled it off.

Despite their differences, they were good friends all through school and even managed to keep in touch for a few years afterwards until Hallie graduated from law school and Amanda got pregnant with her first child. After that, they exchanged Christmas cards and caught up every few years over the phone, always promising to get together and to stay in better touch. But they were both busy, with separate lives, and that just never seemed to happen. She hadn't talked to Amanda in over a year, but she followed her on Facebook, so she knew generally what was going on with her old friend: three kids, all in college, a recent divorce, Amanda's thriving career as a realtor. She promised herself she would call Amanda to catch up and to see how she was doing since her divorce.

She pulled into the front entrance and drove towards the back of the complex. Although the medical examiner had removed the body long before Bridget called her, the scene was still closed off and secured by ominous yellow police tape. Hallie was hoping that she could park unnoticed in the apartments and walk through the trees at the back of the property to get a closer look. She really didn't understand why she felt so compelled to do this. She circled the parking lot, steering her black BMW towards the back of the complex that abutted the trees and thick brush separating the parking lot from the adjacent property. She parked a few spots away from a large, green dumpster and looked for a break in the trees.

"What am I doing here?" she thought, shaking her head as she looked down in her lap, automatically checking her cellphone for messages and emails.

Ever since she was a little girl, Hallie craved a sense of justice. She knew she was going to be a lawyer from as young an age as she could remember, and truly believed she would fight the injustices in the world just like Perry Mason, Atticus Finch and her father. She loved shows like Law and Order and Criminal Minds, because in an hour, the crime was solved, the bad guy was caught, and justice was served. It was amazing how many murderers cracked on the stand and confessed under the relentless questioning of the prosecutor or how many serial killers were caught by the BAU team headed by Agent Aaron Hotchner. While she now realized how unrealistic those scenarios were, they were very satisfying. And although she did become a lawyer, the reality of what paid, what she was good at, and what her family needed meant she took the cases that came in the door, which wasn't quite as righteous or interesting as the cases on her favorite tv shows. But she was still fascinated by criminal law and the psychology behind what drove some people to commit the crimes they did. When she read about or saw a news report about a murder or violent crime in her area, she would read everything reported on it and watch every news account, sometimes doing her own research on-line about the individuals involved to find out more about the victims or their assailants. Maybe because of what happened to her father, she was always looking for some type of resolution, some type of justice or vindication for the victim. But Hallie knew firsthand that crimes were rarely, if ever, quickly and neatly solved, and justice was as elusive as finding the so-called smoking gun.

She grabbed her cellphone and stuffed it in her back pocket, locked her car and started walking towards the break in the trees, believing the crime scene was just on the other side based on the information Bridget had given her. Bridget had told her that the body was discovered nearby the busy Lowes shopping center at the edge of Carrollwood across from the natural, protected preserve. Adjacent to the preserve was a wooden walkway that crossed over a small creek until it connected with the sidewalk on the other side of the narrow waterway. Across the street from the preserve was an abandoned house, its only adornment a wooden sign that read with finality, "*CONDEMNED*," surrounded by thick-trunked trees whose branches reached out angrily in all directions, warning any potential visitors to stay away.

The body was found on the front porch, if you could even call it that anymore, as it seemed to be listlessly hanging on to the house by a few rusty nails. The roof had collapsed at some point into the house, exposing the interior to the relentless summer thunder and lightning storms, rendering it completely uninhabitable. The front porch, which was slanting precariously to the left as if the ground beneath it had given way, consisted of broken floorboards and warped and rotting railings, splintered from years of neglect and rapacious termites who had undoubtedly taken up residence in its wood.

Hallie watched the methodical activity of the remaining investigators and FDLE personnel on the scene, wondering what kind of evidence they had found. As she stood there watching, she also wondered if the victim, who was a young, black female, was killed in the house or killed outside where her body was found. Or was she just dumped there, like Lauren White was in her neighborhood? Bridget mentioned that although it wasn't confirmed, the initial intel was that the body was likely that of a young mother who was recently reported missing by her husband after going for a run in their Carrollwood Village neighborhood. If she was killed in the house, how did she get outside? Did she crawl? Was she dragged from the house after she was murdered? The level of deterioration of the house made both of those scenarios seem unlikely. But if her body had been intentionally dumped on the front porch – just as Lauren White's body had been dumped in the yard where she would be discovered – it was obvious that someone wanted her found, at least by the time she started to decompose, Hallie thought. Her body reflexively shivered as she approached the perimeter of the fear-provoking scene.

As she looked at the remnants of the dilapidated, old house while standing in the side yard outside of the yellow police tape, suddenly Hallie was fourteen again and waiting impatiently for her friend to come out. Oh my God, this was Wayna's house, Hallie realized. She hadn't thought of Wayna since they graduated from high school, but now, standing in her yard, imagining the horrific crime that had taken place there, Hallie couldn't shake the desperate feeling of wanting to know that her old friend was okay. She wrapped her arms around her chest and thought about sitting on that same front porch with Wayna a lifetime ago, sipping fresh lemonade that her mother had made them, lathering their bodies in baby oil and sunning themselves in the backyard, and then taking turns spraying each other down with the hose when their skin felt like it was going to burn right off from the sweltering heat. Those childhood memories would be forever tarnished by the scene before her and the thought of that poor young woman brutally murdered and left to rot on her friend's front porch. She could only imagine how Wayna would feel if she knew.

"Hallie, what're you doin' here?" someone asked her, bringing her out of her reverie of the past.

Hallie jerked around towards the sound of the unable to place, yet familiar voice, the confusion obvious on her face.

The burly, good-looking, officer came walking towards her, "Helll-ooo? Are you okay? What're you doin' here, Hallie?"

"Oh, Jay, it's you. I'm, uh, . . . I'm, well, um, I don't know," Hallie admitted, looking down at her feet.

"Okay, well that clears that up. I can't believe Bridget called you. I'm going to kill her when I get home."

"Don't blame Bridget, it's not her fault," Hallie said, "Ever since that body ended up in my neighbor's bushes, I can't get it out of my head. And then when Bridget mentioned another woman had been found, well, I just had to come."

"Yeah, well, Bridg shouldn't have told you anything. Especially since you were the one who found Lauren White's body. You're a witness. You need to go, Hallie," Jay said more gently than his face conveyed.

"Please, Jay, I can't stop thinking about her. Jesus, she was literally dumped twenty feet from my front door. What if Katie had come home when she was being dumped there, or worse, being killed? And now this poor woman. Do you think it's the same guy, Jay?"

"Look, Hallie, I get it, you're curious. But I could get fired if I tell you anything that hasn't been released to the public yet," Jay said, exasperated. He looked around, making sure no one could hear him and said, "All I will tell you is that based on the similarities of how the women were dumped and brutality of the attacks, it could be the same guy on all three. But that's all I can tell you and I'll deny I ever told you any of this."

"What are you talking about, all three?" Hallie asked, confused. "I thought Lauren White was the first and now this poor woman. Are you saying there is a third victim?"

"Shit. Okay, well, I figured Bridget would have told you that too. Lauren White may not have been the first victim. A young woman was found in Ybor City, beaten and stabbed, just like Lauren White, and found under some bushes next to a parking garage. Last I heard, she hadn't regained consciousness and she's fighting for her life, but she's alive. She was found bleeding half to death by a couple walking home to their loft after a night of partying. The guy went behind the bushes to take a leak and that's when he found her. Lucky they found her when they did or she would have bled out. Anyway, we don't know for sure yet if she's connected to Lauren White or this latest victim, but there are a lot of similarities. We're waiting for the M.E. to compare the victims' wounds to see if the same type of knife was used in all three cases."

"Oh my God, that's terrifying. Why aren't you alerting the public about this? I think people need to know that there's someone out there killing young women."

"Not my call, Hallie, above my pay grade. The media doesn't know about the Ybor victim yet, and they better not hear it from you or Bridget. Look, I've already told you too much and you need to go. Just keep Katie safe, keep yourself safe, and that's all you need to focus on."

As Officer Jay Campbell walked away, Hallie thought she heard him say under his breath, "women," while shaking his head.

Hallie turned and headed back towards her car, trying to convince herself that she must have misheard him, when she stopped to take one last look at the long forgotten, run-down house. The scene was still busy with FDLE personnel and other crime scene techs. Media was starting to gather on the other side of the crime scene tape at the front of the property. If it was the missing Carrollwood mother, Hallie's heart ached for her and her young child whose life was forever altered through no fault of his own.

She got back in her car, sweating from the combination of hot Florida sun and early menopause, and grabbed a hair band out of the middle console of the dash. She tied her long, dirty-blond hair back into a ponytail, and instinctively checked her cellphone. Two missed calls and three texts. One call was from her mother but the other number she didn't recognize, and they didn't leave a message. Two of the texts were from David and one was from Katie, both looking for things that, of course, Hallie would know where to find because she was the only one who put anything away in its place. She quickly responded to their texts, trying her best not to instigate a fight with either one of them, and then called her mother. Glimpsing the activity going on at Wayna's house in her rearview mirror as she drove away, she felt that a part of her childhood was forever lost.

*   *   *

Hallie's mother, Rebecca, answered on the third ring.

"Hi honey," she said in a too-cheery voice as she answered her cell.

"Hi Mom, how are you doing today?"

"Can't complain on this glorious day; how about you?"

"Fine, just busy as usual. Sorry I haven't made it by lately; I've just been swamped with work."

"You work too hard, Hallie. Maybe if that husband of yours helped out a little more, you wouldn't have so much to do all the time,"

"Mom, don't start," Hallie interrupted.

"Fine," she said, dropping the subject. "How's Katie doing with her applications? Do you need me to come over to spend an afternoon or two to help her?"

"Actually, that's not a bad idea. She won't yell at you like she does me," Hallie chuckled, not entirely joking.

"Fine, then it's settled. I'll text Katie and set up a time for next week, one day after school. I'll come down to help her get started."

"Since when do you text, Mom?"

"Since my new boyfriend, Ross, taught me how. Can I tell you about all the things he sends to me? It is quite exhilarating," Rebecca said, giggling like a schoolgirl.

"Good God, Mom, no, you absolutely cannot tell me. I do not want to know. How old is Ross and where did you meet him?"

"Ross is a spry 67 years young, and I met him at yoga a few weeks ago. He asked me out for coffee afterwards, telling me he really enjoyed my downward dog," she said, giggling again.

Hallie couldn't remember the last time she heard her mother giggle, of all things. If she wasn't so weirded out by it, she might actually think it was cute.

"Really, that was his opening? I can't, Mom, I just can't," Hallie responded, horrified at the realization that her 72-year-old mother was probably getting more action than she was.

"What? I thought it was cute, and frankly, he really does like my downward dog for reasons you probably do not want to hear about."

"Oh my God, you're killing me. I'm going now, Mom. I'll call you tomorrow."

"Bye, honey," she heard her mom saying in her singsong voice, as Hallie quickly ended the call, not wanting to imagine anymore yoga positions that her mother and her new beau, Ross, may be practicing.

CHAPTER SEVEN

Lila could hear a steady beeping sound somewhere in the distance. She was cold and hurting all over, especially around her ribs, her neck and her head. She was so confused, unsure of where she was. She could tell she was in a bed but it wasn't her own bed, that she was sure of. She was trying desperately to open her eyes but somehow could not. Now she could hear muffled voices, not too close but not that far away either, but she couldn't make out what they were saying. Her head was pounding as she slowly regained consciousness, unable to move without experiencing excruciating pain, but finally able to slightly open her left eye. She could tell her right eye was swollen shut and she had scratches, welts, and cuts on her face, arms, and legs, not to mention what seemed like a thousand red and itchy bites all over her body. As she strained to take in her surroundings, her broken body started to tremble as the memories of her last waking moments flooded in, causing her heart to race and triggering the monitors next to her bed to alert her keepers of her awakening.

The footsteps outside of her room became louder and quicker as they approached the door of her room, and she instinctively closed her eyes to avoid the blinding light emanating from the hallway as the door opened. Squinting, Lila realized that she was in a hospital and the person coming towards her appeared to be a nurse. The woman checked the monitors, silenced the alarm, and began talking soothingly to Lila.

"Hi, honey, I'm Nurse Patty, can you hear me?"

Lila's breathing and heart rate were beginning to calm as Nurse Patty tended to her, checking tubes and monitors and bandages, all while talking in a soothing voice to Lila.

"You're at Tampa General Hospital and you're going to be just fine, honey. Can you hear me?"

Lila nodded slightly, which sent sharp, shooting pains throughout her neck, and, wincing, she unconsciously reached for her bandaged neck, as a fresh tear trickled out of her eyes, down her swollen cheeks.

"Oh honey, I know you're in pain. I'm going to get the doctor in here right away so we can do something about that. She's going to be real excited that you're awake. I'll be right back, honey, don't you worry," Nurse Patty whispered in her comforting southern drawl, as she covered Lila with a warm blanket and left the room, leaving Lila alone with her terrifying memories.

The night was dark and Ybor seemed unusually empty that night. She remembered walking to her car in the garage after David was a no-show and seeing only a few other cars in the garage at the time. She was almost to her car when a man appeared, wearing a ski mask, and she could see that he was holding a large knife. She tried to get into her car before he made it around to the driver's side but he was too fast. As she tried to open her door, he slammed her into her car with such force, it knocked the wind out of her. She dropped her keys and her purse as she crumbled to the cold, concrete floor, struggling to catch her breathe. When he punched her that first time, her head ricocheted off the concrete and she passed out. When she woke up, they weren't in the garage anymore but behind it, where it was dark and overgrown with brush, and next to what appeared to be a stack of weathered and broken wooden pallets discarded long ago. She noticed the same railroad tracks she had seen earlier and could smell urine emanating from the area where her head rested. He had cut her skirt and panties off and she was laying on the rocky ground on her back while he straddled her. When she started to scream, he laughed and shoved her panties in her mouth to quiet her. She felt like she was going to suffocate or pass out again, but she knew she had to fight or she would surely die.

The door of her hospital room opened, interrupting her terrifying memories, and Nurse Patty came in accompanied by a shorter woman donning a somewhat messy bob who wore blue scrubs and a white coat that seemed at least one size too big while a stethoscope hung loosely on her neck, which seemed to be more of a symbol of her position than a functioning piece of equipment. She had a kind face, especially when she smiled, Lila noticed.

"Hello, I'm Dr. Elligott, and I'll be taking care of you tonight. Do you think you can answer a few questions for me?" the soft-spoken doctor asked her as she listened to her heart with the stethoscope that apparently did work and checked the readings on various instruments and monitors in the room.

Lila held her bandaged neck as she nodded.

"Can you tell me your name?"

"Lila," she squeaked out, quieter than she expected, "Lila Martinez."

"Good, nice to meet you, Lila. You're a very lucky young lady."

"Can someone call my mom for me? I don't know where my cellphone is."

"Yes, honey, I'll call her for you," Nurse Patty responded, "What's her number?"

"It's in my phone. I can't remember it," she stuttered, trying to reach something unattainable in her mind, "why can't I remember my mom's phone number?"

"It's okay, Lila, you just woke up, give it some time," the kind doctor said to her.

"It's in my cellphone, my mom's number is saved in my cell phone. Do you have my purse? My cellphone should be in my purse."

"When you were brought in, you didn't have any belongings with you, no purse, no cell phone. The police found your car in a garage in Ybor City, close to where you were found, but I don't believe they found your purse or your keys. But don't worry, Nurse Patty will track down your mother. What's her name?" the doctor asked.

"Her name is Dina Martinez."

"Okay, don't worry, I'll try to find her right now. Where does she live, honey?"

"Here, in Tampa. We just moved back."

Nurse Patty left the room to find Lila's mother, and Dr. Elligott softly asked, "Do you know what happened to you, Lila?"

"Yes, mostly, I think."

"Lila, do you think you can tell me what happened and who did this to you?"

Lila squeezed her eyes shut, trembling at the thought of reliving her experience, but also wanting to make sure the monster was caught. He had her keys, her purse, her ID – he knew where she lived. The thought that he was out there somewhere terrified her.

"I think so," Lila whispered.

"Okay, good. There is a police officer who has been watching over your room since you came out of surgery and he's right outside in the hallway. He's here to protect you. And a detective who is investigating your case just stopped by to check on your progress.

Would it be okay with you if the detective came in to listen to your story?"

"Um, okay, I guess."

Dr. Elligott introduced Lila to Detective Marcelo Garcia and Lila told them her story, as much as she could remember, answering the Detective's questions when he gently interrupted from time to time. No, she didn't recognize him because he had a ski mask on; no, he didn't say anything to her, just attacked her out of nowhere; yes, she was alone because she was there to meet a friend, but her friend didn't show up.

"Wait, I think he knew my name," Lila said, trying to recall the memory.

"He knew your name?" the Detective asked. "Why do you think he knew your name?"

"Yes, I think so. Right when I first saw him, before he attacked me, I think he said, 'Hello Lila' . . . yes, I'm sure of it. God, why didn't I remember that until just now?" Lila asked, looking up at Dr. Elligott with fear and confusion in her unpatched eye.

"You were knocked unconscious and suffered a great trauma. There might be other things that you forgot or blocked out that you may remember in time or you may never remember at all. It's okay, Lila, it's completely normal."

"Did you recognize his voice?" the Detective with the kind eyes and soft voice asked her, with his pen poised, ready to write down anything Lila could tell them.

"No, I don't think so."

"Did he have an accent or anything distinguishable at all that you can remember?"

Lila thought and suddenly blurted out, "Yes! I remember – the way he said my name, he sounded like he had a southern accent."

"How did you finally get away, Lila?" Dr. Elligott asked gently.

"As I said, I woke up with him on top of me behind the garage, straddling me and pinning me down with his weight. When I screamed, he shoved what I later realized were my panties into my mouth," Lila said in between sobs as she recalled the horrific attack. "I really thought I was going to die, I couldn't breathe. I just wanted to get away from him. All I could think about was would I ever see my daughter again? And then it happened so fast but I saw my opportunity. He got up on his knees, lifting his weight off of me for a second, and let go of my hands so he could unzip his pants. In that instant I brought my knee up as hard as I could between his legs, which caused him to fall to the side for a minute, clutching his balls, and I yanked the panties out of my mouth so I could breathe. As I fought to get out from under him, he grabbed me and pulled me back towards him. I think that's when he stabbed me, but I knew I couldn't give up and so I kicked him again, as hard as I could, and he fell back into the stack of wood behind him. I crawled and scrambled backwards away from him, using the wall of the garage to help me up, and then I just ran, as fast as I could. I hid in some bushes and I thought for sure he would find me, but he never did. That's all I remember until I woke up here."

"Okay, Lila, you did great. We're going to let you get some rest now until your mother gets here, but you push the call button if you need anything at all. Nurse Patty will be back in to check on you in a few minutes."

Detective Garcia handed Lila his card as he said, "Lila, here's my card with my cell phone on it. If you remember anything else at all, anytime, please call me. With your help, maybe we can catch this guy."

CHAPTER EIGHT

As she fought to wake up, caught in that half-conscious place where she wasn't sure if her dreams were reality, she felt warm, moist air wafting over her face. For a moment she dreamed she was smelling the aroma of fresh, brewed coffee, but any hint of coffee quickly vanished, jolting her out of her stupor, as the smell of coffee was replaced with an odor that can only be described as stinky feet or worse. Definitely not coffee. She opened one eye, and quickly shut it. It was too late; she was on to her. Juno stood beside Hallie's bed, wagging her tail, and proceeded to drown her in a pool of slobber as she licked her head and her hands, which got in the way in her futile attempt to cover her face.

"Juno, stop!" Hallie yelled, laughing and mad at the same time. Normally, Hallie woke Juno up to take her out, especially as she got older, but on the rare day she got to sleep in, if you could call 8:30 a.m. sleeping in, this was the ritual. She would sit and wait somewhat patiently and just stare at her, panting, waiting for any sign of life. If she showed any signs of life, such as a stretch or opening of her eyes, that was her cue to breathe in her face and lick her until she got up.

"Okay, okay, okay, I'll take you out, just let me up," wondering where David was and why he hadn't taken Juno out.

Hallie threw on her jeans that were just where she left them, discarded on the never-sat-in-chair in the corner of her room where she often draped her clothes. She slipped her socked feet into her sandals and skipped the bra for the moment as Juno seemed particularly anxious to get outside this morning. She caught a glimpse of herself as she went past her full length mirror, and thought, "God, help me, I hope nobody else is out this morning, that's all I need."

Hallie grabbed her copy of the morning paper off her doormat on her way back into her house. Yes, she was a throwback – she still liked the idea of a real newspaper. Somehow it seemed more credible and permanent than the internet version. She tossed the paper onto her dining room table next to Katie's backpack and the package for her mother she had asked David to mail for her. Rolling her eyes, she picked up Katie's backpack and put it in the hall closet and moved the package to the table on the front foyer so she could mail it later.

Coffee, she desperately needed coffee. As the Keurig brewed her perfect cup of Dunkin Donuts French vanilla coffee, she looked out her kitchen window, catching a glimpse of the yellow police tape still attached to Mrs. Butler's front porch railing -- a stark reminder that her neighborhood was not as safe as she had always believed.

She looked out onto the street; the reporters were no longer camped outside and the only police presence was the rookie officer assigned to drive by periodically and to check with the residents to see if anyone had seen or heard anything unusual since the body had been discovered. The rookie took his assignment very seriously, seemingly pleased that he had graduated from traffic duty to what he self-described "real police work."

The Keurig maker delivered the steaming Dunkin Donuts brew into her favorite cup, and she added extra half and half and stirred it with a knife while admonishing herself for not running the dishwasher more often or buying more teaspoons. She swore David and Katie threw them out. She dropped the knife into the stainless steel sink and sat down at the kitchen counter to read the paper. Smiling, she looked down at Juno who was busy devouring her breakfast, while she lifted her cup to her mouth to savor the first taste of her steaming, hot coffee. She took the paper out of its plastic sleeve and was filled with dread as the frontpage headline registered in her brain:

Missing Lawyer's Body Discovered in Carrollwood
By: Daniel Newman

The beaten and stabbed body of a young woman who was discovered in partially secluded brush next to an abandoned home in Carrollwood last week has been identified as Naomi Banks, 34. Naomi Banks was reported missing by her husband, Steven Banks, after she didn't return home from her evening run. Carrollwood resident, Neal Stoll, discovered the body as he walked to work at Lowes from his home on Orange Grove Drive early Wednesday morning. Stoll explained, "I smelled something really awful, but I thought it was just a dead animal, maybe a dead boar or something." He explained that he looked around and that's when he saw the victim, displayed on the front porch of the broken down old home.

Naomi Banks, a local attorney who graduated from the University of Florida law school, is survived by her husband, Steven, who owns a local landscaping company, and a five-year-old son. Immediately after the young mother went missing, family and friends began searching for her, but she wasn't found until Mr. Stoll stumbled upon her last week. During yesterday's press conference, Tampa Police Chief Patrick Egan confirmed it was a homicide, but explained that the autopsy results, including Naomi's exact cause of death, would not be released until after the initial investigation was completed, which would likely take several weeks. A source close to the investigation who spoke on the condition of anonymity suggested that the latest victim's wounds were similar to Lauren White's injuries, the young UT student found murdered in South Tampa a few weeks ago, and a third victim who has yet to be identified. Does Tampa have a serial killer in its midst? The residents of Tampa deserve to know.

Hallie set the paper down and thought about the young lawyer. Her name sounded familiar, but she didn't know her. But the Tampa legal community was a small community, so perhaps their paths had crossed at some point. The article contained a picture of the young family at Christmas and a picture of the husband at the press conference. He looked devastated and as if he had aged twenty years in the nine months since the family holiday picture. Hallie's heart ached for the young widower and his son. She was jolted from her thoughts by the sound of her cellphone pinging that she had an incoming text.

"Hey babe, sorry I left so early. Fishing with the boys. Didn't want to wake you."

Hallie typed back, "okay but we have a lot to do around here to get ready for the BBQ. I need your help tomorrow."

All she got back was the thumbs up emoji and the letters "CUL".

It drove Hallie crazy the way David used slang acronyms and emojis as if he was the same age as his students. Hallie could figure out most of them, but some of them she had to look up, like "CUL" which she now knew meant "see you later." Did it really take that much longer to type out the words? But David always said, being the principal of a large, very diverse high school, it was his job to be up on the latest slang, texts, and trends so he could relate to his students and know what they were up to. Sometimes Hallie wondered if David tried too hard to be in tune with his students, but she could never say anything to him without triggering a huge fight.

She folded up the paper and rinsed her coffee cup out before putting it in the dishwasher. She had chores to do and a few emails to send but she was so distracted. She couldn't stop thinking about Lauren White and Naomi Banks. What did these two women have in common? How did they both end up murdered? Different ends of town, different ages, one a student, one a lawyer, the only similarities seemed to be the way they each seemingly disappeared and the violent nature of their deaths.

Juno looked up from her spot on the floor next to Hallie as Katie sauntered down the stairs towards the kitchen, yawning and still in her pajamas, which consisted of one of her dad's old concert t-shirts that barely covered the shorts she may have had on underneath and a pair of socks.

"Good morning," Hallie said cheerfully.

Katie grunted and nodded towards Hallie, which was as good as she was going to get on a Saturday morning. Katie's curfew on a Friday night was midnight, which she had been stretching lately, 12:05, 12:10, and last night 12:15. And with what was going on, Hallie didn't like it.

"Katie, your curfew is midnight, not a minute later," Hallie started to admonish when Katie interrupted.

"Please stop calling me Katie, Mom, I hate it. And it was only a few minutes. It's not that deep," Katie exclaimed, with the infamous eye roll.

"It actually is that deep, *K-a-t-e*," Hallie said, emphasizing the pronunciation of her name, "if I tell you to be home at a certain time, that's the time you better be home. So, to show you that fifteen minutes does, in fact, make a difference, tonight, you have to be home at 11:45. And for each minute you're over that, I will continue to move back your curfew until you can't even go out, got it?"

"Oh my God, Mom, you're the worst! It was fifteen freakin minutes! The world didn't end, did it?"

"Okay, now it's 11:30. It's only another fifteen freakin minutes, Kate; it's not the end of the world, right?"

Katie stomped off and loudly up the stairs, mumbling under her breath, until she slammed her door to her bedroom. Hallie was aggravated with herself for letting Katie rile her up and reacting to her the way she did. She wasn't even intending to change her curfew time until Katie mouthed off to her. But she reacted out of anger and, if she was honest with herself, fear, and then there was no turning back. And this summed up her entire relationship of late with Katie. She desperately wanted to keep her daughter safe from all the dangers in the world while Katie desperately wanted to explore her independence. She couldn't wait until they were out of this phase and back to having the loving, mother-daughter relationship they used to have before life got so complicated.

Hallie sat down at her desk to check her emails and pay a few bills. She opened her inbox and quickly scanned through the received emails to see if there was anything pressing that she had to deal with when one email caught her eye:

From: nwc822@gmail.com
Sent: Tuesday, September 17, 2019 10:46 a.m.
To: HMiller@Millerlaw.com
Subject: We need to talk

You don't know me but I know who you are and what you did. Or should I say, what you didn't do. You can't escape the past and it's time you faced it and owned up to what you caused. If you don't respond to this email or take it seriously, you'll leave me no choice but to tell your daughter Kate everything.

Hallie read and re-read the email ten times, trying to figure out if it was a joke or whether to take it seriously. And if it was real, what did it mean and who was it from? She frantically searched through all of her other emails to see if she had any others from the same person. Not finding any, she read the cryptic email again and called Bridget.

"Hey girl, what's up? Still stalking crime scenes and getting me in trouble with my old man?"

"I told you I was sorry about that."

"I know, I'm just fucking with you," Bridget chuckled as Hallie could hear her inhaling on her cigarette.

"Is Jay home?" Hallie asked.

"Yeah, he's out mowing the lawn. What's up?"

"I got a weird email and I'm freaking out a little bit. But maybe I'm overreacting. I need to know if I should take it seriously or just ignore it as some type of spam or phishing email."

"Oh Hallie, please tell me you're not wiring funds to a third world country to get your long lost niece or nephew out of prison? Or maybe confirming your bank account number and social security number with the IRS before they come to arrest you?" Bridget mocked.

"Bridget, I'm serious. This one was addressed to me at my law firm email address and said something about it being time to face my past and own up to something I did or didn't do. They also said if I didn't respond, they would tell Katie everything, whatever that means, except they called her "Kate" not Katie. I don't know, maybe I'm being paranoid, but what if it's not a joke?"

"I know a lot of weird stuff is going on, but it's got to be a joke. Someone just fucking with you, don't you think?"

"Why? Why would someone do that? I can't imagine anyone I know thinking this is funny. Did I tell you my front door was open the other day when I came back from my run?"

"Whoa, back up, what do you mean? No, you failed to mention that, counselor. It was open or just unlocked?"

"Well, both, kind of. I put the key in to unlock it and it just pushed open; so, it was unlocked and wasn't shut all the way. I don't know, maybe I'm losing my mind. Maybe I thought I locked it when I went for my run but didn't and also didn't pull the door shut all the way."

"Those are a lot of maybe's, Hallie. Was anything missing or out of the ordinary when you went inside?"

"No, I don't think so. But this was before Lauren White's body was found next door, so I wasn't as nervous or paranoid. I didn't really look around, just figured I forgot to lock the door."

"Do you ever forget to lock the door, Hallie? Because I've known you forever and that doesn't sound like you."

"I don't know, Bridget. But this shit better stop. I don't know how much more my nerves can take."

"Okay, don't worry, Hal. Let me talk to Jay when he's done mowing the lawn. He'll be done soon and I'll ask him what he thinks and tell him about all the weird shit happening to you. Did they say anything else or threaten you in any way?"

"No, just what I've already told you. They want me to contact them about something that happened in my past and that I better take it seriously. So maybe not a direct threat, but I think just the tone and mentioning Katie by name is threatening."

"Ok, don't worry, it could just be a stupid prank that someone she goes to school with is trying to play on her.

No one bullies in person anymore, like the good ole days, it's all virtual. But I'll talk to Jay as soon as he comes in and we'll call you back. In the meantime, try not to worry too much."

"Yeah, um, too late for that. Call me as soon as you talk to Jay."

CHAPTER NINE

He put Neosporin on the deep scratch that was still healing on his neck, cursing himself for letting the bitch get that shot in. Oh, but she was a feisty one, that's for sure. And so pretty. He did like them young and pretty. And they either wanted to be fucked, the little sluts that they were, or make him miserable with their mean, callous ways. He had learned that from his mother. His wife proved to be no different. Such disappointments. He often wondered if his life would have turned out different for him if his mother wasn't such a drunken whore who obviously ran his father off. He had only one or two memories of his father and they were fleeting. But Momma, yeah, he could never forget her – she wouldn't let him. His grandmother, the only woman he truly ever loved, told him once that his father was a brilliant, successful man, an engineer for NASA or something, and that he could be anything he wanted to be with those genes, maybe even an astronaut. But Momma told her to shut the fuck up and not to fill his head with such nonsense right before she smacked him in the head for not fixing her vodka tonic properly.

"You added too much tonic again, you stupid piece of shit. One of these days you'll learn to make your Momma a proper drink."

But he wasn't eight years old anymore, and the days of getting beaten by Momma were long gone. In fact, once he moved out of Momma's house, he never put up with any shit from any woman ever again. He knew all of their games, too. The way they batted their eyelashes at him, wore those tight jeans or short skirts and cropped tops that barely covered their budding breasts, leaving nothing to the imagination, at least not his imagination. He imagined exactly what was underneath and the punishment he would inflict on them for their naughty ways.

He admitted to himself that he was careless with Lila. But his excitement at seeing her again after so many years made him reckless. At first, he wasn't sure it was her. She looked the same, but curvier and obviously older than the last time he had seen her. He waited for her in that dark garage for almost an hour, hoping no one else would be there when she returned to her car and that she would be alone. He knew it was risky but as his Momma always said, "If a window of opportunity appears, don't pull down the shades."

When she walked into the garage, although he couldn't see her, he knew it was her by the clickety-click of her heels on the concrete. To his great delight, she was alone and the parking garage was still empty at that moment. He hid in the darkness, behind the cement pillar, until she was almost to her car. He easily subdued her and punched her with enough force to temporarily stun her into submission. He half-carried, half-dragged her limp, lifeless body out the back door of the garage, having confirmed in the hour he was waiting for her that it led to a dark, secluded alley next to the railroad tracks where he would not be seen.

Oh, if only Momma could see him now.

"Who would the stupid one be now, huh, Momma?" he asked while looking up at her picture, with her cold gray eyes staring down on him, always judging him, while he took another swig of the cheap, bitter whiskey.

No, he wasn't the stupid one anymore. The women who put themselves in vulnerable positions, like walking alone into a deserted garage at night, were the stupid ones and they deserved whatever they got. But he knew he had to be careful, or he would end up getting caught. And he refused to get caught over some stupid bitch who wasn't smart enough not to walk into a dark, deserted garage by herself. And, of course, he still had unfinished business with his ex.

He realized he had made some mistakes with Lila, due to his uncontrollable excitement, including breaking his own rule of hunting so close to home, but he also told himself that there was no way she could have survived based on the amount of blood on his clothes. He regretted not chasing her down to watch the life drain out of the deep gash he had inflicted on her neck. He would have enjoyed catching her and fucking her hard in her dirty little cooch while she took her last breathes. But that fucking movie had just let out, and he couldn't take the chance of being seen with all that blood on his clothes. He entered the garage through the same door he came out of, grabbed Lila's purse, cellphone and keys off the concrete floor next to her car, and raced up to his car, which was parked on the second floor. He calmly exited the garage as the blood in his throbbing cock finally started to subside, together with his erection, and his breathing returned almost to normal.

As the week wore on, he checked the news each day for anything about her body being found. By week's end, he was surprised that it hadn't been reported on. She had to have been found by now; the area was too busy for her not to be discovered. Maybe she was mistaken for a dumb prostitute killed by a john or a pimp, he thought. The way she was dressed, he wouldn't be surprised. Whores usually didn't make the news no matter what happened to them. Weren't worth the ink, in his opinion. Either way, he wasn't going to worry about it. As Momma always said, "Don't trouble trouble until trouble troubles you."

CHAPTER TEN

Heather poured herself another glass of whiskey, finding comfort in its bitterness as the hint of sherry and oak washed across her palate and warmed her deep inside, and she thought about that horrible night on the beach eleven years before. How many more glasses would it take, she wondered, until the pain subsided or at least numbed her to the point where she didn't care or didn't remember the life she had escaped? The headlights from a passing car reflected off the silver rim of her glass as she lifted it up to her lips once again. Seeing the glimmer sent a cold chill up her spine and she instinctively reached for her throat to shield it from the sharp edge of the knife that was long since gone, its damage permanently etched into her neck and soul.

She thought back to that hopeless night on that empty North Carolina beach when she believed she would not survive the night. Actually, she hadn't. That is to say, the person she was then did not survive. She closed her eyes, silently reliving that last night of her previous life. She remembered how the warm breeze blowing in off the Atlantic felt on her skin as she drifted in and out of consciousness laying on the cool sand that night. Her memories triggered a surge of adrenaline, which caused her heart to race and her breath to come in short gasps. She traced her finger along the raised edge of the scar encircling her neck like the chokers she used to love to wear. The deadened nerve endings created a weird sensation under her skin . . . almost ticklish and tingly but in a painful way. She took another swig of the golden-brown liquor, rolling it around her tongue before swallowing it, and closed her eyes.

"Calm down, focus on the sound of your breathing," she said aloud, trying to follow the steps she had learned in meditation therapy. She was uncomfortably aware that the news reports she heard earlier had triggered her latest anxiety attack and unpleasant trip down memory lane. She replayed in her mind the chilling description of the two victims' injuries and suggestion there might be a third: young women, beaten, knife wounds, possible sexual assault. Any time she heard about crimes like these, she couldn't shake the feeling that it was him – that he was back to get her, just as he promised he would be.

* * *

Heather had fled the Outer Banks in North Carolina eleven years ago after her husband had raped and beaten her in a drunken rage for the last time, slashing her throat and missing her jugular by an inch. She locked herself in their tiny bathroom and escaped out of the window when he started pounding on the door, seconds before he broke it down. She made it as far down the desolate beach as she could fueled by fear and adrenaline before collapsing near the water's edge, hidden by the dunes and the tall sea grass she had passed along the way.

When she came to on the beach on that ill-fated night, she knew she could never return to the small cottage they shared. She made her way in the dark, early morning hours to her neighbor, Julie's house. She didn't know how long she had been unconscious on the beach, but she suspected Bobby was still passed out somewhere in their cottage, as was often the case when he went on one of his drunken binges, the frequency of which had been increasing at the time.

Julie was a kind woman, in her late sixties, with hair as soft and white as the clouds and dark blue eyes that were the color of the cold, Atlantic Ocean in the winter. Whenever she talked about her deceased, fisherman husband and his adventures on the sea, her eyes would sparkle and convey a youthful vitality, which contrasted sharply with the wrinkles on her face, deep and weathered from too many years exposed to the sun and salty North Carolina winds. She would tell the stories as she sold seashells, jewelry made out of shark teeth, and other overpriced trinkets to the tourists who visited her quaint shop located on the dock of the local marina.

Julie tried talking Heather into going to the police or at least the hospital, but she refused both. After they cleaned the dried blood and sand out of the gash on her neck, they could tell it wasn't as bad or as deep as they both first suspected. Julie applied pressure to the slightly bleeding wound with a clean cloth until the bleeding seemed to stop and then closed the wound with butterfly steri-strips she retrieved from the first aid kit she always had on hand from her years of being married to a fisherman. On any given day she wouldn't know when Cliff was going to come home with a hook stuck in his hand or a fresh gash from some mishap on his boat due to the rough seas. She put some antibiotic cream on the closed wound and wrapped Heather's neck with a clean bandage.

Julie pleaded with her young friend one more time to go to the police, but once again, Heather refused.

"I can't, Julie, I know how this system works. How long do you think he'll be in jail? A few days, at most? And what happens when he gets out? It's only a matter of time before he does it again, but worse. I can't live this way anymore."

"Okay, honey, but what are you going to do?" she asked, her concern evident in her warm eyes and soft tone.

"I just need to get away, get out of North Carolina. I have some money saved up in an account that he doesn't know about, left over from my inheritance from when my father died. Can you drive me into Kill Devil Hill? I just need to get some clothes, cash, and a bus ticket out of here."

"Where will you go, honey? Do you have family somewhere?"

"No, it was just me and my dad before he died. My mom died a long time ago. But my dad took me and my mom to Florida once when I was little and I've always wanted to go back. It was the most beautiful place in the world, at least seven year old me thought so," Heather said smiling at the fond memory, which unfortunately re-opened the cut on her swollen lip.

Julie handed her a tissue to blot the fresh blood on her lip while agreeing to drive Heather wherever she wanted to go.

That was eleven years ago and Heather never looked back, leaving everything from her old life on the shores of the Outer Banks. She used about $5,000 out of her $10,000 inheritance to rent and furnish a small bungalow in Indian Rocks Beach, a few blocks inland from the beach. She also bought herself a used bike from one of the local thrift shops she discovered nearby. She lived modestly for the next month, keeping to herself, until all of her bruises had faded. Although healed, the gash on her neck had left a noticeable, ugly scar that might trigger questions she didn't want to answer. She bought a dozen scarves from the thrift shop, in assorted colors and patterns, which she tied around her neck to hide the hideous scar. She got a job at one of the bars near her place and started her life all over again.

Brought back to the present by the pictures of the young women on her television screen, Heather tried to overcome her feelings of dread and terror. Bobby had often told her that if she ever ran away from him, he would find her one day. He would never stop until he found her. Had that day finally come, she wondered? Or was she just being paranoid, she thought, cursing herself for allowing him to still get to her. The only thing she knew for sure was that if he did come looking for her, she would be waiting, and this time, he would be the one who wished he got away.

* * *

Heather woke up the next morning determined not to let her past or her paranoia set her back or ruin her day. She had come too far since those days in North Carolina, and there was no way she was going to revert into the insecure and broken person that she was, living in constant fear that she would die at her husband's hands. She fed her cat, a twenty-two-pound, orange tabby named Oscar, who was more like a dog than a cat, and turned on the TV while she waited for her cup of Earl Gray tea to brew. There was nothing new on the murders in Tampa, but as she thought about what the reporters had divulged, she realized it was her overindulgence in whiskey the night before and her emotional state that allowed her imagination to run wild. In the light of the beautiful Florida morning and her somewhat clearer head, Heather believed that any connection between her husband and the murdered women in Tampa was remote and unlikely. Her therapist warned her that the anniversary of that night would always be difficult for her, and she should try to spend it with friends or in another positive way, not drowning herself in a bottle of whiskey as she recounted each painful memory like she did last night. She chastised herself for drinking so much and jumping to such unrealistic conclusions.

She scratched Oscar affectionately on the head and under his chin, comforted by his soft purring at her touch. She found Oscar outside of her cottage when he was just a kitten in that first month she had arrived in Florida. He was soaking wet from the summer storm that had blown in off the Gulf, and when she found him, he was cowering behind a flowerpot on her front step, unsuccessfully trying to shield himself from the torrential downpour. He was scared and hungry but seemed to instinctively know that Heather would take care of him. Truthfully, at that moment, Heather needed Oscar more than he needed her. Eleven years later, not much had changed.

Heather cherished her weekends, enjoying her solitude and time away from the stresses of the office. She finished her tea and went out back to her tiny courtyard to tend to her garden, her other love besides Oscar. She would get lost in her gardening, tending to her fresh vegetables and flowers for hours like they were her children. She grew arugula, basil, oregano, garlic, and peppers. When the season permitted, she also grew tomatoes but those were harder to maintain with her busy work schedule during the week. Periodically, when she had too much for herself, she would package the excess into cute little baskets with self-made labels and bring them to the nearby farmer's market to trade for vegetables she didn't grow herself. She had come to know the local vendors who were regulars at the Saturday market and they never minded trading her for the herbs and vegetables they didn't grow. Afterwards she would take a walk on the beach on her way back to her little cottage, enjoying the sound of the waves gently rolling onto the beach and the sound of the seagulls that had become a symbol of her own freedom. She worked hard to get to this place in her life, recalling those early years in Florida after her escape from the Outer Banks and her previous life.

For the first few years, with no college degree or references, the only jobs she could get were bartending or waitressing. She took as many shifts as they would give her, shopped at the thrift shops, and rarely went out. With the money she saved, and with a small student loan, she was eventually able to put herself through college at St. Pete Junior College where she obtained a degree in paralegal studies. It took her six years but she was proud of herself and had done it all on her own. For the last two years she worked at Greenlee, Remington, & Stoll, the largest and most respected law firm in Tampa, in the commercial litigation department, assisting about four attorneys at any given moment. It was challenging but she loved it and felt she was good at her job. By far, her favorite attorney to work with was Paige Rhodes, one of the younger partners. She was smart and kind, always taking the time to explain things to Heather. Unlike her male counterparts, she was never condescending or patronizing and seemed to respect and welcome Heather's input.

She met Paige during her third week at the firm. Paige was preparing for an upcoming trial and needed help compiling her trial notebook and volumes of exhibits she would have to present. With the other litigation paralegal on vacation, she had no choice but to use Heather, despite her inexperience at that time. They worked well together and Heather was a quick learner so Paige started giving her more and more work after that. Two years later, besides their working relationship, they had developed a nice friendship too.

A few weeks before, Heather heard Paige arguing on the phone with someone. It was late, after 7 p.m. and most of the office had left. Paige probably didn't realize anyone was still there, but Heather was in her cubicle just outside of Paige's office, catching up on posting her time for the week. She wasn't trying to listen but when Paige started talking heatedly, with her voice rising, at whoever was on the other end of the phone, she couldn't help but hear her side of the conversation.

"No, we can't use that information, no matter what. Look, I hate the motherfucker more than anyone and I don't want to see him re-elected, but there's no way we can leak that information about the rape to help Sarah's campaign. For one thing, we'll be sued for libel or defamation and God knows what else, and two, and more importantly, I have to consider what it would do to Hallie. There's just no way. . . . Oh, thank you for the refresher of law school 101, really? Truth is a defense? Wow, I hadn't considered that. So, genius, ignoring Hallie's feelings for the moment, how are we going to prove the truth that he drugged and raped her that night? Oh, that's right, we can't, which is the same reason Hallie never reported the rape in the first place. I never should have told you about that; Hallie would kill me if she knew. We're done talking about this. . . . I know, I know, but we can't use it. I've got to get out of the office now, but I'll talk to you tomorrow. Hopefully you won't say any more stupid shit that makes me want to punch you. . . . Of course we're still on for drinks on Thursday, the usual place and time. Jesus, Mike, you're always so dramatic. See you then, love," Paige said as she hung up the phone.

Heather tried to gather her stuff quickly and quietly so she could get out before Paige realized she was there. She made her way to the elevator and was waiting for it when Paige came up behind her with her briefcase and a small redwell in hand.

"Oh, Heather, you're still here? I didn't realize anyone was still here."

"Oh, hi Paige, you scared me; I didn't realize anyone was still here either. I was just in the file room catching up on some filing that had gotten behind. I lost track of time." Heather lied.

"Girl, you are too dedicated. So you weren't at your desk just now?" Paige asked, trying to remember what she may have said on her phone call with Mike.

"Not in the last fifteen or twenty minutes, at least," Heather lied. "Since that Stetson wrongful termination litigation involving that crazy librarian who was a convicted sex offender finally settled, I wanted to file all of those pleadings and discovery in the file room to get that clutter off my desk before going home. I didn't realize you were still here."

"Oh my God, that was such a crazy case! I'm sorry that one's over," Paige laughed, "that was a fun one. That librarian was one sick puppy. Seriously, sitting in the corner naked and knitting while her husband raped that poor young girl who answered their ad for a nanny. And then, after lying about her credentials to get the Stetson position, filing a wrongful termination suit against them when they learned of it all? She was a ballsy one, that's for sure. Well, at least Stetson will do better background checks from now on, I'm sure," Paige laughed again as the elevator finally arrived. They arrived at the parking garage, making small talk as they walked to their cars, and said goodbye.

Heather was curious about the phone call she just overheard. Heather got in her car and called her best friend, Natalie Crawford, who also worked at the firm. She worked in the accounting department of the firm, and similar to Heather, had suffered something in her past so she didn't get close to a lot of people. But Heather hit it off with her and eventually they became good friends, neither one of them asking too many questions about the other's past.

"Hey, Nat, what are you doing?" Heather asked when Natalie answered.

"Nothing much, just sitting down to binge watch some Netflix. You're not just now leaving the office, are you, girl?"

"Yeah, but I had some last minute things to finish up. I have to be ready for Attorney Dickhead tomorrow because he has a mediation on Friday so he'll be up my ass all day tomorrow."

"I don't envy you. Nope, let me sit back in my little cubicle crunching numbers and processing check requests. It's boring but no one ever yells at me," Natalie chuckled.

"Well, speaking of yelling, I heard Paige on the phone with someone tonight and she was yelling at him about someone who is up for re-election but he allegedly raped one of Paige's good friends years ago. I don't know who is up for re-election but someone named Sarah is running against him and Paige and whoever she was talking to are on her election committee. Isn't that crazy?" Heather asked.

"That's awful. Wait, I think I know who it is because I processed a check request recently from Paige for expenses related to the Sarah Wilt election committee. She's running for Circuit Court Judge against Judge William Stephens. God, I met him once before he became a judge at some event and he was a real creep. Do you think he really raped one of her friends?"

"Well supposedly. I heard Paige saying something about not being able to prove he drugged and raped her and that's why her friend never reported it, something like that."

"Oh my God, do you know when this happened?"

"No, why?"

"No reason, just crazy to think that a judge is a rapist and he's still on the bench. Do you know who Paige's friend is?" Natalie asked.

"Hallie something, I don't know. A lawyer in town who Paige used to practice with earlier in her career. But whatever, it's not like I know these people. I was just gossiping with you because I don't have anything exciting going on in my own life at the moment. Why are you so interested in this?"

"I'm really not, same as you, this is the most fascinating thing I've heard in a while. But seriously, if this Judge Stephens raped someone, he shouldn't get away with it. Frankly, he should be castrated and should most definitely not be on the bench."

"I completely agree, but enough about that. What are you doing this weekend? Want to get together for a few drinks and watch the next season of Schitt's Creek?" Heather asked, wishing she had never brought it up in the first place.

"Yeah, that sounds good. I don't have anything going on. Let's talk about it at lunch tomorrow," Natalie answered, also welcome for the change of subject.

Heather was annoyed with herself for gossiping about something she overhead from Paige's office and she knew she shouldn't have. She wasn't even sure why she shared it except she really didn't have anything exciting going on in her life, so it was finally something interesting to share with Natalie, truly her only friend. But she probably said too much and she prayed it wouldn't get back to Paige or she might be fired. She vowed to go back to minding her own business and would ask Natalie to forget she ever said anything.

* * *

As she watered her plants and herbs in her garden, she was relieved Natalie never said anything about what she told her. And she hoped she never would.

CHAPTER ELEVEN

Hallie had met David ten years before, after she had been divorced from Katie's father for a few years. Katie was seven years old at the time and spending every other weekend and half of every summer at her father's house. The summer she met David, Hallie had rented a one-bedroom cottage on Indian Rocks Beach for the month Katie was away. She packed up her laptop, files she would need, and Juno, who was just a puppy at the time.

She had gotten into a routine where she would finish her work, go on a run with Juno, and then stop by the local beach bar that was just a few blocks from her cottage. The cute bartender had, in turn, gotten in the habit of having a bowl of water waiting for Juno and an ice cold Corona waiting on the bar for Hallie. He was boyish and funny and, by the end of the second week, it was all Hallie could do to concentrate on her work, counting down the minutes until it was time for her run. It was also no coincidence that her 5k times were getting faster each day.

Hallie learned that David, the cute bartender with the wavy, brown hair, piercing blue eyes, and sexy smile, was actually a teacher. He bartended during the summer to make extra money and to live on the beach. He rented a small studio apartment over the bar just for the summer, which he had been doing for the last three summers. David had explained that the owner of the bar, Jimmy, was a friend of his with whom he grew up. By having someone there he could trust, Jimmy could take trips with his family that he hadn't been able to do without closing the bar. It was a win-win for both of them.

By the third week, David asked Hallie to stick around after he closed up the bar. He grabbed a bottle of wine from behind the bar, opened and recorked it, and took it with them as they walked down to the beach under the moonlight. At some point along the way, he had grabbed her hand and Hallie felt like a schoolgirl, butterflies and all. She was sure if he could see her face, she would be blushing. She fell in love with David that night, sharing a bottle of wine under the stars. He was everything her ex-husband, Kevin, wasn't: carefree, funny, whimsical, full of life. She had met her ex when they were both in law school and he embodied everything she thought she wanted in a partner: strength, intelligence, confidence, a good career, a provider. However, sometime during her five year marriage to Kevin, after Katie was born, she realized that she was married to a controlling, narcissistic asshole and she got out. David was the complete opposite of her ex, and Hallie was ready for a nice man in her life and her heart again.

For the first few years, Hallie had very few complaints, even finding David's childish ways enchanting. When she would start to get mad or resentful that the burdens of taking care of a family and being the primary breadwinner were mostly on her, she would remind herself that David kept her young and got her to do things that she would have never tried on her own: snorkeling on their honeymoon in the Dry Tortugas, an archipelago of coral islands off the coast of Key West; taking a helicopter ride over the grand canyon followed by three booze and gambling filled days in the casinos; and skydiving in Hawaii on a dream vacation for their fifth anniversary.

But always having to be the responsible one got tiresome, especially when David was perfectly content to take his summers off while she felt chained to her desk to keep them living in the manner to which David had become accustomed. No matter how much she made, it seemed David would always find a way to spend it. Around year seven, the fights began, and the resentment settled in deep for Hallie, probably for David too. But by then, Hallie had to shift her focus to Katie, to guide her and keep her on the right path through the tumultuous, angst-ridden teenage years. As she grew more resentful, David grew more distant, in all areas, especially the bedroom. So now here they were, ten years in, just existing and engaging superficially in the niceties of everyday life together to avoid the exhausting fights they used to have or confront the issues in their marriage. Hallie thought she still loved David, at least when she reminisced about the early years, but she didn't feel like he loved her anymore. If she could get Katie successfully off to college, maybe that would relieve some of the tension in the house and she and David could somehow rekindle the relationship they once had.

Hallie was brought out of her memories by the sound of her phone ringing.

"Hi Mom," Hallie answered.

"Hi honey, how are you doing?"

"Not bad, how about you? Still doing naughty yoga with Ross?" Hallie asked playfully, regretting it the minute it came out of her mouth.

"Well, since you asked, he is really quite limber and very enthusiastic, shall we say. I haven't felt this, um . . . relaxed in a long time."

"I'm really happy for you, Mom, I promise, but please, no more details. I can't take it," Hallie groaned, knowing it was entirely her fault for asking the question.

"Fine. So when are you inviting us over for dinner so you can meet him?" Rebecca asked.

"Um, when do you want to come?" Hallie asked, surprised yoga-Ross had made it to the "dinner at the daughter's house" phase so quickly. He really was good, she thought.

"Well, we have yoga tonight and tomorrow night, so how about Thursday night?"

Hallie quickly looked at her work calendar for Thursday, and then said "yeah, Thursday works for me. I'll make sure David comes home right after work."

"Did I mention Ross is a vegetarian?"

"Nope but I guess that goes with the whole yoga-clean life thing. And you haven't converted him yet? You're losing your touch, Mom," Hallie teased.

"Give me time, my smartass daughter, give me time. Anyway, he does eat fish, so maybe do your chicken piccata but instead of chicken, maybe use grouper or a nice tilapia, ok? I've already told him what an amazing cook you are so don't make me look bad."

"Of course not, mother, I live to serve you and impress your dates with my fabulous cooking skills so they know, in turn, what a fabulous mother you must have been."

"You know, Hallie, I think you should consider yoga. It really does help do away with that negative energy, and, did I mention, I haven't been this limber in years. It might do you good."

"You mentioned it, Mom. Gotta go; I have to go catch some fresh grouper or a nice tilapia for Thursday night's dinner," Hallie said as she heard her mother say goodbye and disconnect the call. Hallie hoped that when she grew up she could be as young and carefree as her mother.

* * *

David pulled his cock out and rolled off of the young girl, as sweat dripped down his chest. He kicked the stiff, motel room comforter heaped at the bottom of the bed onto the floor and, panting, reached for his cellphone to make sure Hallie hadn't called or texted him.

"What are you doing, Papi?" the young girl asked him, as she caressed his bare back with her long, pink fingernails.

It was 4 o'clock in the afternoon. He knew he would have to leave soon to make it home in time to avoid a thousand questions from Hallie.

"I have to get going soon," he whispered, while pinching her pink, hard nipples and working his way down to her soft, wet pussy.

"Aye, Papi, you don't have to go yet," she moaned as she helped guide his hand down between her legs.

She was warm and wet to his touch and he felt himself throbbing, ready to pound her again, just as his phone started to ring.

"Shit," he muttered while reaching for his phone and seeing the name "Hallie" come up on the screen. He immediately sent it to voicemail and jumped out of the bed.

"I have to go, Maria, I'm sorry," he said as he quickly slipped into his jeans, pulled his shirt over his head, and sat on the edge of the bed to put his shoes on.

"Please don't leave yet. I skipped cheer practice because you told me we would have the afternoon together," Maria pouted. "Can't you stay just a little longer? I'll be the naughty schoolgirl I know you like," she tempted, licking her lips seductively while twirling a ringlet of her long, brown hair.

"You have no idea how much I would like to stay, but I just can't. Next week, I promise, we'll stay longer. Ok, don't forget, wait at least ten minutes before you leave the room, ok?"

"I know, I know, Principal Miller, I'll be very careful not to be seen when I leave."

David groaned at the sound of his title, bent down, kissed the young brunette, and left the motel room. When he got in his car and started to drive away, he hit the call back button on his phone.

"Hey babe, sorry I couldn't answer before, I was on the phone with one of the faculty members. Someone's always complaining about something," David easily lied.

"That's okay; are you on your way home?" Hallie asked.

"Yes, I should be home soon. Everything okay?"

"Yes, but I was hoping you could stop by Publix on your way home. I'll text you a list. I'm thinking about making Cacio e Pepe tonight," Hallie said.

"Oooh, my favorite! Text me the list," David said trying to sound normal and not like he had just finished banging the school's head cheerleader for the last hour.

CHAPTER TWELVE

"Ay Dios mio, mi amor," Dina Martinez cried as she came into her daughter's hospital room, seeing her daughter's battered face for the first time.

"I'm okay, Mama'," Lila said, trying to keep her voice from quivering for the sake of her mother. "Where's Vera?" she asked, unable to hide her growing concern and angst.

"Don't worry, pobrecita, tu querido hijo esta con Tia Sophia. Who did this to you, my sweet angel?

"I don't know, Mama'," Lila admitted, hanging her head in shame.

"You were going to meet him, weren't you? !Ay, que pendejo! I knew it was a mistake to come back here, mi amor," her mother chastised.

"It doesn't matter, Mama', he never showed up," she cried, no longer able to keep the warm, salty tears from streaming down her cheeks.

"No llores, mi amor, don't cry," her mother said as she stroked her daughter's hair and gently wiped the tears from her face.

"I just want to go home," Lila exclaimed, drying her tears and resolving not to fall apart, "when can I get out of here?" Lila asked, just as Dr. Elligott came into her room.

"Hello, I'm Dr. Elligott; you must be Mrs. Martinez," the pretty doctor said while extending her hand.

"Hello," Dina said while taking the doctor's hand in both of her own, "thank you for saving my sweet daughter's life. Muchas bendiciones sobre ti," she said, with sincerity and warmth in her eyes.

"I've been taking care of Lila. You have a very strong and brave daughter, Mrs. Martinez. You must be very proud."

"Yes, she is my life. When can I take her home, Doctora?"

"Well, we're not ready to let her go home just yet. She has a concussion and a bad wound on her neck that we need to watch to make sure it doesn't get infected. How are you feeling today, Lila?" Dr. Elligott asked, directing her attention towards her patient.

"Sore and very tired, but not as bad as yesterday, I don't think. I really want to get home to my daughter, Dr. Elligott. She must be scared, wondering where I am."

"I'm sure your mother is taking very good care of her while you have to take care of yourself, Lila," Dr. Elligott suggested, looking to Lila's mother for support.

"Si, hija, Vera is okay I am spoiling mi nieta lindo rotten. But I told her you would take her to Disney World when you get home if she's a good girl while you're gone," she said, winking at Lila and the doctor.

"When will that be, Dr. Elligott?" Lila pleaded.

"Probably in about a week, if you continue to heal as well as you have been doing. Beginning tomorrow, we're going to get you up and moving and in some physical therapy. You're lucky to be alive, Lila, and you lost a lot of blood. It's going to be awhile before you regain your strength and energy. In the meantime, I'm prescribing extra iron and protein rich meals. A lot of spinach and red meat. You're not a vegetarian, are you Lila?"

"No, I tried that for a very brief period when I was in high school, but my mother wouldn't hear of it," Lila explained, rolling her eyes.

"Ay Dios mio, who ever heard of such a thing? You would reject your abuela's posta sudada? Ay mi corazon, she would go to her grave never forgiving me."

"Ok, well, Mrs. Martinez, when Lila comes home next week, she will need a lot of pos-ta su-da-da," the Dr. tried to repeat slowly without mispronouncing the Colombian dish, as the three of them shared a laugh.

Everyone left Lila's room so she could get some much needed rest. She was exhausted from the visit and it wasn't long before she dozed off. As she slept, she dreamt about that horrible night when she was attacked in the garage. When she was awake, her memories came in rapid, spurts, matching her fear and her heartbeat. But for some reason, everything slowed down in her dream, like a slow motion movie.

He approached her as she walked towards her car.

"Hello Lila," he said, in that southern drawl.

"He-ll-oo Lii-ll-aa" he said again, even slower, in a more pronounced southern drawl. "I've missed you."

But this time Lila looked into his eyes and saw they were familiar. The same cold, dark eyes she had seen before at some time. She knew them but she couldn't figure out who they belonged to, but she definitely knew them and they terrified her.

"Please no," she said in her dream, right before he slammed her into the side of her car and she fell to the ground hitting her head. His shoes. She saw his shoes. They were black, heavy duty, rubber soled shoes. They looked like work boots, with some type of reinforced toe, and Velcro enclosure. Like stormtrooper boots, Lila thought in her dream. Why was he wearing stormtrooper boots, she wondered?

Next she was behind the parking garage and he was on top of her. This time, she saw his belt. It was a black belt but there was something on the front, some kind of adorned belt buckle. And he was breathing heavy and struggling to hold her down and get his belt unhooked. And he had a ring on one of his fingers. A small silver band. Was it a wedding ring? It looked like a wedding band. What was on the buckle? She could almost see it but then she woke up, sweaty and thrashing around in the sheets, trying to free herself from their entanglement just as she tried to break free from him that night.

She took a deep breath, trying to calm herself. "Just a dream, Lila," she told herself, "just a stupid dream."

At first she tried to shake the dream out of her head, but then realized some of what she dreamt might actually be memories of that night. As terrifying as it was, she tried to remember each part of her dream and quickly grabbed the notepad and pen that was left on the nightstand by her hospital bed. She wrote down everything she could remember just in case it made a difference or any of it was real. For the first time since that night, she was positive that she knew her attacker. In the morning, she would call the detective who left his card with her to tell him what she remembered.

CHAPTER THIRTEEN

He was exhilarated by his latest escapades and kept reliving his evening with Lila and the blondie who was walking down Howard Avenue when he happened to be driving by that night. He knew he was being a little reckless, but he had been so well behaved and careful for so long. Didn't he deserve a little fun? He was enjoying his thoughts when a news report came on about a young mother who was murdered and found in Carrollwood. The newscaster ended with an announcement about an upcoming neighborhood watch meeting scheduled to discuss what the frightened residents planned to do to increase the safety of the neighborhood. He was intrigued and knew he had to attend. Oh, how he hoped the young widower was there; he would enjoy giving his condolences in person and seeing the grief in his eyes.

The meeting was held at the Carrollwood Recreational Center, and most of the attendees were young, truly concerned parents and some retirees who had nothing better to do on their Thursday evening. He blended right in with the group, expressing his shock and dismay at the horror of it all.

"Oh my God, it's like right out of an Alafair Burke novel, I tell you. It's so scary," said the plump mother of two, who mentioned on at least three occasions to whoever would listen that she was also the president of the elementary school PTA and classroom mom. Although she wasn't his type, he would take pleasure in bashing her head in just to shut her up.

He left the neighborhood watch meeting, feeling anxious after all that suburbia, and made his way south to the local college bars. He planned on talking to a few girls and calling it a night when a pretty redhead in wedge heels and a tie-dyed, tank dress, no bra, caught his eye, walking by the bar on her way to the bathroom. When she walked back by him on her way back to her friends, she left a trail of patchouli oil in her wake that further interested him. For the next hour he watched her and eavesdropped on their conversations, learning her name was Chrissy and that she was "fucked up," in her own words, and wanted to go home. He watched as she said goodbye to her friends and left alone out the side door of the bar to meet her Uber driver. He quickly paid his tab, pulled his cap a little lower over his brow, and made his way through the crowd out the door to the parking lot. He knew it wouldn't be difficult to find her. And there she was, looking on her phone, waiting for her Uber driver in the designated spot. God, they made it so easy. He always parked next to the Uber lot so his car was just a few spots away.

He walked up to her, "Chrissy?" he asked while looking down at his phone and around the parking lot at the same time.

Smarter than some of the others, she backed up, checking out her surroundings, and looked at him suspiciously through her glossy eyes.

"I'm sorry, ma'am, I didn't mean to scare you," he said in the sweetest southern drawl. "You must not be Chrissy; I made a mistake. She's supposed to meet me out here," he said, pretending to look at the app on his phone, while continuing to talk and look around the parking lot, "I just ran inside to take a lea . . ., I mean, use the restroom, and I assumed you were my rider," he said as he gestured towards his nondescript, black Honda Civic just a few feet away.

"Sorry to have bothered you," he said, turning away from the confused, somewhat drunk redhead as he started to walk towards his car.

"Oh, wait, you're my Uber driver! You just surprised me, that's all. Yes, I'm Chrissy. Thank you, these heels are killing me -- I'm following you!"

He guided the pretty co-ed to his car, opened the passenger side door for her, and looked around one last time as she got into his car.

"What are you doing?" was all that escaped her lips before he grabbed the back of her head and slammed her face into the dashboard, briefly rendering her incapable of screaming from the shock and debilitating pain she was in.

Semi-dazed and bleeding from her nose and mouth from having her face smashed into the hard surface two feet in front of her, she attempted to catch the blood in the bottom half of her slip dress as she tried to regain her composure. As she started to realize what was happening, she let out a whimper that quickly escalated into a gargled scream. She reached for the door handle as her captor backhanded her, stunning her into submission. Her big, mascara-caked eyes expressed shock, confusion and sheer terror as she began to comprehend the gravity of her situation and she made another futile attempt to get out of the car. The initial fear he saw in his victim's eyes always caused an immediate erection in him and he reached down to shift his growing cock in his jeans.

"My dear Chrissy, buckle up, you're in for quite the ride tonight," he whispered as he fastened her seatbelt and zip-tied her wrists tightly in front of her. The smell of cheap whiskey and cigarettes wafted across her cheek as he reached across her, making her wretch, which triggered another debilitating backhand to her already bleeding face. She hadn't peed her pants since she was five years old but as the warmth enveloped her bottom underneath her, she knew exactly what had happened, further filling her with helplessness and shame. At that moment, she knew she would be raped but somehow had not comprehended that she would also be killed. She started to scream again, realizing her fate as he pulled a large, serrated knife out of

the side compartment of the driver's side door. One last blow to her head with the blunt handle and she was out. He was now able to drive away on the busy, South Tampa street without anyone noticing anything other than an obviously drunk girl passed out in the front seat of the car.

"Ahh, this evening *is* turning out to be delightful, Chrissy" he said with a chuckle and not a hint of the southern drawl his speech had been dripping with previously.

CHAPTER FOURTEEN

Hallie poured herself a glass of wine while she waited for David to get home. While she waited, she texted Katie, "don't be late, honey, 11:30, don't forget."

Katie responded with the thumbs up emoji and nothing more. She knew her daughter was aggravated with her but Hallie wouldn't be able to relax until Katie was home safely for the night. She sipped on the bold Cabernet, reminiscing about her and David's trip to California early in their marriage during one of Katie's spring breaks with Kevin. It was heavenly, visiting all of Hallie's favorite wineries from Sonoma County down through Napa Valley: Rodney Strong, Faust, Chateau Montelena, and finishing their trip with an unforgettable dinner at the French Laundry on their last night. When did they lose their love of travel and adventure, Hallie wondered? Oh yeah, she reminded herself, when life got hard and money got tight.

She sat on her couch, sipping her wine while perusing Facebook and Twitter, with Juno at her feet, when her phone rang. Bridget's name and picture popped up on her phone and she answered right away.

"Hey girl, what's up?" Hallie asked.

"Oh my damn, have you seen the news?" Bridget asked.

"No, not in the last few hours, what's going on?"

"The girl who was attacked in Ybor is alive, thank God. Maybe she wasn't attacked by that same sicko who got the other two girls but, c'mon, three women attacked, the same way? It has to be the same guy. They're not saying much and Jay won't tell me anything anymore because he knows I'll tell you," Bridget snickered. "They're saying on the news that she was grabbed in that parking lot near the movie theater, where she was beaten and stabbed. Somehow, she got away and survived."

"Oh my God, Bridget, that's so scary," Hallie said, before asking, "Who is she? Was she able to identify her attacker?"

"No, I don't think so. He was apparently wearing a ski mask. And, obviously, they didn't give her name on the news because this psycho is still out there."

"What does Jay think?" Hallie asked.

"Jay thinks I watch too much Criminal Minds," Bridget said, rolling her eyes as she exhaled her cigarette into the phone, "and so do you, apparently. But he still wants us to be careful."

"Let me know if you hear anything else, Bridg, I have to take Juno out," Hallie lied to get off the phone.

"Wait, one more thing; Jay heard from one of the detectives that they got DNA off that young lawyer from Carrollwood. Skin and some blood from underneath her nails. If he's in the system, they'll get him."

After hanging up with her friend, Hallie turned on the news to see what she could find out about the Ybor victim. Bridget was right, they weren't releasing her name, but they said she was a Hispanic female, twenty-one years old, born in Miami but had recently returned to the Tampa Bay area. As she was watching the news reports, David walked in.

"Hi, I'm home," he called as he came in the door.

"In here," Hallie replied, "watching the news."

"What's the latest in the world today?" David asked lightheartedly as he brought the groceries into the kitchen and grabbed a beer from the fridge.

"Apparently there was a third victim after all. Remember when I mentioned that last week when I ran into Jay? So anyway, she was attacked in Ybor about a week or two before that poor UT student was murdered. But she lived, thank God. They're saying her injuries are similar to the other two though," Hallie explained as she sipped her wine, never taking her eyes off the TV.

"Oh my God, that's awful. Who is she?" David asked, thinking back to the night he went to Ybor to meet Lila, trying to remember what night that was.

"They haven't said, other than she's a twenty-one-year-old Hispanic girl who recently returned to Tampa."

David choked on his beer, almost spitting it out.

"Are you okay?" Hallie asked, looking up at her husband, as he set his beer down on the coffee table and covered his mouth as he choked.

"Fine . . . went down the wrong tube," he said in between his coughing fit, trying to clear his lungs, and retreating to the kitchen under the guise of grabbing a paper towel so he could regain his composure.

"Yeah, it's crazy," Hallie said louder so David could hear her in the kitchen, "Bridget said she was attacked in the parking garage by Centro Ybor, which is where her car was found too. Can you believe it?" Hallie asked, still looking at the TV, as David returned to the room.

"That *is* crazy. I'm glad the girl survived," David said, trying to sound apathetic while his heart pounded inside his chest and he started to sweat, which thankfully went unnoticed by Hallie.

The newscaster went on to the next story about a senator from South Florida caught in a hotel room with a known drug dealer and a prostitute, prompting Hallie to get up to make dinner. David sat there stunned, wondering how long it would take before the police would be knocking on his door. He tried to calm himself down, telling himself that Lila couldn't be traced to him. He had never texted her and one phone call between them could be innocently explained. He didn't know what to do but he knew he had to calm down. If the police came, he would simply explain that Lila had called him because she was back in town, as a lot of his former students did, but that he had not seen her. He finished off his second beer as he sat watching the news without hearing a word the newscaster said until Hallie called him into dinner.

CHAPTER FIFTEEN

It had been almost a month since the news broke about the Ybor City victim. She still had not been identified in the news by name, but Hallie thought about her often. She wondered if the young girl would be the key to catching the guy who was responsible for so much pain and terror. She also wondered how she was doing knowing she had survived while two other women had not. Hallie remembered reading a book recently about survivor's guilt: the survivor at first is relieved and thankful that they survived some horrible incident or traumatic event but then, upon realizing that others had not been as fortunate, they feel guilty and question why they had been spared. They often feel unworthy and suffer depression and anxiety that can last for years if untreated. Rape victims often suffer a similar conflict, especially when they know their assailants. Through fear, intimidation, or self-preservation, they don't report their attacker; but then if or when they learn that their attacker has raped another or even the belief that they will attack again, they feel responsible and guilty for his actions. Hallie understood this very well.

When Hallie was a young lawyer, after she and her first husband, Kevin Verona, had been married for about a year, she had to attend all types of networking events required by her firm. One of them was the Law & Liberty Dinner, an annual fundraising event for the Hillsborough County Bar Foundation., which was held at the Hyatt Hotel in downtown Tampa. Hallie's firm had sponsored a table at which the honor of her presence was "requested" by the managing partner. The speaker was usually someone famous, such as an author or renowned jurist, who was interesting enough to draw the hundreds of lawyers to the event at $500 a plate. As with most functions attended by lawyers, there was always a cocktail hour with a cash bar (after you used up your two allotted drink tickets) followed by free-flowing, albeit shitty, red and white wine at each table. Hallie was the cute, young associate at her firm's table, which meant she never had to buy herself a drink and never had an empty glass. At the time, Kevin was with the state attorney's office and had a trial starting early the next morning, so he did not go with her. By the time the speaker started, Hallie was feeling unusually lightheaded and knew she had to slow down. She remembered thinking it was strange that she got buzzed so quickly but figured she could easily counteract the alcohol effects by drinking water and eating dinner. Unfortunately, that didn't work, because the last thing she remembered was dessert being served and hearing everyone clapping as the speaker finished their presentation.

She woke up the next morning with a pounding headache, beyond any headache she had ever felt in her life, with her mouth extremely dry and tasting metallic. She was dizzy and disoriented and felt like she was going to be sick. She sat up, trying to focus and clear the fogginess out of her head, while looking around at her surroundings. A sliver of light emanating from the bathroom lit up the dark room enough for Hallie to see her black suit draped haphazardly over the chair in the corner and her black pumps on the floor beneath the chair. As she tried to steady herself and suppress the nausea that was rising within her, she realized she was naked and in a bed that was not her own. She looked over at the naked, hairy-backed man sleeping next to her and snoring loudly, while she came to the horrifying realization that the bald head belonged to the managing partner of her firm, William Stephens. She ran to the bathroom and instantly threw up.

Hallie was no stranger to drinking and could go shot for shot with the best of them, thanks to her large, Irish family upbringing. It was simply impossible that two or three glasses of wine would have rendered her debilitated much less in full blackout mode. She had no recollection of the evening and knew, without a doubt, that she had been drugged. If she went to the police or reported the incident to anyone at the firm, would they even believe her? Would Kevin believe her? She couldn't remember anything past dessert, no matter how hard she tried and her head wouldn't stop pounding. There would be plenty of witnesses to confirm she had been drinking, but what else did she do? She was blonde and flirtatious by nature, even though she didn't mean anything by it, and that would be used against her too. And William H. Stephens, the very, well-respected managing partner of one of the oldest and most prestigious firms in town, would be seen as the victim to this young, predatory associate trying to tarnish his good name to advance her career, no doubt. She feared that accusing him would not only jeopardize her advancement at her current firm but at most other firms in town. One simply did not accuse an attorney of his caliber and reputation of rape, especially when she could not remember anything about the evening past her key lime pie, including how she ended up naked in his hotel-room bed. Her legal career would be over before it even began.

But she knew. As soon as she felt the bruises on the inside of her upper thighs and saw the bite marks and bruises already appearing on her nipples in the reflection of the bathroom mirror, she knew. As soon as she felt the soreness and burning in her raw vagina as she struggled to pee without crying, she knew. And as soon as she realized the blood pouring into the toilet was actually coming from her brutalized rectum, she knew. Hallie knew exactly what had happened to her but she also knew there was a good chance that no one would believe her. She washed her face with cold water, rinsed her mouth with the hotel mouthwash sample, and quietly got dressed. Even if anyone believed her, she knew it would ruin her marriage and her legal career, not necessarily in that order. She slipped out of the dark room filled with shame, fear, and rage, but mostly shame. She looked at the time on her phone, 5:07 a.m., desperately hoping Kevin wasn't awake yet, and quickly typed out a text to him while she waited for the elevator.

"Hey, sorry I forgot to text last night. I had a little too much wine so I crashed at Paige's. Good luck in court today!"

She hoped that Kevin was too wrapped up in his trial to question her or to be mad that she hadn't come home. And then she drove straight to Paige's, calling her on the way.

Through sobs, she told Paige everything that she could remember, but mostly about what she discovered when she woke up and examined herself. Paige listened calmly, trying to suppress her own tears and rage as Hallie told her story, and tried to reassure her friend that it was not her fault. She also tried to convince her to go to the police or the hospital, but finally relented after realizing her efforts were futile. As Hallie showered, Paige compiled a set of clean clothes for Hallie: her favorite, gray sweatpants, a white tank top, her Penn State sweatshirt, and even a pair of her underwear. She placed the folded clothes on her bed and went to the kitchen to make Hallie a hot cup of tea.

Paige Rhodes was an associate in the commercial litigation department of their firm. Hallie and Paige were in the same summer associate group, the only two female associates, instantly becoming fast friends. Paige was funny and brilliant. She was also beautiful, with flawless, sepia-toned skin, high cheekbones, and black hair she wore in long ringlets. Her eyes were a deep, rich brown with flecks of gold and honey, like a warm cup of hot chocolate with drizzles of caramel swirled in. When she looked at you, you felt her warmth and kindness, unless you were opposing counsel, in which case you might feel as if her eyes pierced your soul.

Hallie got dressed in the comfy clothes provided by her friend and wrapped her wet hair up in a towel. She gathered her discarded clothes into a pile and asked Paige for a plastic bag to put them in. She should have just thrown them out then as she was never going to be able to wear them again. She sat on one end of the couch, with her legs criss-crossed, holding the warm cup of tea with both hands, while Paige sat on the opposite end, silently drinking a cup of coffee.

"I'm so sorry I ruined your morning. I couldn't go home and I didn't know where else to go," Hallie whispered, looking down into her tea, having trouble finding her voice.

"Please, don't apologize. You didn't ruin anything. I am *so* sorry this happened to you, Hallie. You are welcome to stay here as long as you want. And if you need me to, I'll stay here with you."

"No, it's okay, thank you. I know you need to get into the office. I'm just going to wait until I know Kevin has left for work and then I'll go home. He normally leaves around 8:30."

They sat in silence for a few more minutes until Paige retreated to her bedroom to get ready for work, leaving Hallie in her living room with her tea and self-blame. When she came out of her bedroom, ready to leave for the office, Hallie was already gone, having left behind a note scribbled on the legal yellow pad on her kitchen table: "thank you, my dear friend. XOXO."

Hallie called in sick for the next few days, trying to overcome her feelings of shame, despair, and overwhelming helplessness, while she curled herself up in a blanket on her Rooms-to-Go sectional couch and binge watched Nora Ephron movies. Kevin was in full blown trial mode so he not only didn't question her but kept his distance when Hallie told him she had come down with the flu. As he said, he couldn't afford to catch anything with the trial going on. Through texting with Paige all week, she was relieved to learn that no one was talking about her at all or seemed to have noticed that she left the dinner with the managing partner or her intoxicated state. As far as what Paige told her, it seemed like everyone believed she had the flu.

A month later, when Hallie's period was late, she should have been surprised but, of course, she wasn't. She remembered waking up on a Saturday morning, feeling nauseous, thinking maybe she had drunk more wine than she remembered the night before. Yet it felt different. And she didn't have a headache. moment she peed on that stick and saw the pink plus sign, she knew she was never going to mention that night to another living soul. And in the seventeen years since then, for the most part, she never had.

CHAPTER SIXTEEN

"Don't forget, I'm going to Bridget's this afternoon, and I won't be home until late tonight. Also, Katie is at Kevin's this weekend. I need you to take Juno out before you go to your card game tonight," Hallie said to David from the bathroom sink as she brushed her long blonde hair up into a ponytail and finished putting her makeup on.

"I know; you've only told me about a thousand times," David responded, annoyed.

"Well, the last time I needed you to take care of Juno, I only told you once and you forgot and the poor dog shit all over my office."

"Are you going to bring that up forever? Jesus, Hallie, let it go."

"Just make sure you take Juno out and feed her before you go to your game tonight, ok?"

"Yes, I got it," he huffed as he left the room and walked loudly down the stairs.

Hallie put on one of her many black tank tops and a fresh pair of jeans. She looked at herself in her full length mirror, noticing every flaw in her body, every wrinkle in her face, and reminded herself that women were more critical of themselves than anyone else was of them. She zipped up her black ankle boots and spritzed herself with her Armani Code before leaving the bedroom.

Hallie drove the six miles from Hyde Park to Bridget and Jay's house in Seminole Heights, stopping at Bodega's to pick up Cuban sandwiches for the three of them. Whenever Hallie was in Seminole Heights, she always had to stop at Bodega's for their to-die-for Cuban sandwich, which was made with lechon (slow roasted mojo pork), ham, swiss cheese, pickles, and mustard, and then hot pressed between two buttered pieces of Cuban bread baked fresh every day from the Alessi Bakery. Her mouth would water as soon as she started to unwrap the plain, brown paper packaging encasing the warm, flat, heavy sandwich. As she took the first bite, the crunchy outside of the warm, buttery Cuban bread would contrast with the savory, delicate roasted pork inside, cheese, and soft pickles that would all melt in her mouth, while the mojo juice would drip down her hand. She would be lying if she said she didn't lick it off when she was alone. Miami had nothing on Tampa's Cuban sandwiches.

As Hallie pulled up to the quaint bungalow, Bridget was sitting on her front porch smoking a cigarette, with a bottle of Windex by her side.

"What's the Windex for?" Hallie asked, as she climbed the wide green steps of the porch, carrying the cherished Bodega's bag in one hand and a bottle of Rodney Strong in the other.

"The mosquitos," Bridget answered, "smells better than bug-spray and gets the job done. You know my mother, Mary, swore by the Windex. There isn't anything you can't use it for," Bridget laughed recalling the memory as she exhaled the last puff of her cigarette while putting the butt out in the sand bucket she kept next to her chair.

They walked into the house and were instantly greeted by Bridget's American Pitbull rescue, Spicoli, and German Shepherd, Sam. Sam was a former, police K-9 but retired at age five when he was shot in the line of duty. After he recovered, Jay was able to adopt him and bring him home where he and Spicoli have been inseparable buddies ever since. At 80 and 120 pounds, respectively, Hallie always teased Bridget that she was living in the safest house in town.

"So, anymore weird emails?" Bridget asked, as they sat down at the table, unwrapping their Cubans.

"Actually, yes, I got one more last night. I knew I was coming over today so I figured I would show it to you both in person," Hallie explained as she retrieved her cell phone, pulling up her email to read it to them.

From: nwc822@gmail.com
Sent: Friday, September 20, 2019 5:23 p.m.
To: HMiller@Millerlaw.com
Subject: We really need to talk

Don't ignore me. I promise this is not a joke. We need to talk. It's important. I know what happened to you. It happened to me too. Maybe if you had done the right thing, it wouldn't have happened to me. Email me back so we can talk or should I just tell your daughter how you failed the women who came after you?

"What are they talking about, Hallie? What happened to you?" Jay asked.

"I have no idea what they're talking about," Hallie lied.

"Oh my God, yes you do," Bridget said, matter of factly, "girl, if you don't think I can tell when you're lying after forty years, you don't know me at all."

"Look, Hallie, if this is some kind of freak or someone dangerous, you need to tell me what you know if you want me to help. I can't help you if you're holding something back," Jay said gently.

"Hallie, spill it. What happened to you that they know and we don't?" Bridget prodded.

Hallie refilled her wine glass, trying to figure out how much to tell her lifelong friend and her policeman husband. The only people she had ever told about what happened to her were her friend, Paige, who she ran to on the morning after, and her sister, Trisha, who knew her better than anyone and had dragged it out of her one drunken night at her place. The only way the email sender could know about that night is if Paige or Trisha had told someone, which wasn't out of the realm of possibilities, she thought.

Hallie took another sip of her wine and began, "This happened over seventeen years ago and I decided I would not give this guy the power to alter my life. I didn't tell you, Bridget, because I didn't want to talk about it with anyone and I didn't want to be a victim. But I did tell two people, so it's possible one of them told someone and that is who is emailing me now," Hallie explained, taking another sip of her wine.

"Who did you tell?" Bridget asked, trying to hide the hurt in her voice.

"Bridget, you're my ride or die, but I didn't tell you specifically because I knew you would have killed the guy yourself. But I'm getting ahead of myself; let me start at the beginning," Hallie said, and then proceeded to tell them all the details about that night that she remembered, including a detailed account of her injuries. Jay asked her a few questions as she told her story, but Bridget stayed silent. The only thing she didn't tell them was who her assailant was, leaving it at "just another lawyer" in her firm. She explained how she woke up sick, bleeding and bruised in the guy's hotel room, and fled to the closest place she knew, her friend, Paige's apartment downtown.

"That's why Paige knows because I couldn't go home in the shape I was in and I also couldn't drive far with the remnants of whatever he gave me still in my system.

Paige was a good friend and lived right downtown," Hallie explained.

"That mother fucker, tell me his fucking name, I'll kill him right now," Bridget said, her voice breaking as she clenched her fist and slammed it onto the table.

"And this is exactly why I have never told you," Hallie said softly, while reaching over and putting her hand over her friend's clenched fist.

"Why didn't you report it?" Jay asked.

"Because you don't understand who this guy is and how this legal community works. It's still a good ol' boys network out there and I was a second year associate. I worked too hard in law school to piss it all away for one unfortunate night," Hallie said, hearing the ridiculousness of her words. "At least that's what I thought would happen at the time. He was very powerful. Actually, still is."

"Does David know?" Jay asked.

"No, I never told him. I promised myself after I recovered, at least from the physical wounds, that I would never tell another person about that night. And as I said, I mostly kept that promise."

"Who the fuck is he, Hallie?" Bridget pleaded.

"For now, it's not important. What we need to figure out is if this person sending the emails actually knows what happened to me and why they're sending the emails. Jay, can you help me?"

They finished their Cubans and took their wine glasses with them out to the back porch. Jay lit the citronella candles and torches as Bridget and Hallie settled into the wicker chairs on the deck.

"I can't believe you never told me," Bridget said softly.

"I just couldn't. I had to move past it and put it behind me. If I told you back then, it would have been too real. And too painful."

"Well, you're right that I would have killed the mother fucker, so maybe it was good that you didn't tell me."

Jay joined them on the deck and they discussed various strategies for dealing with the email sender before finally agreeing on a plan. Hallie would email the person back, agreeing to speak to the person but only over the phone and on a specific date and time. At the scheduled time, Hallie would make the call from Bridget and Jay's house so they could listen in to the call. If the person threatened Hallie in any way or tried to blackmail her, Jay would be there as a witness and then could enlist the help of the police department to investigate further.

After formulating the plan and discussing all the possible outcomes they could think of, the trio went back into the house to watch a movie. Bridget washed the now empty wine glasses and put them upside down on the dish towel to dry. Jay put on a movie they had all seen a dozen times and they half listened, half watched the movie while continuing to chat about who the email sender might be and what they might be trying to accomplish. By the time the movie ended, Hallie was exhausted and drove the fifteen minutes home on autopilot.

When she arrived home and walked into her house, Juno greeted her, anxious to go out. Her empty dinner bowl was on the floor, so David had fed her, which means he also remembered to let her out. But she did seem more anxious than usual. Hallie walked to her back door to let Juno out and was surprised to find it unlocked, which unsettled her a little bit. The house was empty with both David and Katie out, with the kitchen light the only light left on. Before the recent incidents, she would have never given it a second thought. After all, they lived in a very safe, upper middleclass neighborhood. Before a few weeks ago, an unlocked door would not have even registered with Hallie. But things were different now. Juno ran outside, took a quick pee and came back in right away. She ran instantly to the front door and then into Hallie's office, sniffing around and not acting like herself.

"What's the matter, girl? What's going on," Hallie asked, while looking around her house, feeling more than a little spooked.

She took out her phone and texted David, "hey babe, when are you coming home? I'm a little nervous."

After fifteen minutes, he still hadn't responded.

"Hello????" she texted again, beyond annoyed.

"What's up? I'm playing cards!"

"Well, you left the fucking back door unlocked and Juno is acting funny so. . ."

"OMG Hallie, so dramatic as usual. I'll be home soon, we're on our last hand."

"Have you forgotten that a woman's dead and mutilated body was literally dumped thirty feet from our back door? I'm not being dramatic, David, just don't feel like getting murdered tonight!" Hallie typed angrily in response, to which David responded with the thumbs up emoji.

Hallie was so aggravated. If he had just locked the fucking door, she wouldn't be so nervous. But he hadn't. And she was. And she didn't want to go upstairs. She poured herself a glass of wine to settle her nerves and sat down in the living room. She put the TV on and quickly turned off Criminal Minds that automatically came up as the last thing she was watching. She was too nervous for that show tonight, she admitted. She scrolled down the guide until she got to the Food Network and found Chopped. That she could watch, enjoying the chefs' abilities to take seemingly unrelated ingredients and turn them into gourmet meals. Juno finally settled down at her feet, more relaxed then when she had first gotten home.

As she watched, she grabbed her I-pad sitting on the coffee table in front of her. She started searching for anything she could find about Lauren White and Naomi Banks. There wasn't much on Lauren White, other than her Instagram page, which had been filled with heart-wrenching comments posted underneath the last picture she had posted before she was murdered, and her team picture still on the UT volleyball team website. Hallie scrolled through the comments on the Instagram picture, most of which started with "ILYSM, RIP beautiful" or some variation. Hallie quickly figured out "ILYSM" stood for "I love you so much."

Hallie was able to find more on Naomi Banks, including her Facebook page, which was not set on private. Like Lauren's Instagram page, the outpouring of love and grief was evident in the posts to Naomi's page from friends, family, and co-workers. As she continued to scour through Naomi's Facebook page, she saw that they had eleven mutual friends, including her old friend, Paige Rhodes. She also learned that Naomi Banks was a staff attorney in the criminal division of the Thirteenth Judicial Circuit Court of Hillsborough County, where, coincidentally, one Judge William H. Stephens presided.

CHAPTER SEVENTEEN

Katie was looking forward to her weekend with her father for the first time in a long time. She was even starting to tolerate her stepmother, Jodi's, nauseating attempts to befriend her. Her father had started dating Jodi, who was twenty years younger than him, after settling her sexual harassment case against her former employer, the owner of a popular massage franchise, obtaining a six figure settlement for her. Apparently, the owner wanted more than a massage from Jodi in exchange for a better commission rate, which unfortunately for the owner had been caught on his own security tapes. Since he had installed the security tapes himself, he couldn't argue that he was recorded without his consent. Within a year, they were married, and so began Jodi's constant efforts of seeking Katie's approval and friendship. Katie didn't think Jodi was awful, but it bothered her that she was closer to her stepmom's age than her father was. But over the last year, she found that Jodi got on her nerves less and less and she was actually beginning to enjoy her company, not that she would ever admit to that.

For her upcoming graduation, her father had surprised her with a trip to Europe that they would take during the summer before Katie headed off for college. The three of them had decided that they would visit Ireland, Scotland, and Italy. Kevin was of Irish and Italian descent and his ex-wife, Hallie, was mostly Irish, making Katie mostly Irish and a little Italian. Jodi, on the other hand, was of Irish and Scottish descent. Since the trip had been announced, every time Katie would visit her father and Jodi, they would plan their itinerary, researching hotels, bed and breakfast inns, restaurants, and local must-sees. They charted everything out, with Jodi keeping track of it on her laptop, adding to it as they found more places they all agreed they wanted to visit or see.

Sitting at dinner on Saturday night, they were excitedly discussing their trip, with Kevin talking about the places in Italy and Ireland where he thought his great grandparents were from.

"Hey, Dad, we should do those DNA testing kits, like Ancestry.com or 23andMe before we go. Maybe we can track down distant relatives who still live over there and we could meet them; wouldn't that be wild?" Katie asked.

"Oh yeah, I heard about those," Jodi joined in, "my girlfriend, Jen, and her family did it before they went to England last year. They ended up signing up for an organized genealogy tour based on their DNA results, which included a genealogist-tour guide who took them to places where their ancestors had once lived. Not just the towns but the specific houses they had once lived in. She said it was a blast."

"Oh my God, Dad, we should do that! Can we do that?" Katie pleaded, excitedly.

"I don't know, Katie. I don't know how I feel about those companies having all of our private information. Information that we voluntarily submit, I might add, which can then be used for God knows what or sold to the highest bidder. That's how they caught the Golden State Killer last year, by the way. The detectives on that case -- unconstitutionally, in my opinion -- uploaded the DNA retrieved from one of the crime scenes into one of those databases and they found him by tracing his family tree until they eventually got to him, even though he had never voluntarily uploaded his own DNA onto the site."

"How is that any different from matching DNA collected from a crime scene against the FBI database of DNA collected from criminal defendants, Kevin? They certainly don't voluntarily give up their DNA either," Jodi offered.

"Well, I guess if you are in the criminal FBI database, you've already committed some type of crime to be in there, which is different than innocent consumers uploading their own DNA into a non-law enforcement site so they can learn about their ancestry, genetics, and possible family members, which is then used by law enforcement in ways unintended by the consumer. I don't know, as a lawyer, it just seems different and that it may violate someone's Fourth Amendment rights from illegal searches and seizures."

Katie rolled her eyes, "way to suck the fun out of this and go all lawyerly on us, Dad."

Jodi laughed and said, "I'm with Katie on this one. I think we should do it and look into one of those genealogy tours, at least in Ireland where we all three might have ancestors. C'mon, Kevin, it will be fun."

"Oh my God, you two. You know I can't win when you both gang up on me," Kevin laughed, "but don't blame me when you both find out you're related to Jack the Ripper."

"Wasn't he from England?" Jodi replied, enjoying the light sparring with her litigator husband.

"So we can order the kits?" Katie asked, looking to Jodi for support.

"Fine, order the kits. I know I'm going to end up regretting this," Kevin said, unable to resist his daughter's excitement.

Since he and Hallie had divorced, Kevin felt he had a good relationship with Katie until Jodi came into the picture. He knew, from conversations with Hallie, that she didn't accept David right away either, but she was definitely more guarded and unwilling to allow Jodi into their life due to the father-daughter dynamics. It was different with her mother, who she wanted to see happy. But with a father, the daughter, especially an only child, felt she might be replaced by the new woman in her father's life. It was nice to finally see Jodi and Katie aligning together against him for a change and he wasn't going to do anything to ruin that mood, especially seeing the happiness in Jodi's eyes throughout dinner.

Jodi had been so elated at the turn in her relationship with Katie that she surprised Kevin when he came out of the bathroom as they were getting ready for bed. Instead of coming out to see his wife turning down the bed, in her normal tank top and white socks, his wife was standing there in a black lace thong, a pair of 4-inch, red stilettos, and nothing else. Kevin sat on the bed watching his gorgeous wife as she went around the room, lighting candles and changing the playlist on her Bose to the one she had created just for a night like this, playfully titled "All About Me." When the first song came on, 107 Degrees from the Lincoln Lawyer soundtrack, his wife dropped to her knees in front of him and started to stroke him. She took him in her mouth while never taking her eyes off of him and he knew it was going to be a long and glorious night.

The next morning, Jodi got up early, ordered the kits from 23andMe, and went into the kitchen to make her delicious, homemade French toast. As she made breakfast, she hummed to herself along to her Spotify playlist emitting from the nearby Bose player, thinking about how amazing their trip was going to be.

"Good morning, Katie," Jodi said cheerfully, "I ordered the kits so we can do them next time you come over."

"Great, thanks, Jodi," Katie responded, while engrossed with whatever was on her phone.

"Another cup of coffee, honey? You seem a little tired this morning," Jodi teased while winking at her husband and setting a fresh cup of coffee down in front of him.

"I couldn't sleep last night for some reason," he playfully returned, "maybe it was all the excitement of talking about our trip," he grinned, reveling in his thoughts of their last night's sexcapades.

Katie, who never looked up from her phone, was oblivious to their repartee. After breakfast, Katie announced she had to get home to finish some homework before the week began, hugging both Kevin and, in an unprecedented show of affection, Jodi, before walking out the door. He was pretty sure that the unsolicited hug to his wife was going to get him more of what he had enjoyed last night. This weekend couldn't have turned out better, he thought to himself.

CHAPTER EIGHTEEN

After closing the garage door behind them, he carried Chrissy's semi-unconscious body from the passenger seat of his car into his house, past the workbenches and countertops, cluttered with tools, glassware, and various flammable substances. She was starting to moan as he dropped her onto the couch already covered with a plastic drop cloth. He secured her wrists behind and over her head to the metal hook he had anchored underneath the heavy, wooden table next to the couch -- truly one of his best ideas yet. He should have done that years ago; then some of his previous dates wouldn't have been able to run away from him. Confident that this one wasn't going anywhere, he went into the kitchen and came back with a cool, wet cloth and, gently -- as if he wasn't the one who had inflicted the lethal blows -- wiped the blood off of her face and neck. Before returning to the kitchen to pour himself a whiskey, he placed the cool cloth on her forehead, and kissed her cheek, hoping she would be awake when he came back.

She started to cry as she came to, trying to figure out where she was while remembering the terrifying moments in the car before she was brought here. She could hear her captor in the room behind her, presumably the kitchen from the sound of the ice clinking into a glass from an automatic icemaker and the sound of water pouring into a steel sink as a faucet was turned on and off. She knew she would only have a few minutes before he came back into the room so she looked around, trying to memorize her surroundings in case she was able to break free from him and escape.

She looked to her right and could see a sliding glass door but it only led to blackness outside. Unconscious when they arrived, she didn't know if the backyard was fenced in or if the house was in the middle of nowhere. She could only pray that there were neighbors nearby. She looked to her left and could see a dark hallway with at least one closed door at the beginning of the hallway. She had no idea where the hallway led but also did not want to find out, figuring back through the kitchen was probably a more likely way out. In front of her was a wall with a big screen tv mounted to it and a video camera on a tripod in the corner, facing the couch. As she looked around, she could see the living room area was cluttered, with clothes and various boxes scattered throughout. In one corner was a bookshelf, stacked from top to bottom with books on every subject imaginable. She couldn't read the titles but they were obviously textbooks or how-to books, dusty from years of nonuse. There was also a table in the small room, stacked with piles of paper, notebooks, and binders. There were papers everywhere, including the floor and on the nearby chairs, despite the apparent attempt to stack them into piles. She was going to try to remember everything she could about the room in case she survived. It was at that moment that she realized the couch she was on, with her wrists secured somewhere over her head, was covered with a plastic tarp, and she started to scream.

CHAPTER NINETEEN

Hallie sat at her desk, trying to focus on her work. She had so much to do but she couldn't stop thinking about Naomi Banks and the fact that she was a staff attorney in the same court division as Judge Stephens. She hadn't talked to Paige in a few weeks, but it was time to reach out to her old friend. She tapped out a quick email to her:

From: HMiller@MillerLaw.com
Sent: Saturday, October 5, 2019 8:47 a.m.
To: PRhodes@MSLaw.com
Subject: Lunch?

Hey Paige,
Long time no talk! Have time for lunch soon? Would love to get together to catch up. Send me some dates! Miss you!

Hallie XOXO

Paige emailed her back within the hour and they made plans to meet for lunch the following Tuesday at Ulele in Tampa Heights right next to downtown on the

Hillsborough River. Paige said she would have her assistant make a reservation for 11:45 so they could beat the crowd. With the temperatures finally starting to cool off, the tables outside filled up very quickly.

Next, she decided to respond to the mystery emailer just as she, Bridget and Jay had agreed on.

From: HMiller@Millerlaw.com
Sent: Saturday, October 5, 2019 9:42 a.m.
To: nwc822@gmail.com
Subject: Re: We really need to talk

Send me a phone number and I will call you next Saturday at 4:30 p.m. That is all I am willing to do.

Over the next few days, Hallie caught up on work, finally focused out of necessity, and spent the weekend doing projects around the house, including cleaning out her office by scanning and purging old files. The emailer never responded to her email so now they thought maybe the emails were some kind of a prank after all. Hallie hoped that was the case so she could stop feeling so jittery and thinking about the past. She still hadn't told David about the emails because she wasn't ready to tell him about what had happened to her all those years ago. But, just in case it wasn't a prank, she also needed to know if her sister or Paige had ever told anyone about that night.

By Tuesday, the sweltering, stagnant Florida heat had finally given way to some cooler October air coming in from the north. During the day it would warm up to the seventies, but without the humidity, while at night it would drop down into the mid-sixties. This was Hallie's favorite time of the year, and she wasn't alone. Driving through Hyde Park Village on her way to meet Paige, the sidewalks and outdoor tables were crowded with young moms out with their toddlers, meeting up with other young moms, relieved to be out of the house; professionals of all ages grabbing lunch outside, thankful to be out of their offices for a change; and pretty college students thrilled to be wearing their boots or thigh-high knee socks with their Mary Jane Doc Martens for the first time of the season. Hallie was glad they had thought to make reservations at Ulele last week or they would have to wait forever for a table.

She valeted her BMW and walked down the steps towards the entrance of the restaurant while scanning the outside tables to see if Paige had beaten her there. She wasn't even in the door when the fragrant aromas hit her, automatically causing her mouth to water and her stomach to growl. It had to be the charbroiled oysters she never could resist, or maybe the house seafood paella, a Gonzmart family recipe passed down for generations. She realized she was starving.

She walked up to the hostess stand and was about to give her name when she saw Paige sitting on the bench, looking down at her phone, probably reading emails. As she approached the bench, Paige looked up and a big smile instantly appeared.

"Hallie, look at you! All that running has you looking good, girl!" she said, as she stood up and hugged her friend.

"Aw, thank you, Paige. You look stunning as usual," Hallie replied, admiring Paige's cute outfit and signature four inch heels.

They signaled to the hostess that they were ready, and the hostess guided them to a nice table in the shade towards the back edge of the outside seating. They each ordered a glass of wine, chardonnay for Paige, cabernet for Hallie, and spent the next forty-five minutes catching each other up on their families, love lives, and careers.

"So, there is another reason why I wanted to get together with you, Paige," Hallie started.

"I thought there might be," Paige responded. "Does it have anything to do with a certain criminal judge in town?"

"Oh my God, how did you know I wanted to talk to you about him?"

"Well, he's running for re-election and I'm the chair of the campaign committee for his opponent, Sarah Wilt. I know you want him off the bench, for obvious reasons, so I figured you wanted to talk about the campaign."

"Oh, yeah, I saw that. I hope she kicks his ass. I know Sarah. She's a great attorney and will make a great judge. But that's not exactly it," Hallie said.

"Okay, then do tell. Have you finally decided to tell the world about what that creep did to you?"

"No, but it is related to that. Are we okay on time?" Hallie asked, looking down at her phone to check the time.

"I knew we would be drinking wine so I marked myself out for the rest of the day. I have all the time in the world for you, my friend," Paige responded, settling back into her chair and lifting her wine glass to her lips.

Hallie took a sip from her glass too, and then began, "so, I have to ask you, did you ever tell anyone what he did to me?"

"Of course not, Hallie," Paige answered a little too quickly.

"I need you to think, Paige, think back. Anyone at all? Maybe you swore them to secrecy, but you told someone, at some point?" Hallie pleaded.

"What's going on, Hallie? What's this about?" Paige asked, the concern evident in her warm brown eyes.

Hallie told her about the strange emails she received and the plan she devised with Jay and Bridget, including how the emailer hadn't responded to her last email yet.

"Yeah, that sounds a little creepy, Hallie. But it also sounds like it could be a joke. It's so vague, "*I know something. I know what you didn't do. I know what happened to you,*" Paige mocked, making air-quotes with her fingers as she spoke.

"I know, and I agree, but ever since that young college student turned up dead practically in my front yard, I'm just super edgy lately."

"Whoa, wait, that was *your* yard?" Paige questioned.

"Well, technically, she was found in my neighbor's yard, but I was the one who called it in. I, um, well, I smelled her," Hallie said, lowering her voice as she looked around to make sure the older ladies at the next table, sipping on their wine spritzers, couldn't hear her.

"Holy shit, Hallie, that's crazy. No wonder these emails are freaking you out. You don't think they have anything to do with the dead college student, do you?"

"No, not at all. It's just strange timing. And then, that other woman was found. Naomi Banks; she was a friend of yours, wasn't she?" Hallie inquired gently.

"Yes, poor Naomi. I didn't know her that well but we were briefly on a diversity committee for the Hillsborough County Bar Association together. She was really sweet and smart, too. I can't believe she was murdered. In Carrollwood of all places, too. I haven't been able to watch or read anything about what happened because all I can think of is her sweet, little boy. It's just too heartbreaking. They haven't identified a suspect yet, have they?" Paige asked as she motioned for the waiter with her empty wine glass for another glass.

"No, not yet. Did you know she was a staff attorney in the criminal division? You know, the same division where Judge Stephens presides." Hallie said.

"Oh my God, Hallie, you don't think . . .?" she asked, without finishing her sentence.

"I don't know what I think anymore, but all I know is that he is a fucking rapist and she worked there and now she's dead. So it's just so weird; between these poor women ending up murdered, one found in my neighbor's yard, another woman attacked in Ybor, and then I start getting strange emails, I am just a little edgy. And I'm sure none of this stuff is related but my mind is trying to make sense of it all."

"Well, I don't know if it will help you at all, but I actually did tell someone a few years ago about what happened to you, and I'm really sorry for that. I was dating an attorney in the State Attorney's office at the time – do you remember Michael Freeman? – well, anyway, a case came across his desk that sounded exactly like what happened to you, and he was telling me about it one night. But the guy they arrested and charged for the rape kept professing his innocence and lo and behold, the DNA didn't match so they had to drop the charges."

"Okay, but what does this have to do with me and why did you tell him?"

"Right, I'm getting to that. So this young woman, about 27, 28 years old, goes to this event. I can't remember which event it was, but it was a networking event with a lot of professionals: lawyers, CPAs, small business owners. Anyway, she's networking, has a glass or two of wine, and then that's the last thing she remembers before waking up in an empty hotel room on the second floor of the hotel where the event was held, naked, and with almost identical injuries to what you described to me that morning you came to my apartment. Her nipple was practically bit off and she was brutally sodomized and raped. Her injuries and the circumstances were so similar to what you had described to me that I instantly thought of him," Paige explained.

Paige continued after taking another sip of her wine, "security cameras showed her walking out of the event room, past the elevators and then nothing else. She never walked past the next set of security cameras that were in the lobby on the way out to the parking lot. Then the cameras pick up this guy walking in the same direction about a minute behind her and he's not picked up on the lobby security cameras either. So they figured he grabbed her and pulled her into a stairwell, dragging her up into the room on the second floor where she ultimately woke up. The hotel manager identified him as one of the A/C repair guys who was hired to replace the thermostats in many of the vacant rooms of the hotel, which included the room where the woman woke up. After learning he had priors for stalking and domestic violence, they were sure he was their guy. He swore he went out a side door to the back parking lot where his truck was parked and that's why he didn't go through the lobby. When the DNA came back clearing him completely and his Sunpass transponder account showed him on the Veterans Expressway about fifteen minutes after the time stamp on the security camera from the hotel, he was cleared. So, when Michael told me that, I asked him if the event had a list of attendees because what he described was exactly the same as what happened years before to someone who I knew. And that's when I told him about what our not so honorable Judge Stephens did to you. I wanted him to take another look at the attendee list to see if he was on there."

"Oh my God, was he on the list?" Hallie asked.

"No, he wasn't on the list, which is the only reason I was able to convince Michael to leave you alone and your name out of it. I explained that you never went to the police and it would come down to a he said-she said, which is why you didn't file charges against him in the first place. Also there seemed to be no way to connect that case to your case and Michael knew it. But Hallie, he believed you. After my insistence, Michael finally let it go and he swore to me he would never tell anyone. I'm really sorry, Hallie; I just thought it was important at the time."

"I understand, Paige. I would have done the same thing, I'm sure," Hallie reassured her friend. "Did they ever catch the guy who raped that woman? The one at the event? You said they had his DNA."

"Hmmm, I don't know. They hadn't by the time Michael and I broke up a few months later and I never heard anything about that case again. We didn't break up on bad terms and we're actually both on Sarah's election campaign committee. Want me to ask him?"

"Yes, I'm just curious. Let me know if they ever found the guy."

"Ok, definitely, I will. I'm supposed to have drinks with him Thursday night, so I'll ask him."

CHAPTER TWENTY

Jodi was excited when the results from their 23andMe tests came in the mail. She was dying to open them but they had all agreed they would open them together when Katie came for dinner on Thursday night. To keep herself busy when Thursday arrived, Jodi decided to make a big pot of sauce and meatballs, as taught to her by her best friend, Jen, who was taught the family recipe from her Italian mother. The aroma of garlic and olive oil filled the house as she started browning the hot sausages. She poured in the cans of tomato puree, tomato paste, salt, pepper, and crushed red pepper and let it bubble while she made the meatballs. She combined one egg, at least 8 cloves of fresh garlic, parmesan cheese, Italian breadcrumbs, salt, pepper, fresh parsley, and the secret ingredient -- a glass of very cold water -- into the meat, working it with her hands. She had no exact measurements as it was all based on the smell and texture. She browned the meatballs in a large nonstick frying pan in batches as she formed them and then one by one dropped them into the sauce to cook the rest of the way through. When the last one was in the sauce, the house smelled like an Italian café. She cleaned up the kitchen, set the table, and left the sauce to cook for the next three hours.

"Oh my God, that smells delicious," Kevin said as he came in the door after work.

Jodi was in the kitchen, draining the pasta, when she heard Kevin come in.

"In here, babe," she called out, as she poured the steaming pasta into a large serving bowl.

Kevin came in, kissed his wife on the back of her neck and put the wine he had picked up on the counter.

"I'm going to quickly get out of this suit. What time is Katie supposed to be here? I'm starving," he said as he loosened his tie on the way to their bedroom.

"She should be here any minute. She texted a few minutes ago to say she was almost here."

By the time Kevin finished changing, Katie had arrived and Jodi was pouring wine into the two wine glasses on the table. Sometimes they would let Katie have a glass with them, but only when she was spending the night. Since she was driving later, tonight was not one of those nights.

"I can't wait to see our results," Katie exclaimed.

"Me too," Jodi replied, sharing her excitement.

"I don't care about anything except this pasta and meatballs right now," Kevin added as Jodi placed a large bowl in front of him.

As they ate their pasta, they talked about their trip throughout dinner, with Katie occasionally looking up something on her phone about one of the countries they planned to visit. If Kevin had only known what this trip would do for his relationship with his daughter, he would have planned one years ago. But at least they had this now.

After dinner, they all helped clean up the kitchen until it was time to review their results. They moved into the living room and got comfy on the large sectional. Jodi looked at the labels on the envelopes and handed Kevin and Katie their results, while holding onto her own. They all eagerly opened their results and started to decipher them. The first page of their reports, titled Ancestry Composition, showed where their DNA had come from in the world. Above the color-coded diagram, it said "This analysis considers DNA you received from all of your ancestors on both sides of your family."

Jodi spoke first, explaining she was 63.8% Irish, 11% Scottish, 4.2% Scandinavian, 1.3% Finnish, 0.7% French and German, and the remainder Broadly Northern European. Kevin gave his results next, which confirmed he was 32% British and Irish, 12.7% French and German, 42.1% Italian, 6.2% Balkan, 2% Sardinian, and 5% Nonspecific Southern European.

"Wow, I have a lot more Italian in me than Irish. I never realized that but I guess that explains my beautiful olive skin," Kevin laughed, caressing his own face in mock affection.

"So I'm confused. It says it traces it back through both sides of your family but my report isn't showing any Italian, Dad," Katie said, while still trying to figure out her results.

"Let me take a look," Kevin said, also confused. "Okay, let's see," he said, while scanning Katie's Ancestry Composition page, and reading aloud: "British and Irish, United Kingdom, 88%, Scandinavian 5%, Finnish 2.3%, and Broadly Northwestern Europe 4.7%."

They all sat there silent for a moment, somewhat stunned, when Katie finally asked, "What does this mean, Dad? Why isn't my report showing any of my Italian heritage?"

"It's got to be a mistake, a glitch, honey," Kevin said, looking to Jodi for help.

"Yeah, these companies, they're not foolproof, that's for sure. They screwed it up, no doubt," Jodi offered. "Let's put these results away for tonight and I'll contact the company first thing tomorrow to tell them they sent us someone else's results."

She quickly gathered up all of their results and walked out of the room. They got through the rest of the evening ignoring the obvious elephant in the room until it was time for Katie to leave. She hugged them both, holding onto her father just a little longer than usual, and headed out the door.

As soon as she closed the door, Jodi asked, "Kevin, are you okay?"

"What are the chances it's a mistake, Jodi?" Kevin asked, the pain already evident in his eyes.

"I don't know. It could be a mistake but I just don't know. I think we should review the report a little closer and then you need to have a serious conversation with Hallie."

CHAPTER TWENTY-ONE

Lila was relieved to finally leave the hospital. She couldn't wait to see her daughter, having been in the hospital for over a month. She thanked all of the nurses and Dr. Elligott for taking such good care of her and promised she would come back soon to say hello. She and her mother had agreed that it would be too hard for Vera to see Lila in the hospital; frankly, it would have been too hard for Lila too. It was better for Vera to think her mommy had gone away on an important trip. But not seeing her daughter for that long was the hardest thing she had ever done. They wheeled her down to the front of the hospital, with her mother carrying some of the flowers Lila had received, while Lila held the rest and her overnight bag in her lap. She was still weak from the extreme loss of blood but was getting stronger every day.

She had learned since she had been in the hospital that when she came in, her red blood cell count was significantly lower than what it was supposed to be. Sitting upright in the bushes and holding her hand over her neck had likely saved her life. That and the fact that he had missed her jugular veins and carotid arteries by mere centimeters. She underwent surgery to repair damage to the brachial plexus nerves in her neck and received a transfusion. Despite the transfusion, she was still anemic and it was going to take another month or two to replenish all of the red blood cells she had lost.

When they arrived home, they were greeted by her Aunt Sophia, her cousin, Maria, Sophia's daughter, and, of course, her darling Vera. Vera leapt into her arms, causing Lila to drop to her knees on the worn carpet of their West Tampa duplex. She hugged her daughter as tears streamed down her cheeks and smothered her daughter with kisses.

"Mommy, don't you ever go away again," her daughter cried, "never, ever, ok?"

"I won't, baby, I promise you, I won't. Mommy missed you so much."

"Promise mommy? You promise?" the young girl asked, looking up at her with her big, blue eyes.

"I promise, my angel, I promise," Lila said, vowing to make a better life for her and her daughter.

Lila settled in on the couch with Vera kneeling on the floor in front of her, coloring at the coffee table. When Lila got up to go to the bathroom, Vera went to. It was going to be a long time before the precocious four year old let her mother out of her sight. Dina picked up dinner, carne asada, yellow rice, salads, and chicken fingers for Vera from the Latin restaurant, Raices, around the corner from their home. It wasn't *her* carne asada, but it was good and she didn't have the three hours it would have taken to marinate the steak today. After dinner, Dina gave Vera her bath and helped her into her pajamas, despite her protests that she wanted Mommy to help her.

"Aye, mi amor, tu mama' esta cansada de su largo viaje; vamanos, hora de dormir," she said as she gently guided her granddaughter into bed.

"I'm coming to bed too, Vera. I'll be right in after I brush my teeth, my angel," Lila said from the couch, trying to summon the strength to do both.

By the time she made it into the small, bedroom she was sharing with her daughter, Vera was sound asleep and Lila was exhausted. Lila lay down next to her sleeping daughter, snuggling her in close to her chest, inhaling the sweet smell of her lavender baby bath wash. She never wanted to let her go again, she thought, as she fell asleep to the rhythmic sounds of her daughter's breathing.

The next morning, Vera woke her up early with kisses and hugs, obviously relieved her mother's return was not a dream. Lila understood and felt the exact same relief. The entire experience was an awakening for Lila. She realized that if something happened to her, Vera would never know who her father was and that wasn't fair to her daughter. Lila knew what it was like to grow up without a father and she didn't want to do that to her daughter. It was time to call David.

She thought a long time about what she would say. It wasn't going to be easy but it had to be done. She wasn't trying to ruin his life but she had to consider Vera's life. Vera was all she cared about, and it was time he knew he had a daughter, especially after what happened to her recently.

David, it's me, Lila. I have something important I have to tell you. That's why I needed to meet you that night in Ybor. But you never showed up and something terrible happened to me that night and that makes it even more important that you know about your daughter. Her name is Vera, she's three and half years old, and she's amazing. So that's all. That's why I wanted to meet you and what I wanted to tell you. I'm sorry to be doing this by text but you didn't show up the last time. Let me know when you can talk.

Lila hit send and slipped her new phone into her pocket. It was the middle of the day so he probably wouldn't respond until after work. She was nervous but glad she had sent the text. It was time he knew.

She still struggled to do the normal things she used to do without feeling exhausted, like getting dressed or making the bed. Dr. Elligott told her this would happen until her iron and blood levels returned to normal. She looked in the mirror and saw the wound on her neck was healing but it was going to leave a nasty scar. She knew Vera was going to ask questions as she got older that Lila wouldn't be able to explain away with ridiculous answers as she could now.

She didn't want anything from David other than for Vera to know her father. And if he loved her, well, that would be the best thing that could happen in the world.

She was about to leave for her physical therapy appointment when she heard the ding on her phone signifying she had a text. She pulled out her phone and read it.

"Lila, I'm sorry that whatever happened to you did, but there is no way I am your daughter's father. Please don't ever contact me again."

Lila stared at the text, stunned. "What a fucking asshole," she said aloud, thankful Vera wasn't with her at the moment.

Did he think she would make something like that up? She would get a DNA test if necessary to prove he was Vera's father. She never intended to do that or cause him any trouble in his marriage, but all she cared about now was Vera, and Vera had a right to know who her father was. That was the main reason she moved back to Tampa. Her mother tried to talk her out of it or contacting David, but eventually resigned herself to the fact that her headstrong daughter was going to do what she wanted. Fearful for her daughter and granddaughter, she decided to move with them so she could help take care of Vera.

David always told Lila his wife was a bitch and he wasn't happy, so would it be so terrible if she found out? Lila might be doing him a favor or maybe he was afraid his bitch wife would read his texts, she rationalized to herself. She decided she would drive over to the high school right after school let out the following afternoon to confront him in person. Once she showed him a picture of Vera, and he looked into those big blue eyes that were a mirror of his own, he not only wouldn't be able to deny she was his daughter but he would melt, Lila was positive.

CHAPTER TWENTY-TWO

Hallie needed to clear her head after her wine-filled afternoon with Paige. She knew she would be sluggish but a slow run would be better than no run at all. She laced up her running shoes, drank another bottle of water, and pushed play on her running playlist as she left her house, making sure to lock the door behind her.

As she started down her street, the music exploded in her ears and she felt determined and energized. Eminem's *'Till I Collapse,* with his honest, raw raps about never giving up, came alive as she ran, helping her overcome her exhaustion and wine buzz. She ran, her feet mirroring the cadence in the song, invigorating her and helping her think about what she was going to do next. After meeting with Paige, she knew she had to learn as much as she could about Naomi Banks and her relationship with Stephens. She didn't know where to start and she realized she was no detective but after hearing about that woman at that event, she just had to see if Stephens was at that hotel event that night or had anything to do with Naomi's death. She didn't believe in coincidences. If he had drugged and raped her so many years ago, and gotten away with it, why would he have stopped, Hallie concluded. But either way, Hallie was going to find out whether Stephens was connected to any of this.

Hallie finished her run, relieved to find her front door completely closed and still locked. She retrieved her key from her waistband and unlocked the front door, feeling the rush of cold air hitting her sweaty body as she opened the door. Juno looked up from her bed next to Hallie's desk, briefly wagging her tail to acknowledge her presence. Hallie went into the kitchen and poured herself a large glass of water out of the filtered pitcher in her refrigerator. She took her headphones out of her ears, turned them off, and put them in their case that she had left on the counter. She pulled out her phone and instinctively checked her emails.

Just as she finished responding to a client about scheduling a time to meet, she received a text from Kevin. It had been a while since she received any texts or communications from Kevin. Katie was seventeen, almost eighteen, and didn't need Hallie to coordinate visits with her father anymore. The last text she had received was telling Hallie he wanted to surprise Katie with a trip to Europe for her graduation and asking whether her passport was still good. They had agreed a few years before that they would each contribute monthly to a joint account for Katie's college and share all medical expenses for her that weren't covered by insurance, but other than that, neither one paid the other anything. They had always been civil and actually very good co-parents. Hallie was proud of the way they had raised their daughter together, despite their divorce. Needless to say, it was rare receiving a text from him.

"Hallie, we need to talk. Call me when you have a few minutes."

This was weird, Hallie thought. Was something going on with Katie that she didn't know about, she wondered. She immediately dialed Kevin's number.

"Hey, what's going on? Everything okay?" Hallie asked when Kevin answered.

"No, actually, everything is not okay. Can you please explain to me why our daughter's DNA results have zero of my DNA attributes in them?" Kevin asked, the anger and pain evident in his voice.

"What are you talking about, Kevin? I don't understand," Hallie said, no longer feeling the high from her run and feeling as if her legs were about to buckle underneath her.

Kevin explained how they ordered the DNA kits to learn more about their ancestry for their upcoming trip next summer and what the results revealed. He also explained how they contacted 23andMe and were assured the results were accurate for Katie, double checking various internal procedures, including re-running Katie's test as they keep the submitted swabs for sixty days. Hallie sat down, her head spinning and her worst nightmare coming true.

"Kevin, can we meet? I don't want to talk about this over the phone."

"What the fuck, Hallie? Just tell me. Who the fuck is Katie's father?" I can't believe you cheated on me. Oh my God," Kevin exclaimed.

"Kevin, stop. You're Katie's father," Hallie said with conviction. "It's not what you think. Please, I don't want to talk about this over the phone. Meet me at Malio's, in the bar, in a half an hour. It should be empty at this time of day. Bring Jodi. She needs to hear it too because Katie might turn to her; she likes her. And please bring the DNA results for Katie. I'm so sorry, Kevin, it's not what you think," Hallie said as she hung up, not giving Kevin the opportunity to protest or say anything else.

Hallie quickly showered and got dressed, trying to process what Kevin had told her over the phone. She was numb. Unfortunately, she knew this day might come one day, despite convincing herself that Katie had Kevin's smile and his eyes and his stubbornness. Somehow, she admitted, she always knew. But she had also always hoped she was wrong.

The pain and anger in Kevin's eyes broke Hallie's heart, even though she hadn't loved Kevin in so many years. But he was a good father and he loved his daughter and he didn't deserve this. Neither did Katie. And frankly, neither did she. Jodi sat next to Kevin, holding his arm and trying to be supportive, but without any children of her own, the magnitude of what was at stake was overwhelming.

"Kevin," Hallie started, reaching across the table and touching his clenched fists, "it's not what you think. I never cheated on you. Please know that."

"Really, Hallie? The fucking DNA results say otherwise. Who the fuck was it?" Kevin pleaded, his anger barely contained.

"Kevin, I was raped," Hallie said, practically in a whisper, "I was raped," she repeated, looking down, as tears started to well up in her eyes.

"What? What? No, I would have known. You're lying."

Jodi removed her hold on Kevin's arm momentarily, looking compassionately at Hallie, and started to reach out across the table to her, and then quickly pulled back, folding her hands in her lap.

The tears trickled down Hallie's cheeks as Brittany, the pretty waitress who often waited on Hallie when she was there, came to the table, placing drink napkins and silverware settings down in front of each of them. Hallie looked away, pretending to be looking for something in her purse.

"Hi, it's so good to see you again; what can I get you tonight?" Brittany asked pleasantly.

Thankfully, Jodi spoke up and ordered a bottle of wine for the table since Hallie and Kevin were too upset to speak.

"Hallie," Jodi said gently, "what happened? Please explain so we understand."

Hallie told them what happened to her the night of the Law & Liberty dinner eighteen years before and most of the sordid details, including how she was drugged and raped by someone important in her firm and about her extensive injuries. She told them how she went to Paige's the next morning because she was too ashamed and afraid to drive or go home. She reminded Kevin about how it was the same week as his first trial and that she told him she had the flu and slept on the couch for the following week. As insecure and naïve as Hallie was then, not knowing whether Kevin would believe her, it was different now. After raising their amazing daughter together for the past seventeen years, she honestly believed Kevin would know she was telling him the truth. Kevin was smart enough to know that Hallie would have nothing to gain by lying to him now. By the time Hallie finished her story, they were all crying, not only for what Hallie had been through but for the implications.

"Hallie, who did this to you? I want a name," Kevin demanded.

"It's not important now, Kevin. The statute of limitations has run and I'm never going to let him into our lives," Hallie said, afraid of what Kevin might do if she told him who he was.

Kevin reached across the table, taking Hallie's hands in his own, and said, "I wish you would have trusted me enough back then to tell me this."

"I am so sorry, Kevin. I am so sorry. We were so young, both gung-ho to start our careers. When I found out I was pregnant, I really believed you were the father. We had had sex the night before the Law & Liberty dinner, remember? You probably don't remember but I do because you knew you were going to be tied up with the trial for the next few weeks, so we did."

"I remember," he said, solemnly.

"There was as much of a chance that you were biologically Katie's father and I never wanted to know any different. And you are Katie's father. No matter what the DNA analysis says."

"You should have told me."

They sat in silence for a few minutes, somewhat shellshocked, each sipping on their wine, when Jodi finally broke the silence.

"Okay, where do we go from here? What do we tell Katie? She needs an answer and she's confused. She's texted me twice this week asking me if I've heard back from 23andMe about her new results."

"I think we need to tell her the truth," Kevin said. "She has a right to know. But I want to be the one to tell her. I want to make sure she knows that nothing has changed; I am her father, period, even if she has someone else's DNA," Kevin said, his voice cracking and his eyes welling up with tears again.

They all agreed and Hallie had a new appreciation for Jodi, and actually for Kevin, too. She could see Jodi was good for Kevin and she hoped that she would be equally good for her daughter in the coming weeks because Katie was going to need her.

As they were leaving, Jodi hugged Hallie, whispering in her ear, "I am so sorry that you had to go through that alone. I love your daughter and I will be there for her. Thank you for trusting me to be here tonight."

Hallie got in her car, clicked her seatbelt on, and sat there trying to collect herself from the evening. She was absolutely drained. She checked her phone and realized she had missed a call from David. It was time to deal with him, too, she realized. It was time he knew what was going on, regardless of their other issues. She got in her car and hit the redial button.

David answered on the third ring, "Hey babe, where are you?"

"I was with Kevin and Jodi, actually. Are you home?"

"Just got home from school. What's going on, everything okay with Katie?" David asked, genuinely concerned.

"Katie is fine, but, no, everything is not okay You're not going anywhere, are you? I'm picking up a pizza from Sally O'Neals and should be home in about twenty minutes. There's something we need to talk about."

"Yeah, I'm here, not going anywhere. Can you give me a hint? You're kinda freakin' me out."

"Nothing to be freaked out about, babe, I hope. I'll be home soon and then we'll talk."

"Ok, I'll be here. But definitely freaked out until you get here and explain what's going on."

Hallie pulled into the driveway about a half an hour later and David came out to the car to help her with the to-go bags and wine Hallie had picked up from Publix. The streetlights reflected off of Hallie's face as she got out of the car and David could tell she had been crying.

"Hallie, what's going on? I can tell you've been crying," David asked, the concern evident in his voice, as he followed his wife up the steps of their bungalow.

Hallie opened the wine, pouring the deep, red Cabernet into two glasses, as David set the pizza on the table with plates, napkins, and silverware. They sat down and Hallie took a deep swallow of her wine, feeling it warm her insides as it travelled down her throat. She could still feel the lump in her throat from being on the verge of crying again.

"So, something terrible happened to me eighteen years ago that I never told you about," Hallie began, "and in fact, I never told Kevin about it back then either."

"You're scaring me, babe," David interrupted.

"I know, and I'm sorry. Please let me get the whole story out before you start asking me questions. It's hard enough saying it out loud after all these years." Hallie took another sip of her wine, not even pretending to touch the slice of cheese pizza David had put on her plate in front of her.

She told David the story from the beginning, starting with her arrival at the Law & Liberty dinner, taking him through all the things she could remember, to the point where she woke up battered and raped in the hotel room the next morning next to the naked, managing partner. She told him about her injuries, how she was worried about what Kevin would think, her career, her feelings of guilt and shame that somehow it was her fault, everything. She told him how he was now a powerful criminal court judge and about her fears that he probably did this to other women over the years. She paused, wiping the tears from her eyes and taking another sip of her wine to give her the courage to tell him the final part of the story.

"I'm so sorry, babe. What a scumbag, piece of shit. You could have told me, you know? Why is this coming up now, after all of these years?" David asked, as the realization hit him. "Oh my God, Katie," he added, seeing the confirmation and sadness in his wife's blue-green eyes.

"Yes, Katie," Hallie said sadly. "Do you remember how Kevin planned that trip to Europe for Katie's graduation present? Well, they decided they would do one of those DNA testing things so they could visit places where their ancestors came from. Except, surprise, Katie's DNA didn't match Kevin's at all."

"Holy shit, Hallie, does Katie know yet?"

"No, not yet. Kevin and Jodi told her it must be a mistake, a glitch with the test and that they would contact the DNA company, which of course they did only to learn that it is no mistake, no glitch."

"And the scumbag Judge? Does he have any idea?"

"Absolutely not. And actually, I didn't tell Kevin and Jodi that part either. Kevin hates Judge Stephens and has always thought he was unethical. If he finds this out, I'm afraid of what he might do. You're the only person who knows his identity. And I don't want him to ever know or for Katie to ever know of him. He's a rapist and he's dangerous and I hate his fucking guts. But we know Katie's going to ask, and in some ways, maybe she has a right to know who her biological father is, but I'm just not ready for that yet. Kevin and I are still considering what to tell her."

"Can you press charges against him now?"

"No, the statute of limitations has expired, but even if it hadn't, I have the same problem now as I did back then: my word against his. He would have said I got drunk, consented, and cried 'rape' after the fact."

"Jesus. How did Kevin take it?"

"As you can imagine. He's devastated and angry, not as much at me now as at the situation, but he's very sad. I mean, he's not happy with me for not telling him, but I think, maybe, understands a little bit why I didn't at the time. I think Jodi is going to be very helpful to him, and to Katie, during all of this. She seemed genuinely empathetic. How about you? What are you thinking?" Hallie asked.

"Well, I think it all sucks, and I hate that son of a bitch for what he did to you, and I feel terrible for Kevin and what he's going through. Man, he raised Katie her whole life, as his own, to find out now she's not his daughter? Man, that's not right."

"But she is his daughter," Hallie said defensively, "she'll always be his daughter and this isn't going to change that," bracing herself for David to say something to set her off.

"Right, I know, but I'm just saying, it's got to weigh on him, that's all."

"And you don't think it's weighing on me?" Hallie asked, the anger rising within her. "Can you, just for once, take my side and think about how this is affecting me?"

"Oh here we go."

"What does that mean?"

"You asked me what I was thinking. I told you. But I didn't give you the answer you wanted, so now you're going to take it out on me because you want to yell at someone. But I'm not the bad guy here, Hallie. And it's okay if I feel bad for Kevin. It doesn't mean that I don't feel bad for you too and what you went through. I'm just saying, you had a choice whether to tell Kevin back then and you chose not to, so he's kind of been blindsided here, after eighteen years of raising what he thought was his daughter and that has to suck. That's all."

Hallie was so hurt and aggravated at David's reaction and what he said. All she wanted was for him to hold her and tell her everything was going to be okay for a change. But he couldn't do that because he never did that anymore and hadn't in a long time. She was also mad at herself because he was right: she had asked him what he thought and he responded exactly how she knew he would. She just wished that he had the same empathy for her as he did for Kevin. She didn't say another word as she got up and poured herself another glass of wine and went out to the front porch. She didn't have the energy for any more heartbreak or fights tonight.

CHAPTER TWENTY-THREE

She had to calm down, she told herself. The more she freaked out, the more he would be in control. She licked the blood off her swollen, bottom lip, and tried to concentrate on her breathing. She looked around again, shifting on thc plastic tarp she was on top of, and tried to shimmy her wrists out of the bindings holding her to the table to no avail. She had to figure out a way to get him to release her wrists. She knew that was her only chance. She also had to stop thinking about why he had covered the couch with a plastic tarp, because every time she did, she became paralyzed with fear. The only logical explanations did not end well for her.

He came back into the room, carrying the mini Bose player and placing it on the coffee table in front of them. He turned on what appeared to be a preset playlist on his phone, which instantly came through loudly on the Bose speaker and sounded like hardcore, death metal, which added to Chrissy's fear. Then he started to take off his clothes, walking towards her as he danced awkwardly to the music, and she could see he was aroused. His pasty white skin was interrupted in spots by reddish blotches and she could see what appeared to be a long scratch on his neck that was freshly scabbed. She looked up into his dark, angry eyes, trying to avoid looking any lower, and pleaded with him not to hurt her.

"Please, you don't want to do this," she said.

He laughed, beginning to stroke himself standing over her, as he said, "yes, this is exactly what I want to do."

"But wait, please," she begged, trying to stall, "it could be so much better. You're a good looking guy. I noticed you as soon as I saw you. I'm excited that you picked me up. You don't have to do this. I won't resist," she said somewhat quietly, trying to figure out how to motivate him.

"Do you think I'm stupid, whore?" he yelled, angrily, as he backhanded her, but then smiled as she cried out in pain, reveling in her fear.

She turned her face into the couch at the force of the blow, feeling the pull in her triceps with her arms still bound above her head, and screamed from both the pain and her terror. She had to figure out a way to get him to unhook her hands from the table. As long as she was hooked to the table, she had no chance. She was probably going to die either way so she had nothing to lose. As she thought about what to do, she spotted the three pictures in the room, all of them of the same woman. There was one on the wall and two smaller ones on the bookshelf in the corner that held all of the dusty books she had noticed earlier. All three pictures were in black and white and a bit grainy and, despite the dust on everything else in the room, were dust-free and shiny, suggesting they were important to him. The woman in the photos was attractive, with long hair and a petite frame, but with a sinister smirk that seemed to be mocking the photographer. Each picture was positioned in a way so that she could be seen from multiple places in the room.

"I'm so sorry, I know you're not stupid," Chrissy whimpered, "I'm the stupid one. My mother always told me how stupid I was, and now I know how right she was. Oh my God, look at me tied to this fucking table; my mother was always right and I'm an idiot. I deserve whatever you're going to do to me," Chrissy started to sob, "do what you will. My mother told me I was worthless and that I would end up like this one day. She was right, I guess."

* * *

He stood over her, not sure what to do. He got off on their fear, not self-pity. He could listen to fearful cries all day long; in fact, he had even recorded most of his victims begging for mercy that would never come. But sadness and the victim giving up completely? That, he was not used to. He got up and started to pace the room, trying to figure out what to do next. As he paced, he saw the pictures of his mother, another whore who never appreciated him, he thought. Was this one playing him too, he wondered? He had to kill her and he would, but he deserved to have his fun first. But she was getting into his head. He had to make her stop. Or maybe it was the whiskey, he thought. He was very tired all of a sudden and a little confused. It had been a busy month.

He sat down on the couch next to her, brushing her check with the side of his hand. And then, just as quickly, he jumped up, yelling at her while he paced in front of her again.

"Shut up!!! You're not going to play me, stupid bitch!" he yelled, as his angry spit landed on her face. "Don't think you're fooling me. I know what you're trying to do."

Chrissy shifted her weight to try to relax some of the pressure on her wrists. "I promise I'm not trying to play you. But my wrists hurt so bad. Can't you secure them somewhere else? You know I can't go anywhere but my hands are starting to go numb in this position. How can I do what you want if my hands are numb?" she asked.

He could smell the musky scent of her sweat combined with the patchouli oil, obviously intensified by her fear, all of which was starting to make him hard again. He could also smell the urine from when she pissed herself in his car. As much as it pissed him off that he would have to clean that up in the morning, he had to admit it turned him on too. He reached down and ripped her underwear off and lifted her dress. Her nipples were so perky and tan. And other then the little tiny white lines on her hips where her bikini bottoms sat, she had absolutely no tan lines.

"Oh you are a naughty little girl, aren't you," he said, admiring her tight little body.

"Please unhook my hands – I can't do anything. Please, they just hurt so bad," she pleaded again.

He paced again, looking down at her naked body, trying to decide what to do. She was right. Her hands were tightly zip-tied together in front of her so she wouldn't be able to do anything. Even if she wasn't secured to the table, what could she do? She wouldn't be able to get away from him. Most of his previous dates didn't make it long enough to complain about numb hands, he thought, so this was actually very exciting. He decided he could unhook her bound wrists from the table, even if only for a little while just to get her to stop complaining. It was distracting him.

"Thank you," she said, sincerely, after he unhooked her wrists, and she tried to get the circulation moving in her hands again.

"Don't try anything or I'll slit your throat before you can even scream," he threatened, as he pulled out the menacing knife from the sheath still strapped to his calf.

* * *

Chrissy looked away from the sharp knife while trying to get the feeling in her hands to come back.

"I won't," Chrissy lied, desperately trying to figure out what to do next and how to get him to leave the room.

"Come find out how naughty I can be," she whispered, looking seductively into his eyes, which confused him. "Go get me a shot of that whiskey you've been drinking all day. I'm a little thirsty and I need a shot too," she said in her sexiest voice, "and then we'll see what kind of trouble you want to get into."

"Are you fucking with me? I know what you're trying to pull here," he said, the anger and look in his eyes terrifying her again.

"Oh my God, what the fuck does a girl have to do to get a drink around here," Chrissy demanded, mustering all of the confidence she could while trying to hide her fear. "I need a fucking drink after everything that has happened to me tonight. Look, you're going to do what you want to me and I can't stop you. So I would rather have a few shots and make the best of it. If you think you're the first guy I've fucked who I didn't know his name, well . . ." she said, chuckling, trying desperately to appear nonchalant and indifferent, while trying to get him to leave the room.

He seemed taken aback and confused by her assertiveness. She held her breath, hoping she hadn't made him angrier and her situation worse.

"Fine, I'll get us some shots. But I'm warning you, if you're fucking with me or try to get away, I'm going to kill you but even more slowly and painfully than originally planned."

Confused but completely turned on, he left the room to go into the kitchen to pour them both shots of whiskey, and Chrissy let out a sigh of relief, feeling her heart racing. As soon as he left the room, Chrissy jumped up to see if the sliding glass door would open. To her amazement and relief, not only was it unlocked but it opened easily, with the blaring music drowning out any sound the slider could possibly make. She started to run as fast as she could into the darkness, further relieved by the fact that there was no fence enclosing the yard, and never looked back. By the time he finished pouring the shots and returning to the room, she had a three minute head start on him into the complete darkness.

CHAPTER TWENTY-FOUR

Hallie started out on her computer, researching everything she could about the story Paige had told her. There had to be some record or news reports related to the arrest of the air conditioning guy. She was able to pinpoint the year by texting Paige and asking her when she had dated Mike Freeman, which helped narrow down her search. After reading countless articles and refining her search, she finally found an article on the attack:

Woman Raped at Westshore Hotel
By: V. Marie Meister

On the morning of April 23, 2005, a young woman woke up in a hotel room at the Westshore Marriott, naked and brutally raped. She had been at the hotel for a networking event the night before but had no recollection of what happened to her after she left the event. Detectives with the Tampa police department are interviewing a number of potential suspects, including one person of interest who was hired to inspect air conditioning thermostats on the premises, but to date no arrests have been made or suspects identified. The victim, who is not being identified, is a 28 year old woman who was not staying at the hotel but was there for an event in one of the hotel's event rooms and is working with the police to identify her attacker. Meme Mercer, a spokesperson and head of operations for the hotel, issued the following statement: "The safety of our guests is our paramount concern and we are cooperating fully with the authorities to see that the perpetrator of this heinous act is caught. We have turned over all of our security camera tapes to the authorities and will continue to assist in any way we can to see that justice is served." To date, there have been no arrests in the case.

Hallie read and re-read the short article multiple times, hoping to learn something she didn't already know. She did additional internet searches to see if there were any follow up articles published and found one by the same reporter:

DNA Not a Match for Suspect Arrested in Rape at Westshore Hotel
By: V. Marie Meister

The suspect arrested in the rape of the woman at the Westshore Marriott on April 23, 2005, has been released and all charges have been dropped. Bob Martin, the technician hired to replace the A/C thermostats, has maintained his innocence from the time of his initial arrest. He voluntarily submitted his DNA at the onset of the investigation, which investigators have determined did not match the DNA found on the victim or at the crime scene. In addition, Martin's SunPass records confirmed he was on the Veteran's Expressway fifteen minutes after he had been spotted on the surveillance videos, proving he could not have committed this heinous crime. A source close to the investigation who spoke on the condition of anonymity said that they were starting at square one with the investigation and had no additional leads.

The rain fell outside, dancing off the rooftop as Hallie thought about where to look next. Juno nestled closer to her feet, fearing the impending thunder that was likely to come.

"It's ok, old girl," Hallie said as she reached down, petting Juno in her favorite spot behind her ears.

Now that she knew the date of the event, she searched the internet again for local professional networking events that occurred that night. She found a Tampa Bay Metro calendar of events link for the month of April, 2005, that listed the professional mixer at the Marriott as one of the events that month. The description for the event said, "Come mingle with other professionals, including lawyers, accountants, financial advisors, and bankers, for a night of networking. Bring plenty of your business cards to hand out and to submit for the fabulous gift basket that will go to one lucky winner of the night."

Hallie knew from her lunch with Paige that Judge Stephens was not on the attendee list, but what if he was there and just didn't sign in, she wondered. Hallie figured no one looked into that possibility as the only two people who knew that his attendance at the event should be investigated were Paige and Mike Freeman. Hallie had to figure out if he was there. She believed in her gut that if he was there that night, he was the one who raped that young woman, while her pragmatic side told her that, even if he was at the event, it was merely a coincidence. Fueled by her suspicions, appetite for justice, and years of regret, she was determined to figure out if he was there that night.

She started researching everything she could about Judge Stephens. In 2005, when the woman at the hotel was attacked, he was still the managing partner of Behrenfeld Vincent, LLP, one of the most prestigious firms in town, the same one in which Hallie was an associate when he attacked her a few years before. She learned that, in 2006, he ran for the open seat on the bench of the Hillsborough County Circuit Civil court being vacated by Judge Amy Gratzick, who was retiring early after her husband found a rare and priceless diamond while vacationing in the Grand Canyon. This meant that he would have been campaigning in 2005 and early 2006, to make sure voters outside of the legal community knew his name. The Tampa Bay Metro mixer was exactly the type of event he would have attended. He won the election that year and had remained on the bench ever since, running unopposed in most subsequent elections.

Hallie had to figure out another way to determine if he was there. She decided that tomorrow she would go to the public library downtown. They kept hard copies of newspapers, periodicals, and magazines. She might not be able to find it on the internet but the May edition of the Tampa Bay Metro magazine likely had an article about the previous month's events, including pictures from the event. Maybe she would recognize someone in the pictures who she could call to see if they remembered the event and who was there. It was a long shot but it was worth a try.

The rain continued to fall outside as the wind picked up, causing Juno to stir from her position at Hallie's feet, as the rustling of the trees outside grew louder. It was only 8:47 p.m. and Hallie figured it would be a few hours before David came home from his weekly Saturday night poker game. Katie was spending the night at her best friend, Hannah's house, and she had promised Hallie they would not be going out. At this point, Kevin and Hallie had not told Katie about the DNA results or Hallie's rape. They had all agreed they were going to wait until after Katie submitted all of her college applications, because they didn't want to do anything to derail her. They also all agreed that

Jodi would tell her that 23andMe was going to re-run her tests so it would be a few weeks before they would receive the new results, which would buy them a little more time before they had to tell her the truth.

Hallie got up from her desk, deciding she had researched all she could for the night, and went into the kitchen to pour herself a glass of wine. Juno, still fearful of the storm threatening outside, followed close behind. As she looked in her wine rack, considering which bottle she should open tonight, she heard her phone ping from the nearby counter alerting her to a new message. She retrieved a lovely 2016 bottle of Faust, The Pact, Cabernet Sauvignon, which she had received from a client after closing a multi-million dollar deal a few weeks ago. She opened it with her automatic opener, pausing to smell the hint of oak and berries on the cork, and poured the dark, ruby elixir into her glass when she heard the second reminder notification that she had an incoming text. Hallie grabbed her phone and her wine and went into the living room to find something on TV to distract her. When she got situated on the couch, she looked at her phone and saw she had a text from Paige.

"Hey girl, I talked to Mike and he said he would talk to you and tell you what he could remember about that hotel case. And no, they never caught anyone. Let me know when you want to talk to him."

"Thanks! That's great. Can we meet Thursday afternoon for a drink? How about at Ulele again?"

"I'm available. I'll check with Mike and let you know."

She put her phone down on the end table next to her and reached for the remote, sipping her wine at the same time. As she started to scroll the TV guide to find Chopped or something else to watch, Juno's ears perked up and the old dog got up, heading towards the foyer. Hallie looked at Juno and noticed the hair on her back standing straight up as Juno started to growl. Hallie casually put her wine glass down and picked up her phone, ready to call 9-1-1. Juno barked. Juno wagged her tail. Juno did not growl. Suffice it to say, Hallie was nervous. She sat there for what seemed like an eternity, but, in reality, was probably only a few minutes, to see if Juno did anything else or if she heard anything out of the ordinary. Nothing. Within a minute or two, Juno had lied back down at her feet, which was somewhat comforting but at the same time didn't explain what she was growling at a few minutes before. Hallie looked at the time on her phone. 9:03 p.m. David would be so aggravated if she texted him to ask him to come home early. Also, he probably wouldn't anyway. She decided to text Bridget.

"Hey, what are you doing?"

"Living the amazing life of a 48-year-old married woman while my husband protects and serves: working on a 1,000-piece puzzle of a Van Gogh painting. How about you?"

"Home alone too. But a little freaked out. Heard something and Juno did too."

"Where's David?"

"Out. Poker game"

"Are you paranoid or is there an issue? How's Juno now?"

"She's settled down again but she growled, not barked, and her hair was standing up. She never does that."

"Want me to come over?"

"I hate to make you do that . . . but yes."

"Ok, let me put a goddamn bra on and I'll be right over. 20 minutes. Omg so much drama with you lol"

"Thank you! I have wine"

"I wouldn't have offered to come if, one, I didn't already know that, and two, if this puzzle wasn't boring as shit."

Hallie was relieved Bridget was coming over. She knew she was being irrational but her nerves were shot with everything that was going on. She looked at the clock, so she could count down the minutes until Bridget would get there. After about seven minutes of waiting, just when Hallie was starting to relax, having convinced herself it must have been her imagination or the storm outside, Juno stood up and cautiously returned to the front foyer again. Within moments, the hair on Juno's back stood up and she started to growl again while focusing on something *or someone* out of Hallie's sight. Hallie was terrified as she looked around to see what she could grab to defend herself. She noticed the tools next to the fireplace that rarely got used and picked up the poker, which she knew would be useless if the person had a gun. Nevertheless, she stood with her back to the farthest wall where she had a clear view of anyone coming into the room, poker ready, praying that Bridget would get there soon. Juno looked around, sniffing as she explored, walked into Hallie's office, and then back out again, and sniffed by the front door before ultimately returning to the living room and settling down once again.

Hallie looked at the clock, surprised that only three minutes had passed since the last time she had looked. Was that a floorboard creak from upstairs, she wondered, straining to identify every sound she heard. She stood there, frozen, holding her fire poker, as she listened for Bridget's car to pull up into the driveway. She looked at the clock again – another minute down – when the air handler turned on, breaking the silence and causing her to gasp out loud and almost drop her makeshift weapon. Her heart was pounding and she knew she was being irrational but no matter what, she couldn't shake the feeling that someone was in the house. She stood there for the next few minutes, ready to hit send on 9-1-1 that she had dialed into her phone, when she finally heard Bridget's car pull up into her driveway.

She practically flew out the front door, Juno following in tow, never before so relieved to see her friend.

"Well look at these two, greeting me on the front steps," Bridget said, climbing out of her car, "to what do I deserve this grand welcome?" Bridget teased.

"Oh my God, Bridget, I swear I think someone is in the house. Or I'm losing my mind, and so is Juno," Hallie whispered, clearly terrified.

"Well good thing I brought my gun," Bridget said loudly, patting her purse, "and even better that my police officer husband taught me to always aim for the middle of the chest, the kill shot," Bridget finished, winking at Hallie. "Let's go in and have look-see, shall we, ladies?"

Hallie was always amazed at how nothing scared Bridget, nothing, since they were kids. She would stand up to the biggest bully in school without even blinking. As they got older, if some drunken lech wouldn't leave them alone in a bar, Bridget would easily chase him off with her biting tongue and sharp wit. She just never backed down to anyone. She always attributed it to growing up in an Italian Irish household with eight older brothers. She often joked that she came out of the womb fighting with her brothers.

Hallie followed Bridget into the house while Juno went to lay down on her bed, obviously exhausted from all of the excitement.

Nodding over at Juno, Bridget joked affectionately, "maybe I should have brought Sam and Spicoli with me, huh old girl?"

"Juno's a lover, not a fighter – the world needs them too, you know," Hallie said, defending her faithful friend's honor.

Bridget and Hallie checked out every inch of the house, finding no one lurking behind the curtains, under the beds, or hiding in a closet, much to Hallie's relief. They also confirmed that all the doors and windows were locked. Bridget decided to look around outside of the house too. After checking out the front porch area and finding nothing out of the ordinary, she walked around to the back of the house. Using the flashlight on her phone, she searched around the back door and adjacent windows.

"Well, what do we have here," Bridget said, while shining her phone light onto the ground next to the backdoor.

Hallie looked down where Bridget shined the light, seeing exactly what Bridget had seen: plants that once stood a couple of feet high lining the back of the house were trampled and no longer upright with two well-defined footprints in the dirt next to the plants. It looked like someone must have been trying to peer into the back window.

After taking a few pictures with her phone, Bridget said, "Okay, so the good news is, neither you nor Juno are crazy, but the bad news is, someone was definitely trying to look in your windows. Let's go inside and give Jay a call."

* * *

Jay and David arrived at the small bungalow at about the same time. Hallie had texted him at the same time Bridget was on the phone with Jay telling him about the evening's events. David walked through the house, checking everything again just as Bridget and Hallie had, while Jay went out back with his department issued flashlight, which was obviously a lot brighter than Bridget's cellphone, to inspect the back perimeter of the house. Someone had definitely been there, looking in the windows, but neither the door nor the windows looked tampered with. Since the rain had stopped only a few hours before, they could tell the imprints were freshly made. Jay took pictures and told Hallie and David he would write up a report.

"For all we know, this could be completely unrelated to the emails you've received, but until we learn otherwise, we need to treat them as related. I'm going to include them in my report. Hallie, can you print me out copies?"

"Yes, I'll do that right now," Hallie said as she walked into her office, leaving David, Jay, and Bridget sitting in the living room.

She moved her mouse to bring her computer to life and that's when she noticed the handwritten note scrawled on the legal pad on her desk.

You should have told!!

Hallie's loud gasp brought all three of them instantly into the office and she pointed to the legal pad in front of her.

"No one touch it," Jay directed, "Hallie, don't touch anything else on your desk. In fact, let's all leave this room without touching anything else."

Jay called into his precinct and requested a crime scene tech to come out to collect evidence, including the note. Despite not finding evidence of a break in earlier, the discovery of the note on Hallie's desk escalated the potential peeping tom case up to a burglary.

Hallie was officially freaked out. She, David and Bridget sat in the kitchen while Jay and the crime scene tech photographed Hallie's office and collected evidence. Jay had told her that with any luck they would find a fingerprint on the note itself or maybe the pen that was found lying on the desk next to the legal pad and was likely used to write the note. David brought Hallie's wine glass and the bottle of Faust in from the living room and refilled Hallie's glass to calm her nerves. He poured Bridget a glass too and grabbed a beer out of the fridge for himself. They sat around the counter sipping their drinks and tossing around various theories about who could have left the note, none of which made any sense but passed the time while they waited for Jay to finish.

"Okay, we're all done in there, guys. Hallie and David, we'll want to get your prints so we can eliminate any that match yours. Most of the prints were smudged but we did get a few clear ones off the desk, including a partial of an index finger off the pen, although those could easily be Hallie's. We'll see. Since there is no evidence of a break in, I recommend you change the locks tomorrow and think about getting an alarm."

"Thanks, Jay," David said, "I'll call some places first thing in the morning."

Hallie moved to the couch and sat with her legs criss-crossed, hugging her knees into her chest like that morning she sat on Paige's couch, except instead of a hot cup of tea, she sipped on her wine. In some ways, she felt just as violated tonight as she did that morning. But whoever left that note was right: she should have told.

CHAPTER TWENTY-FIVE

Chrissy ran as far and as fast as she could with her hands zip-tied in front of her. She was naked underneath her slip dress and bare foot, the twigs and sharp rocks cutting into her feet as she ran. He had cut her panties off but thankfully had only lifted her dress up to expose her breasts, so at least she wasn't running buck naked through the dark woods. Not that being naked would have stopped her from running away from that fucking sociopath. Her feet were raw and bleeding from the rough terrain, but she kept running anyway. She knew if he caught up with her, he wouldn't just kill her, he would torture her to punish her just as he promised he would. She knew this in all of her being from the look in his eyes, which matched the woman's eyes in the photographs in the room she had just escaped.

Up ahead, she saw a light, just beyond a clearing. As she got closer, she could see the sign that lit up the parking lot and realized she had made it to a 7-11. She felt if she could just get there, she could call the police and be saved. She was running out of the woods, coming up behind the dumpster at the side of the store, when her already battered feet came upon some broken glass, stopping her in her tracks from the pain. She sat down on the curb to try to pull the biggest pieces of glass out of her feet. As she sat, tending to her bleeding feet, she saw headlights from a pickup truck pulling up to the front of the 7-11. She was terrified that it could be him, even though he wasn't driving a truck earlier. She quickly retreated out of the streetlight, cowering behind the dumpster, relieved that she hadn't gone inside the store yet. She had to be sure it wasn't him before she could go in for help.

After a few minutes, while she sat behind the dumpster continuing to pick the broken shards of glass out of her feet, she heard the engine start and the pickup drive away. She peeked around the dumpster, didn't see anyone else parked in front of the store, and hobbled as quickly as she could into the store, blood pouring out of her open wounds and staining the sidewalk and linoleum floor in her wake.

"Please help me," she barely got out before she started to cry uncontrollably.

"What's the matter with you? Are you on drugs? You can't come in here without shoes on," the confused and obviously annoyed clerk said to her.

"Please, hurry, call the police," she begged, all the while cowering behind a display of greeting cards and peering out the front of the store, fearing that her captor would come in at any second, "please, I was attacked," she said in between sobs.

"I don't want any trouble, Miss," the clerk said.

"Just call the fucking police! I'm begging you!" Chrissy yelled, her anger yielding to her terror. Couldn't he see her battered face? Her bloody feet? Her zip-tied hands?

Finally, the clerk picked up the phone and dialed 911.

* * *

Chrissy sat in the back of the ambulance as the medic tended to her feet, cleaning her wounds, removing additional glass and splinters, and closing the largest gashes with sutures. She pulled the warm blanket they had wrapped around her in tighter as her body continued to shiver even though she didn't feel particularly cold. The other medic, the older female one, was asking her if she was allergic to any medications and whether she had consumed any alcohol, pills, or other substances that evening.

"Alcohol. I had a few drinks at the bar earlier, margaritas."

"Anything else?" she asked.

"No, that's it," Chrissy answered, looking down at the markings around her wrists, feeling guilty as if it was her fault she was attacked.

The other medic continued cleaning and dressing the wounds on her feet, bandaging them up when he was done with the sutures, and placing surgical socks over the bandages when he was done.

"Okay, we're all set here. Your feet are pretty bad. You're going to have to watch out for infection and we want to take you to the ER for x-rays to make sure we got all of the glass and debris out of your wounds and to make sure you don't have any other injuries. Is there someone we can call for you to meet you at the hospital?"

"Thank you, yes, can you call my mother?" Chrissy replied as tears welled up in her eyes again, not just from the throbbing pain intensifying in her feet but from the thought of telling her mother what happened to her.

"Chrissy, I'm going to give you a very low dosage, non-opioid painkiller to help with the pain in your feet and to help with your anxiety," the female medic said. "I can't give you much because of the alcohol you drank earlier but it should help ease the pain a little bit. Okay?"

"Yes, thank you. My feet are really starting to hurt and so is my face," Chrissy responded, feeling less judged by the female medic than the male one, although she admitted she could be feeling a little paranoid.

"I imagine they are, especially as your adrenaline continues to subside. Adrenaline is our body's way of protecting us from feeling pain when we're injured and frightened. But as your adrenaline comes down, your ability to feel pain goes up. This will help," she said as she injected the pain reliever into the IV that had already been started on Chrissy's arm to give her fluids.

The medics hopped off the back of the ambulance as a uniformed police officer approached them. Chrissy could only hear part of their conversation.

"How is she doing?" the officer asked them, nodding in Chrissy's direction.

"Pretty shaken up," the female medic said.

"Her feet are jacked up pretty bad," the other medic said, "but they'll heal. Pretty superficial wounds, but that's not to say they won't be painful for her and take some time to heal properly. Psychologically may be another story. She was hysterical when we first arrived, terrified that if we didn't get her out of here, whoever did this to her would be back to get her."

"Any indications of sexual assault?" the officer asked.

"She hasn't said, but she is exhibiting behaviors consistent with someone who has been sexually assaulted, including that she had no undergarments on under her dress and has some unexplained contusions and abrasions on her body around her breasts and on her upper thighs. But we don't do rape exams in the van. Those have to be done back at the hospital."

"Do you think she can answer some questions?" the officer asked.

"She's definitely been through something traumatic, but I think she can answer some questions. She's fairly coherent, but we did just give her something to help with the pain and her anxiety. Also, she sustained some serious blows to the face and head and we don't know whether she lost consciousness or not, so more tests will have to be performed at the hospital. She's still processing what happened to her tonight, so tread lightly."

The officer climbed into the back of the ambulance and introduced herself to Chrissy, "Hi Chrissy, I'm Officer West, but you can call me Catherine. Do you mind if I ask you a few questions?" Officer Catherine West asked her, the empathy and warmth evident in her hazel green eyes.

"No, I don't mind. I'll answer anything. I want you to find the sick son of bitch who did this to me before he grabs someone else. If I didn't get away, he would have killed me, but not before raping and torturing me, I promise you. I was on a fucking tarp for God's sake, a fucking tarp!" Chrissy cried, pulling the warm blanket the medic had wrapped around her up further as the realization of what she had escaped, and what could have been, hit her.

"Chrissy, I'm so sorry this has happened to you, but with your help, we will catch him. But we need to slow down so that I can write down every detail you give me. We need to start at the beginning and work our way through until you made it to the 7-11 to call the police. But the medics want to take you to the hospital so the ER can do a more thorough examination. Would you mind if I met you there so we can talk?"

"No, I don't mind. I'll tell you anything you want to know. You have to catch this guy. He's the real deal, ya know, a real fucking Ted Bundy," Chrissy said, her body starting to tremble again.

They arrived at the hospital and the triage team checked Chrissy out, confirming her vitals were stable and asking her various questions before transporting her to a private bed in the ER. The medics had already removed her dress and put her in a hospital gown, so the ER nurse simply placed two heated blankets on top of her, for which she was extremely grateful. The nurse also attached a fresh bag of fluids to the IV line that had been inserted by the medics, and left the room, allowing Officer Catherine to come in.

"Hi Chrissy, how are you doing?"

"Oh, fabulous; couldn't be better," she said, simultaneously rolling her eyes.

"I'm sorry, Chrissy, I know you want this over as soon as possible. Do you want me to call your mom or dad or someone else to come down here?"

"I gave the nurse my mom's number. I'm sure she's on her way."

"Okay, are you ready to tell me the story, from the beginning? You're our only hope of catching this guy, Chrissy."

"Yeah, I'm ready. I'll tell you whatever I can remember."

"Okay, great, Chrissy. Also, try not to leave any details out, no matter how small or insignificant you think they are, because they could help us catch him. Let's start at the beginning. You told the 7-11 clerk that you were abducted and attacked. Can you tell me where you were when that happened?"

"Yes, I was at MacDinton's in South Tampa."

"Do you know the assailant or did you meet him at MacDinton's?"

"No, I didn't know him. Don't you think if I knew him, that would have been the first words out of my mouth? I've never seen him before tonight."

"Okay, I understand, but I have to ask the questions, Chrissy. Did he speak to you or approach you in the bar?" Catherine asked, trying to guide Chrissy to start at the beginning.

"No, I don't remember even seeing him in the bar, although he had to be in there. He came out after me, out of the same door I left out of, and as he came up behind me, told me he was there to pick up a rider named Chrissy. I thought he was my Uber driver."

Officer Catherine continued to take notes as Chrissy spoke, "Okay, let's back up a second. Did you call an Uber driver?"

"Yes, on the app on my phone. I left my friends to go outside to meet the driver at the pick-up spot outside."

"Okay, and then what happened?"

"A guy came out behind me and said my name. He said he was picking up his rider and went inside to use the bathroom. Oh my God, I'm so stupid," Chrissy said, cursing herself for being so naïve.

"Do you know if he was your Uber driver?"

"No, I don't know. But maybe not . . . probably not. Look, I was a little buzzed. I normally check the make and model of the car when it pulls up and check it against the app, you know, to make sure it's a legit uber driver and everything. But this guy came out of the bar behind me; he knew my name; said he was picking up a rider named Chrissy and just had to use the bathroom. He was so polite and . . . I don't know . . . normal looking. I believed him," Chrissy said, once again looking down and feeling ashamed.

"It's okay, Chrissy. These guys are masters of manipulation; it's not your fault," Officer Catherine offered. "But now it's important that you tell me every detail about him that you can remember so we can stop him from doing this to anyone again. Do you think you can do that?"

"Yes. Absolutely. This guy would have killed me if I didn't get away, no doubt in my mind. I'll help in any way I can so you can catch him. He is pure evil, I promise you. And I wasn't his first victim."

"Why do you say that, Chrissy?"

"Because he was too organized, too confident, and he chained my fucking wrists to some hook he had attached to his end table. And he had a video camera in the corner, pointed at the couch. And I was on top of a fucking tarp – oh my God, are you kidding me? A fucking tarp? What did he need the tarp for?" Chrissy pleaded, looking at the officer, "he's done this before. I know it."

"Okay, this is all important and I know it was terrifying, but let's start from the beginning when he followed you out of MacDinton's. Can you describe what he looked like?"

Chrissy and Officer Catherine talked for the next hour, with Chrissy giving as many details as she could remember. She was so angry at herself for not being able to remember anything about his face except his cold, dark eyes. And his gator hat. She didn't even realize he was wearing a hat until she woke up on that fucking tarp and he was standing over her in that stupid fucking blue and orange hat with the alligator on it.

"Anything else about his face, Chrissy? You said he's white and you estimated about 45-50 years old. What makes you think that?"

It was so weird to her; why couldn't she picture his face? All she could remember was the sound of his voice and the smell of whiskey and cigarettes. Every time she remembered, she could almost taste it, feeling his hot, wretched breath on her face, so close to her. She would have to close her eyes to keep from vomiting from the memory. Catherine explained that people's sense of smell was actually stronger than their conscious visual memory. The visual memory was there, just often suppressed, usually out of fear or self-preservation. Catherine suggested hypnosis with the department sketch artist in the room during the session. When people were in the midst of a traumatic situation, often their subconscious mind remembered things their conscious minds couldn't. Chrissy agreed to it, although she didn't actually think it would work, but she wanted to do whatever she could to help catch this mother fucker before he hurt someone else.

CHAPTER TWENTY-SIX

Judge Stephens sat behind his large, antique mahogany desk in his chambers, the walls on either side adorned with built in bookshelves lined with ancient law books and old classics by Hemingway, Poe, and Steinbeck. His expensively framed diplomas and other recognitions he had earned over the years, evidencing his illustrious and successful legal career, hung on the wall behind his desk so that anyone visiting his chambers would be forced to see them all. There were no windows in his chambers, the only light emanating from the desk lamp he kept on his desk unless he turned on the awful fluorescent overhead lights, which he rarely did. In the corner, he had an old dry sink, which was an antique bar with beautiful crystal glasses kept on top and cabinets below stocked with his favorite scotch, gin, and a few other bottles of liquor he had received as gifts over the years.

He opened his personal laptop and checked into his usual porn sites. Oh, how he liked to see those dirty sluts. The new secretary that started last week reminded him of that hot young associate from so many years ago. Blonde, perky, full breasts, nice, tight ass, just what he liked. What was her name, he tried to remember? That's right, Hallie

. . . Hallie Verona, he thought smiling as her name came to him. She was young and eager, always wanting to please the senior partners. It was a shame she left the firm shortly after the night they spent together. He thought they could have developed a nice little quid pro quo situation: she could hang out with him from time to time and he could help her career. Oh well, she never made any trouble for him so it was fine. None of them ever did, especially the ones who had no idea who he was because he would leave before they woke up, he snickered. The memory reminded him that he needed to reach out to his supplier who still owed him a few comps considering he let him off the last time he came before him on a possession charge. He took out his prepaid burner phone, which was untraceable to him, and quickly sent a text: *"30 Rf; usual p/t"*, which stood for, need a supply of 30 roofies, to be delivered at the usual place and time. He had learned a lot about the criminal underground since he became a criminal court judge and it served his needs well.

Oh Hallie, yeah, he remembered her fondly, even though he had to admit what he did that night was a little reckless, even for him. But he was already high when he got to the dinner and she was so damn flirtatious with her lowcut blouse, just begging for him to look. He dropped the roofie into her glass so easily, as they passed the bread, if he recalled correctly, and no one even glanced over. She didn't notice either and she drank it right up. By the time the dinner was over, she was out of her mind and all he had to do was guide her. He made it seem like he was walking her to her ride, the caring, protective managing partner. Instead, he guided her right into that elevator and up into his room. She passed out almost instantly but he didn't care. It felt the same either way, and actually he liked it when they were completely incapacitated, as if they were dead. He could do whatever he wanted then with no objections.

He was surprised when he woke up the next morning and she was gone. He was a little worried at first that she would accuse him of taking advantage of her or worse, but she had been drinking, to which others in the firm could attest, and he would say it was consensual. When it came down to "he said, she said," with no other proof of any wrongdoing, what "he said" would be more credible than some flirtatious, drunk associate, especially when the "he" was the managing partner of the firm. He remembered that she had called in sick for the next few days but then returned to the office the following week without saying a word to anyone, including to him. Within a month, she resigned and went to a new firm, which was probably better for him in the long run. It would have been hard to resist her if she had stayed.

Naomi, his latest young aspiring attorney, was completely the opposite of Hallie, but just as exciting. He would watch her when she delivered her analysis about a case, trying so hard to be articulate and composed, but inside, he knew she was so nervous in his presence and all he could focus on was her hard nipples from the 67 degrees he insisted on keeping his chambers. He got slightly aroused every time he saw her. He felt she was turned on by him, too: his power, his brilliance, his distinguished career. She would always retreat quickly or make an excuse to leave the room whenever he turned the conversation personal, but he knew that was just her way of playing hard to get. He couldn't wait to be alone with her.

And then, out of the blue, a few weeks later, as he sat on his back patio enjoying an evening cocktail, there she was: running right past his house on the pedestrian/bike path that ran just behind his property line along the golf course. He had no idea they lived in the same neighborhood in Carrollwood Village.

As he sat behind his great antique desk, he thought back to that night. Whenever he watched porn, he thought about his conquests, but Naomi, wow, she was going to be hard to top. He remembered he was just sitting on his patio, sipping his scotch, hoping for her to run back by. Just as he was about to give up, he spotted her walking back down the trail, presumably towards her house after her run. He went out his back screen door just as she was approaching and called her name. Startled, she stopped in her tracks and looked up at him, obviously confused, pulling out her earbuds as she tried to register how she knew the large man in front of her.

"Naomi, I'm sorry, it's me, Bill Stephens. Did I startle you? I had no idea we lived in the same neighborhood."

"Oh, Judge Stephens, hello," Naomi hesitated, "I'm sorry, I just didn't expect to see you here," Naomi said nervously, while trying to regain her composure and catch her breath.

"Please, call me Bill. We're not in court," he said, smiling, "can you join me on my patio for a drink?"

"Um, no, I'm sorry, your Honor, I have to get home to make dinner. Another time?" Naomi asked, walking onto the grass in an attempt to get around him.

"Of course, I understand, no problem. Oh, but since you're here, would you mind helping me for one minute? I've been trying to upload my Order on that frivolous motion filed by that unethical attorney, Mark Harrison, all night and I'm having trouble with the portal. I won't keep you, I promise, but I just can't get the damn thing uploaded. I'll give you a nice cold bottle of water for your troubles," he offered, smiling and trying to sound charming.

She hesitated for a moment but then reluctantly agreed, obviously not wanting to seem unhelpful, and followed him onto the patio and into his house.

He never meant to hurt her but once she came into his house, he just couldn't control himself any longer. She was so beautiful, and he was turned on by her energy and the smell of her sweet sweat emanating off of her body. They were standing in his kitchen and he had just handed her a cold bottle of water when he grabbed her and pulled her in close for a kiss, while squeezing her tight ass. He was shocked at how mad she got, pushing him off of her, while saying things about ruining his career and reporting him to the Florida Bar and to the police for assault. He tried to calm her down, telling her it was a misunderstanding, but nothing he said seemed to work. She got angrier with every excuse or explanation he gave, especially when he said he must have misread her signals. She was heading for the back, sliding glass door, still threatening who she was going to tell, and he panicked.

He just wanted to stop her from leaving so he could convince her it was just a mistake and that it would never happen again. But when he grabbed her arm to pull her back, she pulled away so forcefully, she tripped over her own feet and hit the marble countertop with the side of her head on the way down. As she hit the ground, she was completely unconscious and there was blood starting to trickle out of one of her ears. He knew he should call an ambulance immediately, but now his situation was even worse. He paced around his kitchen, looking at Naomi's crumpled body on his kitchen floor, trying to figure out what to do next. How would anyone believe him now? He was in a complete state of panic, yet he realized he was equally turned on: seeing her lying face down on the cold floor gave him a new kind of excitement and rush, much more so than the girls who he incapacitated with alcohol and roofies.

Instead of calling an ambulance, he dragged her limp body into his living room and pulled off her shoes and running shorts to expose the hottest, sweetest pussy he had seen in a while. She had a nice racing strip down the center and nothing more, just as he had imagined. He pulled her tank top and running bra up to expose her beautiful, brown tits, instinctively biting one of her nipples, as he liked to do. He unzipped his pants and started stroking himself as she regained consciousness, the confusion in her eyes instantly replaced by horror. She started to scream and he silenced her by placing one of his large hands over her mouth while trying to control her flailing arms with his other as he straddled her. He was so aroused he couldn't see straight. She struggled to get out from underneath him, punching and scratching him in her desperate attempt to get free, which only turned him on more. He had never been so hard in his life. He placed his weight completely on top of her and started choking her with his right hand, feeling her body struggle as she fought to breathe. He just needed to calm her enough so he could control her, but she was fighting too hard. He tightened his grip on her throat until she stopped fighting him and he felt her body go limp beneath him.

At first, he thought she was just unconscious again but upon further examination, he realized he had killed her. It should have horrified him but it only excited him more. He left her on the floor and took her phone and earbuds off of her and immediately submerged them in a bucket of hot water in the kitchen. He paced the kitchen again, taking a long swallow of his scotch that was still sitting on the counter from earlier, contemplating what to do. And then he returned to the living room and fucked her warm, dead body for the next hour, making sure to never cum inside her, both disgusted and exhilarated by what he had done.

Eventually, as the thrill and buzz of the evening started to wear off, reality set in and he started to freak out. The first thing he had to do was to get rid of her body. If he got caught, he would end up in prison with the scum he had sent there along the way, which would not end well for him, he knew. He often had death threats against him from the offenders he had put away over the years. As he tried to think of what to do, he remembered reading about some recent murders of young women in the area and overhearing an officer in his courtroom talking to his bailiff about the cases and the women's injuries. He would make it look like Naomi was just another one of the victims of the same guy, he thought, pleased with his quick thinking.

He grabbed an old shower curtain from his garage and rolled Naomi's lifeless body on top of it. He went to the kitchen and grabbed a sharp knife, remembering that all of the victims had been stabbed in the neck. Before he could think about what he was doing, he stabbed and slashed Naomi's neck, hopefully in the same way as the other women were stabbed. He also made some random slices on her palms so they would look like defensive wounds. He was surprised by the relatively small amount of blood that came out of the wounds, which in some places didn't bleed at all. She already had bruising around her eyes, probably from when he choked her, but to him, she looked like she had been beaten. He rolled her body up in the shower curtain and put her in the trunk of his car in the garage. He cleaned everything up in his house, showered, and got dressed in all black. He threw Naomi's running shorts, panties and his clothes that he had on before into the washer and washed them on high heat. He would discard them later, but at least he would wash all of the evidence off of them first. Or maybe he would keep them, at least the panties. He would definitely keep those. He cursed himself for washing them.

It had only been a few hours since Naomi had come into his house, but it was already dark outside. He had to get rid of her body before anyone started looking for her. He headed out of his Carrollwood Village neighborhood, making sure to stop at every stop sign and red light, and to obey the speed limit so as not to cause any attention to himself. He considered dumping her by a pond or maybe in the lake where a hungry alligator could destroy or compromise any potential evidence. He crossed over Dale Mabry, heading east on Fletcher, as he remembered Lake Carroll as a possible spot to dump her body. He turned onto Orange Grove Drive and headed south. Just as he passed Stall Road, he looked to his right and remembered that abandoned old house that sat back off the road in overgrown brush and trees surrounding the property. As he thought about it, he realized it would be better if someone found her so they would assume it was the same guy who had killed those other two girls. He passed the dilapidated wreck of a home and turned into the next driveway he came to on his right, which was the back entrance to an apartment complex. He drove around to the right to the farthest part of the parking lot that backed up to the brush and trees separating the apartments and the adjacent property. He backed his car into the spot closest to where he could cut through the trees to get to the house and turned off the car, including the lights, and waited, watching for any movement or signs of people around.

The closest building, a brown and tan three story remnant of eighties construction, was situated so that all of the windows and balconies faced away from where he was parked. Judging by the years and makes of the cars in the parking lot, the residents were likely middle to lower income, working class folks. The small balconies, with their faded and weathered wooden railings and ripped screens, were further evidence of the condition of the complex and probable social status of the residents. As long as no one was coming or going when he took her body out of the trunk, he should be able to make it through the woods behind the complex without being seen.

His car was secluded on one side by a large dumpster and some low hanging tree limbs on the other. Everything was quiet. He put the latex gloves on that he brought from his house, got out of his car and popped the trunk while he looked around one last time. He picked up Naomi's body, which was still somewhat warm but beginning to show early signs of rigor mortis. She was heavier and more awkward than he expected as he tried to position her so that he wouldn't drop her. He quickly retreated through the brush behind him, thankful for the darkness and lack of any streetlights.

He arrived at the house and realized the front porch would be the best place to leave her. He situated her body so that in the daylight, she should be seen from the street if someone looked directly at the house. He carefully pulled the shower curtain out from under her and tucked it under his arm. He retreated quickly through the darkness back to the where he cut through the trees, threw the shower curtain in the dumpster, and drove away, only turning on his lights once he was closer to the entrance where he had come in. He drove home, once again obeying the speed limit, stopping at every red light and stop sign, tossing Naomi's waterlogged phone and earbuds out his window, one by one, along the way. Once he got rid of her things, he breathed a sigh of relief, pulled off his latex gloves, shoved them in the glove box of his vintage Mercedes, and drove the rest of the way home until he was safely parked back in his garage. Once inside his house, he poured himself a large, fresh glass of Macallan, and drank, feeling the warm liquid gold travel down his throat, instantly settling his frayed nerves. He sat on his couch, sipping on his scotch, thinking about what had happened over the last few hours.

* * *

As he relived the events of that night while sitting in his chambers, including how he had dumped her body on the porch of that abandoned house, he felt his cock starting to get hard again and he decided it was definitely time for a scotch. He poured himself a tall one, surprised that his hand was slightly shaking when he picked up his glass, and realized he was still excited from the rush of it all. He had never felt such power like he did that night. As a judge, he was the most powerful person in the courtroom: holding people's fates in his hands. But holding someone's life in his hands, like when his hands were around Naomi's neck? It was exhilarating. And now that he had tasted it, he knew that he had to experience it again, even if only for a moment.

CHAPTER TWENTY-SEVEN

The first cold front of the season finally blew in, cooling the temperatures down to the high sixties during the day and the fifties during the night. David wore his tight black dress slacks with a charcoal gray, long sleeve, Italian waffle-knit crew neck sweater. He usually wore more conservative dress slacks with a button down dress shirt and a tie, always keeping one or two jackets behind his office door in case he needed to throw one on for an unexpected visit from a parent or the superintendent, but today, being the Thursday before the Thanksgiving break, he dispensed with the more formal attire. As he walked down the crowded hallway on his way to his office, he heard a few students whistle at him while hearing one say, "Lookin' good Principal Miller." He loved every minute of it.

He arrived in his office feeling particularly chipper, forgetting for the moment about all of the things that had been weighing on his mind lately: namely the recent break in at his home, Lila, her attack in the garage, and her recent text revelation about a child. He logged into his computer and checked his emails while halfheartedly listening to the morning announcements over the intercom. He went out to the area where Mrs. Gilbert, the administrative secretary who had worked at the school for the past forty-five years, always kept a hot pot of coffee brewing.

"Good morning, Principal Miller," Mrs. Gilbert said towards his back while he poured himself a large cup of coffee at the coffee station.

"Good morning, Mrs. Gilbert," David returned, having given up many years before on being on a first name basis, "Ready for Thanksgiving?" he asked trying to be polite but not really interested in her reply.

"Oh yes; I've done all of my shopping and all my grandbabies are arriving this weekend," she replied cheerfully, "my children too, but it's those grandbabies I can't get enough of."

David smiled as he headed back into his office, sipping on his coffee to avoid engaging in any further small talk with Mrs. Gilbert. He was only back in his office about five minutes when Bobby, the P.E. coach, came into his office.

"Hey, Dave, gotta minute?"

"Sure, Coach, what's up? C'mon in," David said, gesturing to the red vinyl, padded chairs in front of his desk.

"I wanted to talk to you about the equipment for the football team. We've got one of the best teams in the County but the worst equipment. My boys are playing with old, worn footballs, shoulder pads that we're constantly patching back together, and helmets that have been worn so many times, they stink. We need new equipment, Dave," Coach Bobby pleaded, "I ask every year but somehow it never makes it into the budget."

"I understand, but the budget was tight this year. How much are we talking?"

"Truthfully, we need like $10,000 for everything, but I could get by with $5,000."

"Okay, let me see what I can do. I think I have a little extra in my miscellaneous fund that I can maybe squeeze out from there and there might actually be some left in the sports budget. No way can I come up with ten but I think I can get you the five."

"Thanks, Dave. I knew I could count on you. The boys will be really thankful. They work hard and, for some of them, this is their only shot at going to college. Take Sam Hebert, for example. Sam is a bright, hardworking kid, but the only way he's going to college with his family situation is if he gets noticed on the field."

"What's his family situation?" David asked.

"It's tragic, frankly. His mother was murdered six years ago when a recently fired co-worker came into the office building where she worked and opened fire, killing thirteen people, including his mom. From what I heard, Sam's father, Carl, couldn't handle the pressure of raising two kids by himself and ran off with a stripper two years later. Sam and his brother have been raised since then by relatives, but it has not been an ideal situation. His older brother, Ben, took a wrong turn after high school and I really don't want to see the same thing happen to Sam."

"All right, Bobby, I know, it's important. Submit a detailed request with estimate to Mrs. Gilbert and I'll approve it. You're doing a good job with those boys, Coach. Keep it up," David said as the two men fist bumped and Coach Bobby left his office.

David continued to work in his office, thankful for no further interruptions, until it was time for lunch. There were three lunch periods, with most of the freshmen and sophomores assigned to the first two lunch periods and the juniors and seniors assigned to the third. He always made it a point to walk through the lunch periods to make his presence known and to see who was looking at him. He hoped he would see Maria, the head cheerleader, during third period lunch so she could see what he was wearing today and so he could see what she was wearing. He hoped she was wearing one of her miniskirts, a tight sweater, and her knee-high boots, now that the temperature had dropped a little bit. Maybe they could have a little rendezvous after school.

He finished up his lunchroom tours, disappointed that he didn't see Maria, and stopped by the faculty lunchroom on his way back to his office. There were only a few teachers still in there, including Ms. Dickens, the hot new IB Biology teacher who took over for Mrs. Horvat who was out on leave after being asked by the FDLE to assist on a cold case she had worked years before she left the FDLE to teach at the school. No one knew what the case was, but the rumors were running rampant that it was related to the young women who were recently murdered and attacked. Mrs. Horvat's credibility just rose a few notches with the students, that was for sure.

"Hello, Ms. Dickens, how are you settling into your classes?"

"Very well, Principal Miller, thank you," the pretty blonde teacher responded.

"Call me David. Most of the faculty go by first names unless the students are around."

"Oh, okay, well then, please call me Alecia. The students are great, so eager to learn. It's quite refreshing."

"That's because you get to teach the smart students," came a raspy voice from across the room. "Try teaching the traditional students and let's see how refreshing it is," the gray-haired woman sitting at the other table chuckled as her laugh turned into a wheezing cough.

"Don't listen to her, Alecia; Sheila is just bitter because her students think she's boring," said the curly haired, bearded man sitting across from her doing a crossword puzzle.

"Shut up, Evan, at least my students learn something in my class, unlike yours," the woman they called Sheila with the smoker's voice retorted.

"Oh please, Sheila, science fiction writing is an art, and some of my students are probably going to go on to successful careers in Hollywood, thanks to my class," the sci-fi teacher shot back.

"That's one elective class, Evan, the rest of the time you're teaching shop," Sheila, the smoker, countered, while she continued to laugh or choke to death.

"Whatever, Sheila, jealousy does not become you," Evan said, never lifting his eyes off his crossword.

"Can you believe they're married?" David whispered to Alecia, as he winked and headed towards the door.

David left them to their banter and returned to his office. He worked for the rest of the afternoon, finishing up various reports he had to send to the superintendent before Thanksgiving. He logged out of his computer and re-organized his desk to get ready to leave, just as Robert, the chemistry teacher, poked his head into his office.

"Hey, got a minute?"

"Sure, Robert, but only a few minutes unless it's urgent. I promised my wife I would get home early today," he easily lied, anxious to get out of there to see if he could find Maria.

"Thanks, this should only take a minute or two. I'm sorry to bother you, but I was hoping you could help me with an issue I'm having," Robert began reluctantly.

"Student issue or faculty issue?" David asked, somewhat bored as if he'd heard it all before.

"Um, actually, neither. It's more of a personal issue."

David looked up, his interest now piqued, "what type of personal issue?"

"Nothing sinister or deviant," Robert laughed, nervously, "but I am having an issue with one of my neighbors and a fence I want to install, and someone in the faculty lounge mentioned your wife is an attorney."

Bored again, David replied, "yes, my wife is an attorney. Here, let me give you one of her cards. Give her a call."

"Don't you even want to know what my issue is before you send me to your wife?"

"Nah, it's fine. I handle student, faculty and parent issues. Neighbor issues are my wife's area," David chuckled as he retrieved one of Hallie's business cards from his desk.

Robert took the card as he stood up, looking at David a little strangely. David didn't care. He had no interest in being Hallie's marketing assistant or promoter or whatever title she wanted to give him. At least he handed out her cards from time to time. More importantly, why would he want to listen to any faculty member's bullshit personal problems? What did he look like, Oprah fuckin' Winfrey or Dr. Phil? No, he didn't have time for that shit.

Robert was walking out just as Mrs. Gilbert came in to tell David he had a visitor, a former student named Lila Martinez.

David saw Robert glance back at him, still with the strange look on his face, and then back down at his wife's business card, and walked out of his office. Mrs. Gilbert looked at him expectantly, waiting to see what she should tell Ms. Martinez.

"I'm sorry, what did you say her name was?"

"Lila Martinez."

'I just don't recall her," David lied, "What year did she graduate?"

"I don't know, Principal Miller. She said she was a former student and that you were expecting her. Do you want me to have her fill out a questionnaire?" Mrs. Gilbert asked sarcastically, somewhat suspicious of David's response.

"No, of course not, fine, send her in. I just don't remember her is all. Maybe I will when I see her face," David said, trying to salvage the moment.

"Yeah, maybe her face will ring a bell," Mrs. Gilbert said as she rolled her eyes and walked back to the front office, knowing better than most whether the rumors about David and his student relationships were true.

"Ms. Martinez? Principal Miller will see you now."

Lila walked into David's office and stood awkwardly in the doorway for a moment before David motioned her to one of the chairs in front of his desk.

"Come in, Ms. Martinez. It's very nice to see you again," David said loud enough for Mrs. Gilbert to hear him as he shut the door behind Lila.

"Hello Principal Miller," Lila said coldly.

"What are you doing here Lila?" David whispered so Mrs. Gilbert couldn't hear him, as he sat back down behind his desk.

"You gave me no choice, David," Lila responded, in a tone not quite as hushed as David's.

"How did you expect me to react when you send me a text like that? Is this some kind of a joke?" David asked, noticing the fresh scars on Lila's face and neck for the first time. "Oh my God, you *were* the girl who was attacked in Ybor that night, weren't you? The night we were supposed to meet?"

"Yes, David, I was. When you didn't show up, I walked back to the parking garage by myself, and that's when I was attacked."

"I am so sorry, Lila. I truly am. But I realized it was a mistake to meet you. I am a married man, and the principal of this school. I can't be meeting students, even former students, in sketchy bars late at night."

"Well, maybe you should have told me you weren't going to make it so then maybe I wouldn't have been walking away from that sketchy bar at eleven o'clock at night by myself into a deserted garage," Lila retorted angrily.

Seeing her anger rising and fearing that Mrs. Gilbert was going to overhear them, David suggested they go off campus to Al Lopez Park, which was only about ten minutes away, where they could talk. There were closer parks, but he was afraid there could be students at those parks, participating in after school sports or other activities, who might recognize him. They agreed she would leave first and he would leave a few minutes behind her. They agreed to meet in the parking lot off of the Himes Avenue entrance where they used to meet up when she was a student.

"Goodbye, Lila; thank you so much for stopping in. Please say hello to your mother for me," David said a little too loudly to fool anyone, while waving at Lila as she left his office.

Lila looked over her shoulder and nodded while looking down at her feet to avoid Mrs. Gilbert's knowing gaze. Lying was as hard for Lila as it was easy for David and Mrs. Gilbert wasn't fooled one bit, Lila knew. Lila left the office and headed down the long corridor towards the faculty parking lot where she was parked. As she passed the gray steel lockers and industrial beige cement walls, thick from years of painting over the old, she was reminded of the last times she walked these halls, usually on her way to David's classroom filled with butterflies and excitement of what was to come. How different the hallway looked now: so small and cold and not intimidating or exciting in the way it was when she was a student.

"Lila, is that you?" came a familiar voice from behind her.

Lila turned around at the sound of her name to see Mr. Johnson, her old chemistry teacher, standing in the doorway to the old lab.

"Oh, Mr. Johnson? Yes, it's me, Lila Martinez. How are you? I'm surprised you remembered me."

"How could I forget one of my favorite students? Of course, I remember you. What brings you back here?"

"I'm thinking about applying to HCC to get my AA degree, so I stopped by to get a copy of my transcript for my application and to see if Principal Miller would write me a letter of recommendation," Lila partially lied, once again looking down at her feet. The part about applying to the local community college was actually true, just not the part about getting a letter of recommendation from David.

"Good for you, Lila. If you need a letter of recommendation from anyone else, I would be happy to write one for you. You were always such a bright student and always prepared. I never forget those students, believe me, you're a rare breed," Robert said.

"Thank you, Mr. Johnson. I appreciate it and I'll let you know. It was nice running into you," Lila said as she continued on her path to the faculty parking lot.

"You too, Lila. Good luck and welcome back. I hope to run into you again soon," Robert said as he winked at her.

Lila looked back over her shoulder at him as she walked away. Something about his voice bothered her but she couldn't place it. Maybe it was just the way he was looking at her, including the creepy wink, she thought. Mr. Johnson was no different than a lot of middle-aged men who looked at her curvy body, but he was harmless – just another science geek who spent way too much time in his lab, Lila thought. By the time she reached the parking lot, she had forgotten all about Mr. Johnson and was already thinking about meeting David in the park. She heard the last bell ring while students poured out of every exit of the two-story, historic brick building. She was relieved that she made it out of the hallway before the classes let out. She would have been overwhelmed with all those students filling the hallways, just as she was when she was a student, and picked up her pace as she made her way to her car across the parking lot.

She exited the parking lot onto Central Avenue, automatically taking the familiar route towards Al Lopez Park, reflexively getting butterflies as she passed Principal Miller's black truck in his reserved parking space on her way. She tried to remind herself that she was a teenager when he seduced her; he, as the adult, should have stopped it. But she couldn't help herself; she was excited to see David again and knew she still loved him. He looked even better than he had when she last saw him: he was in better shape, more confident, and distinguished. Like George Clooney, she thought. She reminded herself once again that this wasn't about her and David – those days were probably over. She was here about Vera. No matter what, she was going to make sure he recognized Vera as his daughter.

As she headed for the park, she noticed a black car behind her that seemed to have been following her since she left the school. She was sure it was just a coincidence but since her attack in Ybor, she was nervous and hyper alert about everything around her. She glanced again in the rearview mirror just as the car turned off onto a side street and she chastised herself for being so paranoid. She pulled into the park entrance, pulled down the vanity mirror to put on her fresh pink lipstick, and waited for David.

CHAPTER TWENTY-EIGHT

Officer Catherine West finished her interview with Chrissy, believing they had a serial rapist or worse on their hands. Chrissy was lucky to have gotten away and was extremely credible. She wondered if there was any connection between Chrissy's attack and those recently murdered women. Chrissy certainly fit the profile: young, attractive, picked up in the same area of Lauren White, and brutally attacked. But Chrissy escaped before she became another sad statistic, thankfully. One of the detectives assigned to the serial murder case was one of Catherine's best friends, Marcelo. She texted Detective Marcelo Garcia to see if they had any leads and to tell him about Chrissy.

"I think my s.a. victim could be the one that got away from your guy. You need to check it out," Catherine texted.

"Tell me more. Meet me at Four Green Fields at 5:30. Wanted to see you anyway."

"Ooh, is this your way of asking me out on a date?"

"You always have to make it weird. Just meet me 4GF at 5:30 weirdo."

Catherine smiled at the text, thinking about Marcelo's kind eyes, his full beard that she was always teasing him to shave off, and their last dinner out. Not a date but still, a delightful interaction. Marcelo had asked her out shortly after they first met two years ago, and, admittedly, Catherine thought their first date went well. But having just come out of long tumultuous relationship at the time, Catherine told him she just wanted to be friends. The ever respectful Marcelo accepted that but continued to invite her out, always as friends, much to Catherine's confusion. So now they were the best of friends but Catherine secretly regretted putting the brakes on the relationship and hoped at some point they could grow out of the friend zone.

"Always playing hard to get. Fine, see you at 4GF at 5:30," Catherine texted back.

Four Green Fields was a small Irish bar near downtown Tampa. It was often frequented by lawyers due to its strong drinks and proximity to the many law offices downtown and in Hyde Park. Occasionally officers and detectives from TPD headquarters, which was also downtown, would come in. Marcelo was sitting at a table near the empty stage where they would have live Irish music on the weekends, with two light beers already on the table.

"Have you been here long?" Catherine asked, looking at the time on her phone, worried she was late, as she often was.

"Nah, but my last interview went a lot shorter than planned when the guy lawyered up in the first two minutes," Marcelo responded, "so I got here a few minutes earlier than I thought I would. Got your favorite," he said, motioning towards her pale, blonde ale sitting in front of her.

"I see that, thank you."

"So, tell me about this latest sexual assault victim you've got," Marcelo directed, getting right down to business.

Catherine told him everything she could about Chrissy and what had happened to her, pausing now and then to answer his questions.

"DNA?" Marcelo asked.

"We don't know yet. We've sent the handcuffs out to the lab and we swabbed her face because she said he got pretty close to her, so we're hoping maybe he spit on her and we were able to collect it, but it's a longshot. She escaped before he could rape her, thankfully. How about you?"

"Yeah, we sent the fingernails from the young mother found in Carrollwood to the lab and then uploaded it to CODIS and the FDLE."

Catherine knew that the lab must have come back with enough of a DNA specimen from underneath the victim's fingernails to enter it into the FBI Combined DNA Index System (CODIS) and the Florida Department of Law Enforcement's statewide DNA database. That kind of lead could break this whole case wide open.

"Wow, that's awesome, Marcelo. I hope you get a hit and can nail this sick son of a bitch."

"Well, we got a hit from a cold case from 2005, brutal rape at a hotel, but the guy was never caught and it didn't match to any known person in the system," Marcelo said, obviously frustrated.

"What about those DNA genetic testing sites? You know, the ones to find relatives. That's what they did to catch the Golden State Killer, you know. They uploaded DNA from the crime scene into one of those sites and then found him through some relative match," Catherine offered.

"Does that hold up in court?" Marcelo asked.

"Yes. There was even a case recently where the court ruled it was not a violation of the defendant's constitutional rights and allowed the DNA analysis in as evidence. You should try that, seriously."

"Hmmm. Maybe I will. Let me run it by the Captain. What are the best sites, do you know?"

"Well, I've heard a lot about Ancestry.com and 23andMe. Those are the two big ones, I think."

"Thanks, Cat, that's helpful. So, tell me what else you've been up to besides fighting the good fight and solving the sadistic crimes of Tampa Bay?"

Catherine looked at Marcelo, about to respond, when she looked into his eyes and felt those familiar butterflies in her stomach. Jesus, why did this guy get to her? Sometimes she felt like he was looking through to her soul and knew all of her secrets, which unnerved her and aggravated her at the same time.

"You know," she stammered, "the usual," looking down into her almost empty pale ale.

"So, are you ready to let me take you out on another date one of these days?" Marcelo asked, never taking his eyes off of her.

Catherine blushed, thankful for the dark lighting in Four Green Fields, hoping he wouldn't notice, while her heartbeat kicked up a notch or two. "There you go, confusing me with your tactics again," Catherine replied, trying to figure out if he was serious or not.

Marcelo laughed, "Cat, I've been ready to take you out on another date since our first date, but you weren't ready. I've been patiently waiting for you ever since. So, my question to you is, are you ready now?"

"Well, when you put it like that, well, fine, yes, I'm ready for our second date," Catherine responded awkwardly, which only made her more endearing.

"Awesome. Our second date begins now," Marcelo said, confidently, reaching over and briefly squeezing her hand.

* * *

Marcelo went to the precinct early the next morning and started researching the DNA genetic testing sites and the Golden State Killer case Catherine had mentioned. The Golden State Killer was a serial rapist and murderer who committed at least twelve murders and over fifty rapes in California over a ten-year period beginning in 1976. Investigators had collected DNA from the crime scenes and victims but had not been able to match it to a suspect. The brutal murders and rapes abruptly stopped in 1986 and the case went cold. In 2018, more than thirty years later, a cold case detective teamed up with a retired attorney who helped adopted people find their birth families through genealogy sites to see if they could link the DNA to a suspect in the same way. They created a profile and uploaded the perpetrator's DNA into GEDmatch, one of the only genealogy sites that allows law enforcement to upload DNA and search the profiles of its users in connection with the investigation of violent crimes.

After uploading the DNA from the cold cases, they were able to identify a number of individuals who were third cousins of the perpetrator. Through painstaking and meticulous research, including using birth and death certificates, marriage announcements, and other public records, they built a family tree from the known third cousins to ultimately identify a common ancestor. From there, they worked forward until they were able to narrow down relatives who fit the profile of the Golden State Killer, including approximate age based on the time of the killings and geographic proximity to the area where the crimes occurred. Eventually, one person, Joseph DeAngelo, a 72-year-old grandfather and retired police officer, emerged as the likely suspect. After further investigation of him, he was arrested and DNA collected from him on his arrest connected him to ten cold case murders in California and a number of unsolved rapes.

Marcelo felt he had enough to take to his captain. He went to his captain's office and was happy to see she was in her office.

"Hey, Captain, got a minute?"

"Of course, Detective, come in," Captain Jackie Mastandrea said.

Captain Mastandrea was a force no one fucked with, but she was also fair and kind. She didn't take shit from anyone but didn't give any either unless someone deserved it or challenged her. She was honest and direct, which her officers appreciated. They always knew where they stood with her and she had earned the respect of most of the department over the years.

Marcelo explained his research and the work of the detectives in the Golden State Killer case. He also explained how they had retrieved DNA from under Naomi Bank's fingernails but it didn't get any hits on CODIS or with the FDLE and that he wanted to upload it to GEDmatch.

"Do you think you can get a warrant?" Captain Mastandrea asked.

"Wait, what do you mean? A warrant for what?"

"Well, if you get a judge to give you a warrant that you can serve on all of these genealogy sites, maybe you can upload the DNA you got from Naomi Banks and search them all. And then we may have a better shot of connecting the DNA from our victim to a suspect. Also, if it does lead us to a suspect eventually, then maybe, if we had a warrant from the get-go, the results might hold up in court."

"Actually, only GEDmatch lets you upload the DNA we collected from the victim. The other sites send you a kit that you have to use and will only take saliva. I think we need to start with GEDmatch and see if we get anywhere from there. Also, GEDmatch doesn't require us to have a warrant."

"You don't want to try to get a warrant first?"

"No, because if the judge denies it then we can't even try. There's a lab in Virginia that offers this service to law enforcement around the country. They have an expert genealogist on staff that analyzes the data after they get the DNA results from GEDmatch to create a family tree."

"How much does that cost?" the Captain asked him.

"I don't know but I'll find out. I wanted to run it by you before I proceeded."

"Ok, find out. Let's see if it's doable. Sounds like a good way to go if we have room in the budget."

"Thanks, Captain, I'll find out and let you know."

Marcelo walked out of her office and returned to his desk. He picked up his phone and texted Catherine.

"I had an awesome time last night. I hope u did 2. Also thanks for the lead re DNA sites. I think the captain is going to let me run with it. This could be the break we need."

He waited a few minutes, no response. Well, she might be out on a call, he reminded himself, or she could also be freaking out at the progression of their relationship. When

Marcelo walked her to her car last night, before she opened her door, he leaned into her and kissed her deeply on the lips. She didn't back away and he confessed to her how long he had wanted to do that. She nervously admitted that she had wanted him to do that for a long time too. He found the dichotomy of Catherine, the badass police officer, compared to that Catherine, a little shy and awkward, completely adorable. He hoped she wasn't having any regrets.

He sat down at his desk and pulled up the contact information for GEDmatch. After a few minutes of researching, he heard his phone ping, signifying he had a message.

"Hey you, I had a great time too. Not sure where we stand. Not going to lie, this is kinda freaking me out. But I also want to see what happens next."

"Baby, you overthink things. Meet me at 5:30 at FGF and we'll talk. No pressure. But this is how it's supposed to be. You'll see in time."

Marcelo put his phone down on the desk, smiling at Catherine's messages. She was so secure in her job and all other things, but not with him. He couldn't wait until she felt more comfortable with him. He had liked her from the first time he met her and knew she was special. He loved her analytical mind and how she always tried to stay up on the latest investigation techniques. He never would have thought of the genealogy companies to try to match the DNA found under Naomi Bank's fingernails had Catherine not told him about it. He opened his personal MacBook Pro, went to GEDmatch.com, and registered. He filled out all of the information, including that he was uploading the DNA of an unknown perpetrator for law enforcement purposes. As noted on the site, law enforcement may only use the site in connection with violent crimes, such as murder, aggravated rape, and other similar violent crimes. At the end of the registration, he was able to upload the DNA raw data profile he received from the FDLE.

GEDmatch finds matching segments of DNA from among its 1.3 million users, regardless of which kit they originally used, such as 23andMe or Ancestry.com. He learned that within 24-48 hours, by using the "one-to-many" tool on the site, he would be able to see if the perpetrator's DNA that he uploaded matched any other user on the site. Any such matches would be assigned a number to show the degree of relationship between the DNA match, such as 1 for parent-child, 1.2 for sibling, 1.4 for half sibling, uncle or grandparent, and 2 for cousin, all the way up to 4 for a more distant relative.

* * *

A few days later, Marcelo logged into the account he created on GEDmatch to see if there were any matches. At first, he didn't understand the data that came up on the one-to-many tool, as it generated a spreadsheet with a bunch of numbers in various columns. But the tutorial he found helped explain what each column represented and how to interpret the information. The most important columns included the relationship factor and an email address for the user who uploaded the DNA that matched his perpetrator's DNA. From these columns, he found three significant matches: a potential relative with a 1.0 match, meaning a potential child or parent, a 1.2 match, and a 2.0 degree match. The rest were more distant relatives that could be related by five or more generations up the ancestral chain. He jotted down the email addresses for the three users and any other information he thought could be helpful.

He emailed the user with the closest match, wording his email carefully:

To: jam86@gmail.com
From: mgarcia@TPD.org
Date: November 14, 2019
Subject: DNA Match – Profile #37042A

Hello. I am an officer with the Tampa Police Department. Your DNA showed up as a possible match through a familial relationship to DNA we collected from a recent crime scene. I can assure you that you are not a suspect as it did not match your DNA, but it would help us tremendously if we could speak with you. Please contact me as soon as possible on my cell phone number provided below. Thank you.

Officer Marcelo Garcia
Badge # 2670
Cell: 813-264-1600

He sent an identical email to the other users, each with their respective profile numbers, hoping he would hear from at least one of them soon. If any of them had any relatives who lived in the Tampa Bay area, he might be able to come up with a list of suspects who matched the profile developed by the behavioralists. At this point, they had nothing else to go on other than the similarities of the crimes, the possible connection with the 2005 rape victim, and the statements from the two victims who got away. It would be a start, he thought, just as his cell phone started to ring.

CHAPTER TWENTY-NINE

Hallie's phone started to vibrate that she had a message before her alarm even went off, although she was awake as she often was at that time just relishing the last few moments of calm before the chaos of the day would begin. The only person who messaged her that early was her mother, Rebecca. Her mother had finished her sunrise yoga lesson with Ross and apparently remembered she promised Hallie she would help Katie with her college applications. Why she felt the need to reach out to her at 6:30 a.m. to let her know she hadn't forgotten was a mystery to Hallie. Her mother probably wanted to take the opportunity to mention Ross was still in the picture.

Hallie lay in bed, scrolling on her phone as David finished in the shower. She liked to read the latest news blurbs, emails and check Facebook before getting out of bed to start her day. She texted her Mom back, telling her she was glad Ross joined her at yoga and looked forward to having dinner with them again soon. She also told her to text Katie directly about helping her. As she lay there, she checked her email messages, seeing the usual advertisements and other messages that filled her inbox on a regular basis but luckily nothing from the anonymous emailer who seemed to have gone dark. When her phone started to ring, she assumed it was her mother.

"Hey Mom," she answered without even looking at the phone.

"Bitch, I'm the same age as you, don't start calling me mom," came Bridget's unexpected voice in her ear.

"Good God, why are you calling me this early? Everything okay?"

"Yeah, everything's fine; I saw you were active on the Facebook so I knew you were awake."

Haley couldn't help but smile at her best friend's reference to "the Facebook." It always amused her when she called it that, as if she was so out of touch. "Jesus, I haven't even had my coffee yet, Bridget. Also, I'm not buying it. What's up?"

"Okay, well, Jay might have a lead on who is sending you those weird emails. I'm not supposed to tell you, but he got an address from the search warrant on the IP address."

"And???" Hallie asked, impatiently.

"I don't know anything yet because Jay won't tell me because he knows I'll tell you," she laughed, "but as soon as I hear anything else, I'll let you know. The only thing I might have overheard is that it may have originated from one of the office buildings downtown."

"When will he know something do you think?"

"I don't know, maybe later today? I think they're going to check out who works in the office that matches the IP address. I'll let you know if I hear anything else."

They said their goodbyes just as David came out of the bathroom, dressed for work.

"Who was that this early? Everything okay?" he asked.

"Bridget. She said they may have gotten a match on the IP address where the weird emails originated. Possibly coming from an office downtown."

"Anything else?"

"No, that's all she knows right now. She'll let me know if she hears anything else."

"Okay, well, I'm heading into work. Let me know if you hear anything else. Also, I have a faculty meeting after school today, so I'll be late. And a few of us might grab a beer afterwards so don't worry about dinner for me tonight."

Hallie was annoyed but didn't let him know, not wanting to trigger an argument before she had even had her coffee and ruin her morning. It seemed there were more so-called faculty meetings in the past few months than she ever remembered before. In her gut, she knew he wasn't being honest with her, but she didn't have the energy to deal with it yet. After the holidays, she was going to confront David about working on their marriage by going to counseling or separating. She couldn't keep living this way.

She climbed out of bed as Juno looked up at her from her bed on the floor and then rested her head back down, knowing the routine. It wasn't time to go out until Hallie washed up, brushed her teeth, put her contacts in, and got dressed, not that Juno knew what Hallie was actually doing. But Juno had learned that the final step in the routine was when Hallie sat in her chair to put her tennis shoes on, which was Juno's signal to get up. Juno bounded down the stairs ahead of Hallie and waited for her by the front door. There was a time when Juno would have to be on a leash, but those days were over. Juno wasn't going anywhere and would stay in the front or side yard close to the house. Every once in a while, one of the neighborhood cats would venture into the yard while Juno was out there, and she would put on a show of chasing them out of her territory. Hallie thought the cats did it to humor the old girl.

The fall weather had returned again after the recent heat spell, and the morning temperature was perfect: no humidity and about 65 degrees. But cool enough that she was glad she put her Tampa Bay Lightning hoodie on this morning. She looked up into the trees, still holding onto their leaves, and at the palm trees in the distance as the sun beamed through from the blue, cloudless sky. This was the weather that made up for the brutal summers, Hallie thought, and was a perfect morning for a run on Bayshore. Juno followed her up the weathered steps of the front porch into the warm bungalow where Hallie fed her breakfast, made herself a cup of coffee and went upstairs to change into her running clothes. It was still early enough to get a quick run in before she had to shower and face the work waiting for her at her desk.

Sometimes when she ran, she had absolute clarity of thought and could see things in a different light or from a different perspective she hadn't considered before. Today was one of those runs. Her heart pounded, her breathing regulated into its familiar rhythm, and she thought about Katie, her precious only child. She knew the news about how she came to be in this world was going to devastate her, and she was thankful that Kevin and Jodi were going to be there to support her and help her deal with it. But how was it going to affect her relationship with her daughter? Would she be angry with her for not telling Kevin or anyone else about the rape? If she had told Kevin what happened back then, he would have questioned the paternity, as anyone in his position would have. And Katie would have grown up without a father, Hallie was sure of it. Kevin couldn't have handled it back then.

Now he has loved Katie as his own for almost eighteen years – as he said, she's his daughter and nothing can change that. For that alone, for having Kevin, who was a good father, in Katie's life all these years, Hallie had no regrets. She and Kevin agreed that although they would tell Katie about what happened, they did not intend to tell her who her biological father was. But Hallie knew that one day Katie might try to find out on her own. Her daughter came before everyone and everything else in her life and

Hallie realized she was not responsible for Judge Stephens' actions before or after he raped her. She refused to succumb to survivor's guilt or to absolve him of any responsibility for his crimes. She didn't do anything to cause him to rape her nor did any of his other victims, and she certainly wasn't responsible, her silence or not, for anyone he raped after her. He had to bear that responsibility alone. And she was going to make sure he did. She picked up her pace as she ran along the Bay, feeling the cool salty air against her face and seeing the charcoal fin of a dolphin break the surface of the water, and she knew exactly what she had to do.

CHAPTER THIRTY

"Detective Garcia," Marcelo answered, not recognizing the incoming 813 number.

"Hello, Detective, my name is Hallie Miller, and I'm an attorney here in Tampa. You recently sent an email to one of my clients about some DNA results. Is this a good time to talk?"

"Yes, Ms. Miller, of course."

"Please, call me Hallie."

"Thank you for contacting me, Hallie. Is your client willing to talk to me?"

"Well, it depends. To be honest, I'm just here to gather a little more information from you before my client will talk to you."

"Are you a criminal defense attorney? As I assured your client in my email, your client is not a suspect, so I'm not sure why he felt the need to lawyer up, I'm sorry, I mean, retain the services of counsel."

Hallie laughed easily as she responded, "he didn't have to lawyer up, as you say, because I'm his regular corporate attorney, not a criminal defense attorney. So, when he got your email, as with most things, he immediately sent it to me to get my input. I figured I would call you to see what we're dealing with here and how my client can possibly help."

"Okay, counselor, makes sense. I can't tell you much because it's an active investigation, but we have a series of unsolved rapes and murders in the area. We have obtained DNA from some of the crime scenes and may have a match of the suspect, through a familial relationship, to your client. We just want to ask him some questions to see if he has any relatives who live in the Tampa Bay area who may fit the profile. That's all; as I said, your client is not a suspect as his DNA does not match."

"Wow, that's actually really interesting. I was reading something about that recently. Isn't that how those detectives in California solved that Golden State Killer case?" Hallie asked, genuinely interested.

"Um, I don't know anything about that case," Marcelo lied, diverting the conversation away, "but we have this possible lead and we need to follow it. Is your client willing to help us or not?"

"Let me talk to my client. Can you tell me this, is this connected to the women who have been murdered recently? Lauren White and Naomi Banks?"

"I'm sorry," he stuttered, caught off guard when Hallie mentioned the two women's names, "I'm not able to tell you anything more at this time. But your client's help could prove invaluable in ensuring no other women are killed or raped by this guy if we can catch him," Marcelo said, hoping he didn't convey anything he shouldn't have.

"Ok, Detective, thank you. I'll call you back after I speak with my client."

Hallie hung up, thinking about how the detective hesitated and stumbled over his speech when she mentioned Lauren White and Naomi Banks. It was obviously related to those murders and she wondered how her client was possibly connected to them or the guy who hurt them. She also didn't correct the detective as he kept referring to her client as "he" when her client is actually a "she." Her client, Nicole Rodriguez, who was the founder and CEO of an investment group that invested in local, high-end restaurants, had called her that morning to tell her about the strange email she received from the detective. She asked Hallie to call him back because she would always want to help if she could, but she wanted to make sure it wasn't a scam. Hallie called her to let her know what she knew and that it was not a scam; she had validated Detective Garcia's credentials and spoke to him personally.

"So, what do you want to do? Do you want to call him or do you want me to arrange a meeting? I can attend with you, but I do believe it's legit."

"Oh my God, this is terrifying. To think one of my relatives might be responsible for some kind of violent crime. What do you think I should do, Hallie?" Nicole asked.

"Well, I think we should at least meet with the detective to see if you can help. Do you have a lot of family in this area?"

"Well, my ancestors originally came from Cuba on my father's side and England on my mother's side, believe it or not. But we are third generation in Tampa. So yes, I have so many cousins, aunts, and uncles in Tampa, some of whom I've never even met, frankly. But if I can help, obviously, I want to help. Set up the meeting."

* * *

The next day, Hallie accompanied her client, Nicole, to the police headquarters in downtown Tampa on Franklin Street to meet with Detective Garcia. Hallie parked her BMW on Madison Avenue in a metered spot. She pulled up the Park Mobile app on her phone and paid the meter for two hours. She and Nicole walked across the street, past the park in front of the police headquarters. Hallie noticed the contrast of the businessmen and women in their suits, sitting on benches to steal a moment away from their cold, stark offices to relish the Florida weather, and the vagrants sitting in the grass or near trashcans, hoping for a meal or a little cash to get through the day and colder night. The contrast was always there but never as obvious as when the temperature dropped resulting in the paths not only crossing but overlapping, especially in the park in the center of downtown.

Detective Garcia met them at the front desk. Hallie noticed his gentle manner and kind eyes, instantly and uncharacteristically trusting him for some unknown reason. He escorted them back into what was likely an interrogation room, which was devoid of any furniture or other aesthetics other than a bolted down, industrial wooden table that had probably been there longer than Hallie had been alive, and four plastic, uncomfortable chairs that served their purpose but little else.

"Thank you for coming in, Ms. Rodriguez. So, I think the best way to do this is to tell you about the person we think might be responsible for a number of crimes in our area – violent crimes – and if you can think of anyone you're related to that might fit that profile, or um, description, you let us know. Would that be alright?"

"Yes, I will try to help in any way I can, but as I was explaining to Hallie, as a third generation Tampa native, I have a ton of family in the area, so this might be difficult."

Detective Garcia nodded, as if to say he understood, while he opened a manila folder he had placed in front him on the wooden table. He retrieved the printout of the profile the Behavioral Analysis Unit of the FBI had prepared on the unknown offender who the TPD now suspected had attacked Lauren White, Naomi Banks, Lila Martinez, and Chrissy Wright.

Reading from the report, he began:

"The suspect is likely a white male, between the ages of 45 and 60, middle class, college educated, and probably holding a job where he can do his job by rote, such as an accountant, bookkeeper, mid-level office worker, or other job where he goes unnoticed as long as he does his job. He kills for revenge, to punish his victims. His victims represent his anger at all women who have slighted or rejected him in his life, which likely started with his mother and which he projects onto all women. He probably did not have a strong male figure in his life growing up and his mother may have been promiscuous, further leading to his disdain of women and lack of significant relationships with men in his life. He has likely been arrested for domestic violence at some time in his adult life, and possibly stalking or voyeurism, especially in his teenage years. At times he can be methodical and charming, but he has impulse control issues, so this individual probably has a volatile and violent temper that he tries to hide but is unable to control once unleashed.

Lauren White, Lila Martinez, and Chrissy Wright all fit the same victimology: attractive, college-age young women, long hair, similar body types, all three leaving bars late at night by themselves. The offender's mother was likely an alcoholic, may have been a stripper or prostitute, or at least engaged in other behavior that put her at risk for unwarranted attacks by men, which could have been witnessed by the offender from a young age. Instead of blaming the men his mother came in contact with, he blamed her and judged her for her inappropriate and dangerous lifestyle. The offender wants to punish these women who were out drinking in bars late at night, leaving by themselves, just as he wanted to punish his mother for her choices that scared him as a child, although he probably never did. It should be noted that Naomi Banks doesn't fit the victimology, and although she could have been an impulse attack, it is more likely that she is a copycat victim, killed by someone else who staged the attack to look like the same offender but who is motivated by something completely different."

After he finished, Detective Garcia looked up at Nicole and Hallie, "so, Ms. Rodriguez, can you think of any male relatives who are white, between the ages of 45-60 and fit the description at all? Anyone at all that you can think of?"

Nicole compiled a list of the male relatives she could think of who were in the right age range, although she didn't think many of the other characteristics matched. In all, she gave the detective a list of about thirteen names, which consisted of cousins and two uncles, one on her mother's side and the other on her father's side. When she finished, she asked the detective to give her a few minutes to talk to Hallie alone before she turned the list over to him.

The Detective left the room and Hallie turned to Nicole, "what's up? Are you having second thoughts about turning over the list?"

"Well, I just wanted to ask you, none of these people can sue me or cause any issues for me for identifying them, right? All I'm doing is giving them a list of family members' names, right? But what if they find out the information came from me? Is there anything they can do?"

"Hmm, good question. No, legally, there is nothing they can do, but I don't know who your family members are. You're simply cooperating with a police investigation, and if they aren't connected to the murders or attacks in any way, then they probably won't ever learn you gave the police their names. But if any of them do turn out to be involved, well, I suppose it could come out during a trial. But I think we're getting ahead of ourselves; is there anyone on the list that you're particularly concerned about?"

"Well, actually, just one, although I never thought he was anything more than just my creepy uncle. He also might be older than the range in the profile but I'm not sure how old he actually is. Anyway, I never saw any signs of violence from him, but he's always just made me uncomfortable. Also, everyone in his family, including his mother, are pretty heavy drinkers. But he's a judge, so I'm concerned about what he could do to me if he finds out I included his name on the list."

"A judge? Which judge?" Hallie asked, holding her breath as she knew who Nicole was going to say before she answered.

"Judge William Stephens, one of my mother's brothers. Do you know him?"

CHAPTER THIRTY-ONE

Heather picked up dinner from Forbici and a bottle of red wine for her girls' night in with Natalie. She picked up all of her favorites: their amazing wings, fregola sarda, and a marguerita pizza, with the best sauce and fresh basil Heather had tasted on a pizza since she moved to Florida. It reminded her of the pizza she used to have with her dad when they visited New York City. Thinking about it brought back warm memories.

As Heather carried the food over to the small dining room table, Natalie scrambled to clear away the papers and newspaper clippings that were arranged in stacks on the table. Before she cleared it away, Heather realized that what she was trying to clear away were articles about Judge Stephens and a pile that seemed to be about a woman named Hallie Miller.

"What's all this?" Heather asked, looking closer at the papers Natalie was gathering.

"Just some research I was doing," Natalie answered.

Heather read the names written on the yellow legal pad in front of her: Judge Stephens and Hallie Miller, "why are you researching Judge Stephens and Hallie Miller? Who is she? Oh my God, is this about that story I told you about in the office a few weeks ago? What's going on, Natalie?"

"Nothing, the story just interested me."

"Nope, not buying it," Heather said as she put the food down and started to open the bottle of wine. "What's really going on?"

"Really, it's nothing, please pour our wine. We're starting season six tonight, right?" Natalie said, trying to change the subject.

"Fine, I'll open the wine, and yes, we're starting season six, but not until you tell me why a random story of office gossip has you so intrigued you're doing your own research," Heather said, as she simultaneously uncorked the wine and filled the two glasses that Natalie had sitting on the table.

"Okay, can we sit down? I haven't shared this with anyone in many years. But I trust you, Heather. And after I tell you, I think you'll understand why I felt it was more important than just a little office gossip."

"You're scaring me, Natalie," Heather said as she kicked off her sandals and settled back into Natalie's couch with her glass of wine, eagerly anticipating what her friend had to share with her.

Natalie took a deep breath and began, "it was April 22, 2005, and I went to a networking event at the Westshore Marriott hotel. It was a mix of lawyers, accountants, and other professionals and I thought it would be good for my career to go. I remember distinctly only having one glass of wine, which actually wasn't even that good, so I wasn't drinking it very quickly. Around the room they had all those high top bar tables that people would gather around as they chatted about people they knew, what they did, what they could do for each other. I remember I put my drink down a few times to get my business card out of my purse to hand to someone who I was talking to. At one point, I also left my drink and asked the woman I was chatting with to watch it for me while I ran to the bathroom, which she did. When I returned, I finished my one drink while I continued to mingle with a few other people. But it wasn't long before I started to feel dizzy. I remember looking for somewhere to sit down because I was really feeling woozy. And that was the last thing I remembered before I woke up the next morning, alone in a hotel room, naked, and bleeding from having been brutally raped and sodomized. From tests at the hospital, they determined that I had been drugged with a large dose of Rohypnol, more commonly known as a roofie. And for all of these years, I had no idea who could have done this to me. Until now."

"Oh my God, that's awful, Natalie, I'm so sorry that happened to you."

"Thank you. It's taken me a lot of years but I'm finally coming to terms with it, and getting closure, finally, after all of these years is certainly helping."

"Wait, what do you mean, until now? You don't think your attacker was Judge Stephens, do you?"

"Yes, I do. It all makes sense now. He was there that night. He talked to me. I never put it together until you told me about what you overhead Paige saying, but he was there, and he was creepy."

"Natalie, this is all just a huge coincidence. I understand wanting to have closure and hold the person who hurt you responsible -- believe me, more than you know, I do understand. But I think you're just, well, I don't know, jumping on a story I told you, which we don't even know is true, to connect it to what happened to you so you can blame someone. You have to let this go, for your sake."

"No, listen, maybe you are right about how this started but I really think there's a connection after all of the research I did. I learned that Hallie Miller, the attorney who worked with Paige Rhodes at Behrenfeld Vincent when they both first started out, was one of the firm's rising stars and on a fast track to partnership when she abruptly left the firm in 2002 to join a small, unknown firm. Turns out, Judge Stephens was the managing partner of the firm at the time and continued to manage the firm until he ran for his seat on the bench in 2006. It makes no sense why an attorney with such a promising career would leave such a prestigious firm so abruptly for a position far less promising unless something happened. He obviously did the same thing to her, as you overheard Paige talking about, but she never reported it or did anything about it. And because of her, how many other women, including me, were raped by this monster?"

Heather had to pause for a minute to make sure her own words didn't sound too confrontational, "so, am I hearing you right, you are blaming this Hallie person for what happened to you because she didn't come forward back then?"

"Yes, you're damn straight I am. I mean, don't get me wrong, Judge Stephens is the sick son of a bitch who is ultimately responsible and has to pay, but she is responsible too. If she had reported what he did to her, maybe he would have gone to prison and then he wouldn't have been around to rape me or whoever else he did this to. Do you have any idea how that night ruined my life?"

"It's a horrible thing that you went through; believe me, I do understand, and I'm so sorry you went through that," Heather said, instinctively reaching for the scar on her neck, "but you don't know that her reporting it would have changed anything. He was a very powerful lawyer at the time, the managing partner of one of the most prestigious firms in town, and she was just a lowly associate, so I can imagine that had to be so frightening and intimidating for her."

"Well, we'll never know because she didn't even try to stop him from hurting anyone else," Natalie said, the anger evident in her tone and her eyes.

"So, what are you going to do now? Are you going to tell the police what you've learned?" Heather asked, dumbfounded at her friend's blaming of the victim and wanting desperately to change the subject and get out of there.

"The statute of limitations has run on my case, so I'm not sure the police can do anything. But if he's done this to anyone else more recently, maybe the information can help them. I will tell the police eventually but before I do, I'm going to confront Hallie Miller, in her perfect little house and her perfect little life in Hyde Park, where she sits with her husband and daughter and pretends nothing ever happened and doesn't take any responsibility for the fact that she didn't tell anyone what that bastard did to her. I'm going to see what she has to say for herself."

"Oh, Natalie, I don't think that's a good idea. Just tell the police what you suspect and let them investigate it. You don't actually know anything, by the way. It could have been anyone at that event or even just visiting the hotel who did this to you. Just because he was there and I overheard some random conversation about an alleged rape doesn't make it fact," Heather pleaded, trying to talk some sense into her friend.

"Look, you don't know what I've been through. And I just know in my heart that Judge Stephens raped me, just as he raped Hallie Miller years before, and she could have done something about it. I'm just going to ask her why she didn't tell the police or do anything to try to stop him from hurting anyone else. I think I have a right to know."

"No, you don't know that, Natalie. And you certainly don't have a right to torment this poor woman and bring up these painful memories for her, if they're even true, which are based on a one-sided conversation I overheard!" Heather yelled, completely losing her temper.

"I'm sorry but I've been tormented with the memories of waking up bloody and battered for the last fourteen years, always wondering who did it to me and why it had to happen to me. After all of this time, I'm finally going to get the answers I deserve so maybe I can stop the nightmares once and for all. If you don't understand that, well, just be thankful you've never had to go through anything like I've had to go through."

"Once again, you're wrong about so many things. I have to go. I can't talk about this anymore. I'm sorry I ever said anything to you," Heather said, frustrated and angry that she couldn't get through to her as she picked up her purse and car keys and stormed out of Natalie's apartment, slamming the door a little too loudly behind her.

As she drove home, she couldn't figure out if she was angrier at Natalie or herself for sharing the gossip with her in the first place. If she was being honest, she was angrier with herself. She knew better. But it had been so long since she had a close friend, someone she could share secrets with, confide in, and she thought she and Natalie were reaching that stage. She trusted her.

"Look where that got you," she said aloud, shaking her head. Now she had to worry about her job if anyone traced Natalie's story back to her and the conversation she overheard outside of Paige's office. At one time, she thought she could tell Natalie about her own past with Bobby and how she fled in the middle of the night to start a new life. How for years she lived in constant fear, always looking over her shoulder. How she had only started to let down her guard and feel stronger in the past few years. Now she knew she could never share her story with her. Natalie would never understand, because, like Hallie, she just ran and never looked back. Fear and self-preservation motivate people differently and Natalie didn't have the right to judge Hallie or her for their decisions. Heather was sad at the realization that she and Natalie would never be the close friends she thought they would be, especially in light of the night's events.

She drove over the Howard Frankland Bridge towards her cottage in Indian Rocks Beach, leaving the lights from the Tampa skyline behind her in her rearview mirror. The Gulf under the bridge was rough tonight, splashing up against the concrete barriers at the bridge's lowest points, the first hint of the impending storms rolling in overnight.

CHAPTER THIRTY-TWO

Monday morning, Kevin left for the office right after breakfast, kissing Jodi goodbye while she was loading the dishwasher with their breakfast dishes. She had made him his favorite this morning, avocado toast with two fried eggs, over medium, with a side of real bacon. She finished cleaning the kitchen, poured herself a second cup of coffee, and sat down at the kitchen counter with her laptop. Still in her bathrobe, she wanted to go through her emails, twitter feed, and Facebook before jumping in the shower since she hadn't been online in a few days. Friday morning, Kevin had surprised her by taking the day off and renting a room at the Sand Pearl for the weekend, complete with spa treatments for both of them. It was an unexpected treat and a nice break from the stress of the last few weeks since they received Katie's DNA test results and Hallie's revelation.

Most of Jodi's inbox was filled with advertisements, coupons, and other unimportant notifications from various senders. She found an email from her favorite aunt with an Amazon gift certificate and a note:

Happy belated birthday, love! Finally catching up on things since returning from my cruise and saw I missed your birthday. I hope it was wonderful!

Love, Aunt Claire xoxo

She was almost done deleting all of the spam emails when she came across an email with a subject line and sender that caught her eye. Ever since she had ordered the DNA kits through 23andMe, she was constantly receiving unsolicited emails about genealogy and ancestry or family tree tracking services, but this one didn't seem like an advertisement, and she was right. She read the email twice before fully understanding its import:

To: jam86@gmail.com
From: mgarcia@TPD.org
Date: November 14, 2019
Subject: DNA Match – Profile #37042A

Hello. I am an officer with the Tampa Police Department. Your DNA showed up as a possible match through a familial relationship to DNA we collected from a recent crime scene. I can assure you that you are not a suspect as it did not match your DNA, but it would help us tremendously if we could speak with you. Please contact me as soon as possible on my cell phone number provided below. Thank you.

Officer Marcelo Garcia
Badge # 2670
Cell: 813-264-1600

Jodi went into the office and retrieved the three DNA test results she, Kevin, and Katie had received from 23andMe. The unique profile number assigned to each test result was listed at the top of each page, although all three tests were tied to her email address because she had been the one to order the kits. The top righthand corner of Katie's test results reflected that her profile number was #37042A. Jodi picked up her cell phone and called Kevin.

After telling Kevin about the email, they agreed they should speak to Hallie before calling the detective. Kevin sent a text to Hallie:

"Hey, can you talk? Jodi received an email from a detective we want to run by you before we call the detective back. When you call me back, I'll explain."

Kevin's phone rang about ten seconds after he sent Hallie the text.

"Wow, that was quick," Kevin said as he answered.

"Kevin, is the email from a Detective Garcia at TPD?" Hallie asked, sounding alarmed.

"Yes, that's exactly who it's from; how did you know that? Did you get one too?" Kevin asked, confused.

"Shit. Can you and Jodi meet me downtown? Meet me at Hattrick's in an hour. I'll explain everything."

Hallie hung up and tried to process all of the information she had learned over the past few days and how it fit with everything she now knew. Judge Stephens was a brutal rapist who had raped her eighteen years ago and was the biological father of her daughter, Katie. DNA from one of the crime scenes was uploaded into a genetic database that matched to her client, Nicole, who happened to be Judge Stephens' niece, and now also matched to Katie, his biological daughter. There was no question the DNA collected from the crime scene belonged to Judge Stephens and she had to tell Detective Garcia what she knew. But she also had to consider how this was going to affect Katie. Before they did anything else or notified Detective Garcia, she knew she had to tell Kevin who Katie's biological father was.

As she was locking her front door to head out, Hallie's phone rang but she didn't recognize the number, which had a 252 area code. She decided to answer it just in case it was important.

"Hello?"

"Hi, can I speak to Hallie Miller?"

"This is her."

"Oh, Mrs. Miller, my name is Robert Johnson and I work with your husband, David. He gave me your card as I'm having an issue with one of my neighbors and the

HOA and David said you might be able to help me. Is this a good time?"

"Please, call me Hallie. I was actually just running out the door to a meeting. But if you want to tell me a little about your problem while I'm driving, I can see if it's something I'll be able to help you with," Hallie said as she got into her BMW and switched her phone to her handsfree.

She listened to Mr. Johnson tell his story about wanting to put up a six foot privacy fence surrounding his backyard but only four foot chain link fences were allowed in the deed restricted community. He had applied to the HOA for an exception but one of his neighbors objected and his only recourse was to appeal to the HOA and show why it was a necessity and wouldn't decrease the property values in the neighborhood.

"Is this something you can help me with?" he asked when he finished his story.

"Actually, this is more of a land use issue and there are attorneys who specialize in HOA disputes. One of my good friends, Paige Rhodes, used to handle these types of cases all the time and may still handle them. You'll be in much better hands with her or she can refer you to someone who can help you. Are you calling me from a cell phone?"

"Yes, this is my cell."

"Okay, when I get to my destination, I'll text you her contact information. Just let her know that I referred you.

If she can't help you, I'm sure someone else in her firm can," Hallie said, not wanting to take on a new case at the moment anyway.

"Thanks, Mrs. Mill--, I mean, Hallie, I really appreciate your time."

She was about a half an hour early and Hallie found a parking space on the same block as Hattrick's. Must be her lucky day, she thought. She pulled up her Park Mobile app, paid the meter for two hours, and turned her car off. She quickly forwarded Paige's contact information at the firm to David's colleague and went to get a table at the often crowded, popular restaurant/sports bar. While she waited for Kevin and Jodi at the table, after ordering an unsweetened iced tea from the waiter, she sent Paige a text to let her know the PNC, which was short for potential new client, would probably be calling her.

Hallie's text to Paige was brief. It said PNC and included his name, number, and that he was one of David's colleagues. She also disclosed that it wouldn't be a huge case so to feel free to punt to an associate if she wanted.

"Thanks, Hal. We're all set for drinks Thursday night at Ulele with Mike if you're still interested in talking to him," Paige texted back.

"More than ever. I have some intel to update you on too. 4:30?" Hallie responded.

"Sounds good, see you in a few days."

CHAPTER THIRTY-THREE

Heather hadn't seen Natalie since she stormed out of her apartment last Friday evening. They had briefly exchanged texts over the weekend, short and to the point, both apologizing to the other and just basically agreeing never to discuss it again. But Heather realized that Natalie had some serious opinions about things that were diametrically opposed to Heather's own views, so she decided she would just keep her distance and let that friendship dwindle. She just couldn't get past how Natalie seemed angrier at and wanted to blame the victim more than the person who allegedly hurt her.

Paige called out to Heather, as she often did instead of using the phone intercom, "Hey, I'm expecting a call from a PNC referred by my friend, Hallie Miller. If he calls, set up a thirty-minute, free phone consultation on my calendar."

"Okay, what's his name?"

Reading from Hallie's text, Paige responded, "Robert Johnson."

"Okay, you got it. I'll let you know if he calls," Heather answered as she wrote his name on the yellow legal pad she kept by her desk phone. She worked for the next few hours preparing the pleadings binder for a mediation Paige had scheduled the following week. She completely lost track of time and realized she hadn't taken her lunch yet.

She brought the pleading binder into Paige's office and dropped it in her inbox on the corner of her desk, as she said, "Here's the pleading binder for next week's mediation in the Marotta case. Let me know if you want me to add anything else to it or organize it differently."

"Great, thanks for getting to that. I'll take that home tonight to review."

"I'm going to run and grab a late lunch. Do you need anything?"

"No, I'm good, I had a protein bar in my desk, but thanks for asking."

Heather left Paige's office, grabbing her purse as she made her way to the elevator. She wasn't even that hungry but she wanted to take a break and maybe take a walk outside. She stood in front of the elevator, waiting, watching the numbers above the door as if watching them would make the elevator arrive faster, until the elevator finally arrived on her floor. The elevator doors opened and as she went to step on, there was Natalie, returning from her own lunch, Heather presumed.

"Oh hey," Natalie said, awkwardly, as she tried to walk past her to get off of the elevator.

"Oh sorry, should've let you off first but didn't see you. Just heading out to grab a late lunch. One of those weeks, you know?" Heather responded as she sidestepped Natalie to get on the elevator. The doors closed without either of them saying another word, but the exchange left Heather feeling just as uncomfortable as she had Friday night.

* * *

Heather came back from her late lunch, thankful she didn't have another weird elevator exchange with Natalie, and saw she the voicemail light blinking on her desk phone to let her know she had a message.

She sat down, put her purse in her bottom desk drawer, and got situated. She picked up the receiver and pushed the voicemail button to listen to the message, pen in hand, ready to write down any important information:

"Hello, my name is Robert Johnson, and I was referred to Paige Rhodes by Hallie Miller. I would like to set up an appointment with Ms. Rhodes to see if she can help me with my case. My number is 252-647-6328."

Heather dropped the receiver onto her desk with a loud thud, instantly feeling nauseous. She looked up and down the length of the hallway that she could see from where she was sitting in her cubicle, terrified to stand up or look anywhere else. She hadn't yet regained her composure when Paige came out of her office to drop some files on her desk.

"Oh my God, Heather, are you feeling okay? You're white as a ghost. Are you sick?" Paige asked, genuinely concerned.

Heather was frozen, unable to speak while she tried not to hyperventilate, her breathing erratic while her trembling hands were sweaty and clammy. Paige threatened to call an ambulance, suspecting Heather was having a stroke or a heart attack, when she finally got her breathing under control and tried to convey to Paige with a hand gesture that she was okay. She instinctively placed her hand over the scar on her neck, looked up at Paige, her hazel eyes welling up with tears, and whispered in the most terrified voice Paige had ever heard:

"It's him."

CHAPTER THIRTY-FOUR

Robert was shocked to see Lila sitting in the front office when he came out of David's office. She looked as beautiful as she did that night in Ybor when he followed David to see who he was going to meet. He had no idea it would be Lila and was pleasantly surprised when he saw her get out of her car. He had always had such a crush on her. She reminded him of his wife, who ran away from him in the middle of the night many years ago, the fucking bitch, he thought. One day he would find her again, just as he had promised her, and then they would be together forever. Lila definitely looked like her, with her long, curly brownish-red hair, and big brown eyes, and, well, her amazing body, which is what drew his attention to her in the first place. When he saw her in Ybor that night, he just couldn't contain himself. He was exhilarated and knew it was his only opportunity to finally have his way with her after she abruptly left high school a few years before. But then, the little slut ran away from him before he could finish the job. He assumed she had died that night, but now, here she was, alive and well, waiting for Principal Miller, just like her high school days, and he had a second chance. The thought excited him beyond belief.

He waited in his classroom until he saw Lila pass by in the hallway. He opened his door and called her name. She turned around, smiling as she recognized him, and saying hello to him. That pleased him very much and he made a mental note to remember that later when he was killing her. They had a brief conversation and then she headed towards the exit that led to the faculty parking lot.

He locked up his classroom and went out the side exit, which got him to the faculty parking lot before Lila could have gotten there. He got in his car and waited. Within a few minutes, Lila came out of the school and got in the same white car he recognized from that night in Ybor. He followed her out of the parking lot, a few cars behind her, until the cars in between turned off, closing the gap between them. As soon as they went a few blocks and he realized the direction they were heading, he suspected she was meeting David at the park, just like her high school days and David's favorite spot to meet his conquests. Robert often followed him and watched, sometimes recording David's trysts for his own enjoyment and for security should he ever need it in the future. That's how Robert discovered David was fucking Lila. She should have been fucking him, not David, that he also knew. But, like most of the sluts at the school, she just batted her eyelashes at him, shook her ass a little bit, always trying to improve her grade or get out of some lab assignment. And, of course, it worked, Robert chuckled to himself. But Lila was different, mostly because she looked like his wife, except his wife's eyes were hazel, not brown. The resemblance was uncanny, and she piqued his interest as soon as she came into his classroom that first day. But then one day, she just left and moved back to South Florida with her family. He thought he would never see her again, and then there she was, walking in that tight, short mini skirt and high heels in a deserted garage in Ybor City. Fate, he thought.

Thinking back on that night, he realized that his excitement caused him to make some mistakes that he would not make again when he got the opportunity to be with her again. He would plan things perfectly and take his time with her. He couldn't wait to watch the life drain out of her, drop by glorious drop. He thought about his wife, too. From a phone call he received a little while after she left North Carolina, he believed she was somewhere in Florida. He didn't know exactly where but he would find her one day. And then he would punish her for running away from him in the middle of the night, just like he would punish Lila for running away from him too.

But for now, he just had to wait. He would follow Lila home from the park so he would know where she lived. And then, she would be his. As the sun started to go down in the distance, he sat in his car underneath the trees where he had a clear view of David and Lila talking outside of David's truck. He thought about her big brown, terrified eyes that night in Ybor and he thought about how he straddled her and stuffed her own panties into her mouth to keep her from screaming, all of which made him rock hard. He closed his eyes thinking about that night and started to stroke himself, confident she would be his again. Next time, though, it wouldn't be her panties that he stuffed in her mouth, he chuckled, as he continued to stroke himself and watch her in the distance.

"It's just a matter of time, darlin, just a matter of time," he said aloud, staring at Lila in the distance, not even trying to mask the southern drawl that was usually hidden, just under the surface of his speech.

CHAPTER THIRTY-FIVE

Hallie hadn't seen Bridget and Jay for a few weeks. They had agreed they were long overdue for Bodega's and a game of Phase 10, a card game that was similar to Rummy but requires each player to complete ten different phases, with specific requirements or matches for each phase. It was a nice way to get her mind off of everything going on in her life at the moment, Hallie realized. She grabbed a bottle of Cab out of her wine rack, picked up the Cubans from Bodega's on the way, and arrived at her friends' Seminole Heights bungalow just after 7:30 that following Wednesday night. Bridget was sitting on her front porch, waiting for her, smoking a cigarette.

"What, no Windex tonight?" Hallie teased as she walked up the front steps.

"Not necessary; that last cold front chased the mosquitos away. Mary always said not to use the Windex after October. You don't want them building up a tolerance. It's one of those rules, like not wearing white after Labor Day."

"Well, Mary didn't know about global warming, so you may have to adjust that October date going forward," Hallie smiled, always enjoying the Mary-isms, as they had called them since they were kids. Whatever Mary said, those were the rules, period. And apparently, you did not spray mosquitoes with Windex after October.

"Let's go inside, bitch, I don't want my Cuban getting cold," Bridget said to her lifelong friend, warmed by the memory of her mother but never wanting anyone to see her soft side lest they see it as a weakness.

It always amused Hallie, because Bridget was the most giving, kindest, truest person she had ever known, but she never wanted anyone to realize it, so she could also be entirely terrifying and came across as abrupt if you didn't know her. As Hallie learned on the playground in elementary school, Bridget never backed down from anything, never showed fear, and always had your back, period. All of the qualities you wanted in a best friend and she was never fooled by the exterior layer Bridget liked to present to the world.

The Cubans from Bodega's did not disappoint, as they never did, and as Hallie was savoring the last few bites of roasted pork, she was thankful for this evening. She hadn't realized how much she needed it until she was sitting at the table enjoying the remnants of the savory pork, pickle and crunchy, buttery Cuban bread, and laughing with Bridget and Jay.

"So, before we get to the cards, I did want to give you an update on the weird emails and break-in at your house," Jay started.

"Do you have anything?" Hallie asked, having forgotten about those damn emails lately with everything else that had gone on.

"Well, we've narrowed it down to an office downtown."

"So that's good, right? Should be easy to figure out from there, I would think," Hallie interrupted.

"Not exactly," Jay said, "it's a large law office, takes up three floors in one of the biggest buildings downtown. So it could be coming from anyone in that office."

"Which law firm?" Hallie asked.

"Greenlee, Remington & Stoll," Jay answered, as he looked down at his feet, knowing full well the implications of what he said.

"No, not possible," Hallie responded, defensively, "no way. I know what you're suggesting here and it's just not possible."

"Are you sure, Hallie? I know Paige is your friend, but she works at that firm and, by your own words, she's the only one who knew what happened to you that night," Jay said.

"No, no fucking way. It's not Paige. As you said *yourself*, it's a large firm and takes up three floors in that building. It could be anyone. I'm telling you right now, it's not Paige."

"Fine, fine, calm down," Jay said, which only ignited Hallie's anger further.

Hallie started to respond when Bridget jumped in to save Hallie from losing her shit on Jay, "Jesus Christ, Jay, have you learned nothing from being married to me for um, well, forever? How has 'calm down' ever worked out for you before? Hallie, don't you worry about the stupid shit he says, because he just doesn't understand female friendships. And I agree with you. Notwithstanding your questionable track record with men, your record with friendships is impeccable, so if Paige has been your friend as long as she has, and you trust her, well then, I trust her and nothing else needs to be said about that. Jay, figure out who the fuck else in that building is sending Hallie these emails because it's not Paige."

"You're lucky I adore you, Bridget, or I might taser you right now for how you constantly emasculate me and tell me how to do my job," Jay said affectionately, winking at Hallie as his own form of an apology.

"Oooh, promise, Officer Campbell?" Bridget replied seductively, their cute, affectionate banter reminding Hallie of all of the shortcomings in her own marriage.

"Look, if you guys want to call it a night, we can play cards another night. I don't want to intrude on this lovefest," Hallie offered.

"No fucking way," Bridget replied, "I'm ready to kick both of your asses and neither one of you are going to weasel your way out of it."

"Fine, let's play cards," Jay said, "and Hallie, don't worry, I'll figure out who else works in that office. You're right, there are a lot of people and it could be anyone."

"Thanks, Jay," Hallie said, "but I'm still going to kick your ass."

They all laughed as they cleared the brown paper wrappings from their Cuban sandwiches away, refilled their wine glasses, and got down to the serious business of Phase 10.

* * *

Hallie woke up the next morning, smiling at all the laughs and silliness she shared with Bridget and Jay the night before. She really needed that break. Jay promised to figure out who else worked at that firm who might be responsible for sending the emails to her. They all agreed that whoever sent the emails had likely been the same person who broke into her home and wrote the angry note on the legal pad on her desk, which was the more alarming intrusion into Hallie's life. Juno looked up from her bed, wagged her tail as Hallie got out of bed to walk into her bathroom, and then yawned, scratched behind her ear with her back paw, and settled back down into her bed until Hallie gave her the signal it was time to go downstairs.

After many weeks, Hallie finally had a productive, billable day. She responded to existing clients, worked on a transaction that was closing at the end of the month, and even engaged a new client, Trinity Palmer, the daughter of an old colleague, and her best friend, Kathleen Henry.

Trinity and Kathleen were fascinating, smart and talented. They had a promising rap career and were on the verge of signing a multi-million dollar deal, as the modern day Salt-N-Pepa, but had the good sense to seek the advice of counsel before signing anything. The fine print would have crushed them and left more money in the producer's pockets than their own. A few years before, Hallie had taught with Trinity's mother when Hallie was an adjunct professor at USF and Trinity's mom, Mahisa, was a tenured professor, who taught a black women's study seminar and had published significantly on the subject. Hallie remembered when Trinity would accompany her mother to class and sit in the back row coloring or playing with whatever toys she brought with her for the day so her mother could teach. Hallie was so impressed with Mahisa, and how she seemed to juggle everything with such grace and calmness, unlike Hallie who always seemed a bit of a chaotic mess when it came to juggling her career and Katie. She was thrilled with Trinity's success and so glad that they had called on her to help them.

She had just finished her last phone call of the day and realized it was time to meet Paige and Mike Freeman at Ulele. She ran upstairs, fixed her makeup, switched out of her normal uniform of very worn in, comfy jeans and a black tank top to a more respectable, tighter pair of jeans that hugged her ass, her cute, black four-inch heeled boots, and a different black tank top that she paired underneath the new, light leather jacket she had recently ordered from White House Black Market that had arrived that afternoon. It really was beyond cute and fit her perfectly.

Hallie arrived at Ulele right at the time she was supposed to meet Paige and Mike, which was technically early as far as Hallie was concerned as she was usually at least ten minutes late everywhere she went. She pulled up to the valet, got her ticket, and made her way down the stairs towards the entrance of the restaurant, always enjoying seeing the restored figures from the lost Fairyland theme park that was once part of Lowry Park Zoo, a favorite attraction from Hallie's childhood. The theme park had contained life-sized scenes from several popular nursery rhymes and Grimm's fairytales, including "The Three Little Pigs," "Humpty-Dumpty," "Snow White and the Seven Dwarfs," "Little Red Riding Hood," "Rapunzel" and "The Old Woman Who Lived In A Shoe," and had been a favorite attraction for children during much simpler times. Fairyland and the beloved statues had disappeared during a complete renovation of the Zoo in 1996, and, unbeknown to most, sat outside exposed to the elements for the next twenty-plus years in a City of Tampa storage yard.

Richard Gonzmart, a Tampa native for many generations and the owner of Ulele and other treasured Tampa restaurants, such as the Columbia in Ybor City, learned about the existence of the treasured relics and decided to buy them from the City. He paid $30,000 for all eleven Fairyland scenes, paid a local artist to restore them, and then set them up on the expansive Ulele property fronting the Hillsborough River. No matter how many times Hallie dined at Ulele, seeing the fully restored Fairyland scenes made her happy and nostalgic, often triggering a memory from her childhood when her mom would take Hallie and her siblings to the Zoo during the summer.

She was seated at her table for only a few minutes when she saw Paige and Mike walking in together and Hallie waived them over to the table. Seeing Paige standing next to Mike, Hallie thought they made an interesting and somewhat adorable couple, even though Paige said they were no longer dating. But he was cute, with short, black hair, sprinkled with a little salt and pepper at the temples, a friendly smile and warm gray-blue eyes that pierced through his vintage tortoiseshell frames. He was nerdy but in a really attractive, Clark Kent kind of way. Hallie could see why Paige had been attracted to him and wondered what went wrong, other than the usual things that break up two career-motivated, type A, lawyers on the ramp up of their careers trying to start a new relationship together.

"Hallie, this is Mike; Mike, this is Hallie," Paige introduced, "I can't believe you two have never met in person."

"I know, I can't believe our paths have never crossed before either. Nice to meet you in person, Mike, but I feel like I already know you from Paige talking about you all these years," Hallie said.

"Likewise," Mike said, "it's nice to put a face to the name after all this time."

They all sat down and ordered some appetizers and a few drinks, Hallie ordering a glass of Charles Krug Cabernet. Ulele was one of Hallie's favorite restaurants because not only was the food delicious, but they had a decent wine list including good wines by the glass. Also, unlike most restaurants, Gonzmart didn't believe in marking up the price of the wines beyond what you would pay if you bought them at retail, which meant you could enjoy a decent glass of wine at a very reasonable price.

After they all had their drinks in front of them and Mike and Hallie figured out who their common friends were, besides Paige, Mike pulled some files out of the leather backpack resting by his feet that he had brought in with him.

"So, Paige tells me you have a renewed interest in this case," Mike said, trying not to state the obvious about why Hallie might have an interest in the 2005 hotel case.

"Well, yes, I do. Some things have come to light of late that, well, have renewed my interest in that case and I was hoping I could ask you a few questions."

"This case has always bothered me because the police were never able to identify the assailant, despite collecting DNA, and for the sheer brutality of what he did to that poor woman. The victim in this case had a mental breakdown afterwards, understandably, and it's just one of those cases that I've never been able to get out of my head. I've always hoped that they catch the son of a bitch, even if we can't prosecute him for this case. But, having said all that Hallie, I'm here as a favor to Paige, and I know she trusts you implicitly, but if I divulge confidential information, I could lose my job with the State Attorney's office."

"I would never do anything to jeopardize your job or career, Mike, and I appreciate you coming here today. I don't know how much Paige has told you, but it's been the strangest few months of my life and it's hard to not think some if it is related, including to that 2005 case."

"Paige has told me some of what's happened to you, but why don't you tell me, starting from the beginning, so I get the whole picture, firsthand," Mike said, as he picked up his blackened grouper sandwich and bit into it as he gave Hallie the floor.

Hallie told him everything she knew, starting with her rape by Judge Stephens in 2002, the discovery of Lauren White's body in Mrs. Butler's yard, Naomi Bank's murder and the fact that she was one of the staff attorneys in the same division as Judge Stephens, the weird emails she received, including Jay's revelation that they originated from somewhere within Paige's firm, the note left on her desk at home, and how the DNA collected from a recent crime scene matches the DNA collected from that 2005 rape case. For the moment, she decided not to mention the DNA connection between Nicole Rodriguez and Katie to Judge Stephens.

"Okay, so let me see if I follow what you're saying," Mike said, "You were raped by Judge Stephens in 2002. This we know and there is no question as to who attacked you. You believe he drugged you because you had no recollection of the events that led to you waking up next to him in a hotel room bed or how you sustained the injuries you discovered you had. In 2005, there was another brutal rape that was very similar to your experience except the victim had no idea who her assailant was as she was drugged, and he was gone by the time she woke up, alone, battered, and brutally raped. They collected DNA allegedly from the assailant in the 2005 case, but until recently, had not been able to connect it to a suspect or another case. Right so far?"

"Yes, so far, so good. Keep going," Hallie directed.

"Now we jump to the present and we have a series of murders, presumably victims who were sexually assaulted prior to or during their attacks that resulted in their deaths, and one of those cases has linked the DNA collected from the crime scene or the victim to the 2005 rape case. The only thing I'm confused about is how, other than Lauren White's body ending up in your neighbor's yard, any of this is connected to you or what happened to you in 2002. In other words, how did you or anyone else connect your 2002 rape by Judge Stephens to any of the recent cases or the 2005 case, other than your own suspicions? I feel like there's a piece missing, Hallie," Mike finished, as he looked at both Paige and Hallie.

"You're right, Paige, he is smart. Okay, there's a final piece that I haven't shared with you, which I will share with you now. But there is more at stake with this information than your career or any case, because it involves my daughter."

Up until this moment, Paige had been listening but not wanting to interrupt, but now it all became clear to her as she was friends with Hallie back when she had announced her pregnancy and at the time had wondered whether it was the result of her rape. But Hallie never brought it up, so she never brought it up, and, truthfully, had never given it another thought after Katie was born. Until today.

"Holy shit, Hallie, when did you find out?" Paige asked, placing her hand on her friend's arm.

"Just recently," Hallie said, looking down and taking another sip of her wine.

"Okay, wait, I think I know where this is going," Mike said, "but let's back up. Connect the dots for me."

"I have a seventeen-year-old daughter, Katie, who I had when I was married to my first husband, Kevin Verona. He's also an attorney, and in fact, used to be a state prosecutor for many years. Maybe you know him?"

"Yes, I know Kevin. He's a good attorney and a good guy," Mike offered.

"Yes, he is. I never told Kevin about what happened to me, not back then anyway, so when I found out I was pregnant, I decided I never would. There was just as much of a chance that Kevin was the father, and I was young, scared and also in denial, so I convinced myself that the possibility that Stephens was the father of my unborn child was minimal. And after she was born, I thought she looked like Kevin and I honestly never gave it another thought. But all of that changed recently when Kevin, his wife, Jodi, and Katie decided to do one of those DNA ancestry kits so they could learn more about their heritage for an upcoming trip to Europe they are planning as a graduation gift for Katie."

"Oh shit, Hallie, I'm so sorry, hon," Paige said.

"Yes, you guessed it, Kevin learned from Katie's results that he is not her biological father. Katie doesn't know yet as we're waiting to tell her when we think the time is better, not that there can ever be a right time, but we don't want to derail her as she's finishing her senior year and applying to colleges."

"How did Kevin take it?" Paige asked gently.

"Better than I would have expected. He adores Katie and is a great father, so he said that is not going to change. As far as he's concerned, Katie is his daughter and that's that. He, of course, was furious when he first found out, believing I must have cheated on him, betrayed him, but after I told him about the rape, he understood, as much as he could understand. I have a whole new appreciation and fondness for his wife, Jodi, who has actually been really great through all of this. I think she will be very helpful to Kevin and Katie as we navigate these unchartered waters going forward."

"I'm really sorry, Hallie," Mike said genuinely, "what a horrible ordeal. But I guess I'm still confused as to how those DNA results are connected to the latest crimes and the 2005 rape."

"Right, of course. So when you submit your DNA to those genealogy sites, you have to give an email address and you also have to consent to law enforcement being able to use your DNA results in connection with investigations of violent crimes, such as rape and murder, or you can opt out, so the results can't be used or even seen by law enforcement. Most people don't opt out though because they haven't committed any such crimes so they're not worried about it. When you get your results, it tells you if there are other people in the database who are related to you and to what degree. Law enforcement has started uploading DNA results from their cold cases into the one site that allows it and then analyzing familial connections to see if they can find a suspect through links to relatives who have submitted their DNA. It's complicated but that's basically it. One of the detectives did that here in Tampa. He uploaded the DNA results collected from one of the recent murders, which he had already determined matched the suspect who committed the 2005 rape, and found a number of familial matches. Although the sites don't divulge who the results belong to, the participants have the option to publicize their email address so potential family members can reach out to them. Believe it or not, this is how a lot of adopted children have connected with their biological parents, and vice versa," Hallie said, pausing to eat a French fry and take a sip of her wine.

"Did Katie get an email from the detective?" Paige asked, genuinely fascinated by Hallie's story.

"Well, thankfully, no, because Jodi had used her email address for all three tests. So Jodi received the email. Coincidentally, so did a client of mine, who called me to confirm the email was legitimate. Before I learned that Jodi received an email, my client called me and I actually accompanied her to her meeting with the detective. She comes from a huge family in the area, so she had a list of about twelve or thirteen men who potentially fit the profile the detective described to her, but it turns out Judge Stephens is one of her uncles and was one of the people on her list. And then Kevin and Jodi called me about the email they received from the detective inquiring about Katie's results, and I realized Judge Stephens is the common denominator in all of this."

"Wow, that's incredible. Have you told the detective all of this yet?" Mike asked.

"No, not yet, I will but we're trying to do it in a way to keep Katie's name out of it, if that's even possible."

"Okay, so what do you need from me?" Mike asked, tapping the stack of manilla folders he had in front of him.

"Just a name," Hallie said, looking at him square in the eye. "I just need to know the name of the 2005 victim so when I tell my story to the detective, I connect all of the pieces. I want to see if she knows Judge Stephens and can place him at the networking event in 2005. If she does, then there is no question that he is the monster and predator we think he is. But Judge Stephens is still a really powerful man in this town, and I don't want him to get away with this. It's important that there are no possible ways for him to wiggle his way out of this."

Mike understood, nodded, and looked down, "I could get fired for this," he almost whispered.

"I promise you I will never divulge to anyone where I got her name, but I need justice. For me, for her, for my daughter, for Kevin, for what this man did and is obviously still doing. We all deserve justice. As I know you know, the statute of limitations has run on both of our cases. The law on sexual battery and new DNA discovery in Florida didn't change until 2006, so in 2005, the prosecution was still limited to, at most, 10 years to file criminal charges. She wasn't a child, so the civil statute of limitations is even shorter. By giving me her name, you're not doing anything that could jeopardize her case or the State's case because there is no case. Please, I just want to talk to her," Hallie pleaded, looking to Paige to see if she could add anything to sway him.

Before Paige had a chance to speak, Mike held up his hand and said, "Counselor, you made your case but I can't help you. I took an oath and for me to divulge the name of a rape victim in a case would be an ethical violation I would not be able to live with, despite the cause," as he tapped the manilla file under his short, manicured fingernails, once again. "I need to go to the restroom. When I get back, we can discuss this further," he said as he got up, leaving Paige, Hallie, and the unattended folders at the table.

"If you don't sleep with that man tonight, I just might," Hallie whispered to Paige when she was sure Mike was out of earshot. They opened the file and quickly learned the victim's name was Natalie Crawford and it was Paige's turn to gasp.

"Holy shit, wait, I know her, she works in my office!" Paige exclaimed, as the implications of Paige's statement hit them both.

CHAPTER THIRTY-SIX

Hallie called Detective Garcia to set up another meeting with him. He assumed it was about the list that Hallie's client, Nicole Rodriguez, had given him and maybe she thought of someone else she wanted to add to it. He agreed to meet her at 11:30 at the downtown precinct but Hallie declined and asked him to meet her instead at the rooftop bar above the Epicurean Hotel on Howard Avenue. At this time of day, it would be pretty vacant and Hallie could make sure no one would overhear them. She didn't trust the precinct where their conversation could be recorded.

When she met with Kevin and Jodi at Hattrick's, after Hallie explained her meeting with her client, Nicole, and the detective, they all agreed that they wanted to do whatever they could to keep Katie out of it. The plan was for Hallie to meet with Detective Garcia on behalf of an anonymous client, the biological mother of Profile Number 32047A, who did not want to be identified or come forward yet, if at all. Hallie would tell the story of her client, including how her client was raped eighteen years ago by Judge Stephens, which produced an offspring, #32047A, so that the Detective could focus his investigation on the judge. If and when he could tie the judge to the attacks and murders of the young women, then Hallie's client would come forward and be willing to testify against him, if necessary.

She met Detective Garcia on the roof of the Epicurean. It was a beautiful day but still warm out in the sun. Hallie had ordered an orange seltzer water on ice and sat at a table at the far end of the patio where they would not be overheard. Detective Garcia joined her, ordering a diet coke from the waitress when she came over.

"So, Ms. Miller, what's with all the cloak and dagger?"

"Please, call me Hallie, and I'm sorry but I have attorney-client, sensitive information, some of which I have been authorized to disclose to you, but I wanted to make sure there was no chance it could be recorded or overheard. And to that end, Detective Garcia, you do not have my consent or permission to record this conversation, so please refrain from doing so."

"I'm not recording you, Hallie," the detective offered, looking her directly in her eyes.

For whatever reason, Hallie believed him. From the first time she met him, she got a sense that he was honorable and a good detective. There was something in his eyes that conveyed honesty and integrity, Hallie thought, and she trusted him.

Hallie told Detective Garcia her story, except she phrased it so that it was about an anonymous client. She explained about the DNA results and how her client had received one of his emails and she contacted Hallie, just as Nicole Rodriguez had. She explained that unlike the 2005 rape victim, her client knew her rapist who attacked her eighteen years ago, and that rapist was Judge William Stephens, who her client now confirmed was also the biological father of her client's daughter as a result of that rape. She also reminded him how Judge Stephens was one of the relatives listed on Nicole Rodriguez's list of relatives who could be potential suspects. After she finished, she felt she had adequately connected all of the evidence and relationships to show that Judge Stephens was likely responsible for the recent attacks and murders.

"Wow, Counselor, you've been busy," Detective Garcia said. "I just have one question."

"What is it?" Hallie asked.

"Isn't your daughter, Kate, almost eighteen?" he asked, giving her a knowing look.

The question caught her off guard and she almost choked on her seltzer water she was sipping when he asked the question.

"Look, I'm not here to cause any issues for you, Hallie, but you've been invested in this since the beginning and I always wondered if there was a more personal reason for that. I will keep your name and your daughter's name out of it for as long as I can, hopefully permanently, since we have other information leading us to Judge Stephens. And I do appreciate you coming forward to try to help, Hallie. All of this information is really helpful because it gives me a suspect to investigate and direction to take the investigation, but I need to take it from here."

"Thank you, Detective. I appreciate that. My daughter doesn't know yet so if anything happens that you think the information is going to come out, please call me first so her father and I can prepare her and tell her before she hears it from someone else."

"Absolutely, I promise."

* * *

Paige sat Heather in her office and got her a glass of water. Her paralegal's color had finally returned to her face and she had stopped trembling.

"Heather, you have to tell me what's going on. You are terrified. Who are you afraid of?"

"My husband, Bobby, who I ran away from when he almost killed me eleven years ago," Heather said, while pointing to the scar on her neck, "He did this to me and much worse."

"You said, 'It's him', what did you mean? Did he call you? Did he threaten you?"

"He's on my voicemail. The PNC from your friend, Hallie. It's him, no doubt in my mind, although he hid his southern accent somewhat. But it's him. And that means he's here and he's going to find me and kill me, just as he promised," Heather said, matter-of-factly.

"What did he do to you, Heather?" Paige asked, the concern evident in her warm brown eyes.

"He raped me, sodomized me, and tried to slit my throat, but missed by an inch, thankfully, probably because he was so drunk. I escaped out of a bathroom window and never looked back. He vowed that he would never stop looking for me and would kill me when he found me again. He has a penchant for sharp knives and necks, by the way. He says he likes to the watch the blood drip out of the veins in women's necks. He's an absolute sadist and he's here to finish what he started."

"We need to call the police, Heather,"

"No, they can't help me. I just need to run away from him again."

"No, you can't keep running. I'm calling my friend, Hallie, to see what she knows about him since she referred him to me. Maybe he doesn't know you're here yet. Let's call Hallie."

* * *

Paige called Hallie and told her everything Heather had told her about her estranged husband, Bobby Jackson, now obviously going by the name, Robert Johnson. Hallie called David to find out what he knew about Robert Johnson, confirming that he had started at Hillsborough High School about ten years ago. The timing matched Heather's story.

"David, have you ever seen anything to suggest he's violent? From what Paige told me, it sounded like more than just a domestic violence situation. According to Heather, he raped her and tried to kill her the night she ran away. The guy apparently has a thing for sharp knives."

As she described what Heather had told them, Hallie remembered the profile Detective Garcia had read to her and Nicole Rodriguez at the precinct that day. He definitely seemed to fit the profile, she thought.

"No, not that I ever saw."

"I wonder if he knew any of the victims," Hallie said, while also wondering whether he had any connection to Judge Stephens.

"Oh my God, yes, actually, that Ybor victim. I just learned that she went to school here a few years ago," David lied easily. "He would have been her chemistry teacher as he was the only one we had," David offered, remembering for the first time that Robert had left the school at the same time as he did that night he was supposed to meet Lila in Ybor. Is it possible that he followed him? Did he lead him right to Lila, he wondered?

"I'm starting not to believe in coincidences, David. I'm going to call Detective Garcia. He needs to know about all of this."

"Hallie, one more thing," David said before they hung up, "Robert called in sick today and isn't in school."

CHAPTER THIRTY-SEVEN

Detective Garcia headed back to the precinct after his morning meeting with Hallie Miller, calling Catherine on the way.

"Hey, babe, how's it going?" he asked when she answered.

"You know, living the dream on the cold, hard streets of Tampa Bay. How are you doing?" she asked.

"Making progress with this crazy case and may have just caught a break because of that DNA tip you gave me. But I need your help. You available?"

"Sure, I would love to help. Anything we can do to get this scumbag off the streets. What do you need me to do?" Catherine asked?

"Do you think you can get your s.a. victim that you told me about to come in to look at some pictures? She's the only one who actually saw the perp's face, even if she doesn't think she remembers it clearly. I want to show her a picture of someone."

"Yeah, I don't see why not. I'm sure she won't mind coming in. Let me call her and see if she's available. If she's available, when should I bring her in?"

"Give me an hour and then meet me at the precinct,"

Marcelo responded, feeling the excitement of the case progressing for the first time in months.

When he got back to the precinct, he updated Captain Mastandrea and got help from one of the other officers, Officer Tracy McCrink, to put together a photo lineup, including the headshot of Judge Stephens that they downloaded off the court's website. They made sure all of the photos looked similar and that you couldn't see the Judge's robe or court attire in the photo.

He thought he should see if Lila Martinez could come in too to see if she could possibly identify him as her attacker, although she was in much worse shape when they found her than Chrissy Wright was, so he wasn't too optimistic about her being able to identify him from the photos. But it was worth a try. He pulled her case file and found Lila's new cellphone number she had given him the last time she called him. He dialed the number and after several rings, it went to voicemail. He would try again later.

Just then, his cell phone rang, and he saw Catherine was calling him back.

"What's up, babe, are you bringing Chrissy Wright in?"

"Yes, but not for a few hours. She's at work but said she would come in when she finished at 3. I'll bring her by then, okay?"

"Ok, I couldn't reach the Ybor victim by phone, but now that I have time, I might grab the photos and run by her place to see if she's around. Maybe I'll catch her. Want to go with me and then we can grab some lunch?"

"Yeah, sure. I'm about ten minutes away from the precinct. I'll meet you there and then you can drive."

"Sounds good, my car is in the back parking lot. I'll wait for you in my car."

Marcelo gathered up the photos, put them in a folder in no particular order, and headed to the back lot, letting the Captain know what he was doing.

"Make sure you record it, Detective, just in case she does recognize him. By the book, got it?"

"You know it, Captain. No mistakes."

He met Catherine in the parking lot of the police precinct downtown. She looked as beautiful as ever and Marcelo tried hard to maintain his professionalism when they were both working. They got in his department issued black mustang and headed towards West Tampa.

"We'll check in on Ms. Martinez and when we finish with her, we can grab lunch at Raices on Spruce," Marcelo said.

"What's Raices? I've never eaten there."

"Oh my God, only the best Spanish food in West Tampa, mi amor," Marcelo said affectionately, just as his cell phone started to ring.

"Hello, Counselor, did you remember something else that you forgot to tell me?"

CHAPTER THIRTY-EIGHT

Lila was looking forward to her day off. Since recovering from her attack, she had gotten a job at a daycare center near their home, which allowed her to bring Vera to work with her every day. Even on her days off, she was allowed to drop Vera off so that she could run errands and get things done without Vera under foot. Lila was making her own money and Vera made friends, so it was the best situation for both of them right now. She had submitted her application to HCC and planned to start taking a few classes, part-time, beginning in January. She felt like she was finally getting her life under control and moving in the right direction for her and her daughter.

She dropped Vera off at the Rosa Valdez Day Care Center that morning, said goodbye to her sweet daughter who was excited to see her friends, and headed west on Albany towards Howard Avenue to return to the West Tampa duplex on W. Spruce Street she shared with her mother and daughter. Her mother had already left for work by the time she got back so she had the small house to herself, which was rare. She enjoyed the solitude and was looking forward to just having a little time by herself to recharge. On the advice of one of her physical therapists, she had recently started yoga and found that it was really helping her come to peace with what had happened to her in Ybor that night, in addition to helping her get stronger, physically.

She changed out of her jeans that she had thrown on to take Vera to daycare and changed into her yoga outfit. She gathered her hair up into a bun on top of her head and popped one of the yoga DVDs she had checked out of the West Tampa Library into the player that was built into the old TV they had picked up from a secondhand store when they arrived. She moved the Ikea coffee table out of the way to give herself more room and set up her mat in front of the tv. She was just about to get started when she heard a key opening the lock on the front door.

She looked up, expecting to see her mother come in the door, but was confused by the familiar face standing in front of her, "Well hello, Lila."

"Mr. Johnson?" she stuttered, "What are you doing here?"

With one sudden move, Robert shoved Lila back and off her feet, slamming the door behind him. Before she had a chance to scream, he had jumped on top of her and placed duct tape across her mouth, while pinning her hands and wrists above her head and quickly secured them together with zip ties. Lila was confused and momentarily stunned from the air being knocked out of her when her back slammed against the floor. But as Robert straddled her and she saw his cold, dark eyes, everything became clear to her and she realized they were the same cold eyes she had seen the night she was attacked. She tried to scream but was unable to with the duct tape covering her mouth. She also couldn't get enough air in and out of her nostrils in her current exasperated state. She could taste the glue from the duct tape and smell the stale cigarette odor coming off of Robert. She was sure she wouldn't survive another attack like the one she suffered in Ybor. What would happen to Vera, her poor sweet, Vera, she thought, as the tears started to pour down her cheeks.

"Now, darlin', don't you start crying on me. You got away from me last time, you little rascal, so we can't let that happen again, now can we?" Mr. Johnson asked her in a voice she barely recognized. It had that same southern drawl she remembered from the night in Ybor. He could tell she was struggling to breathe.

As he smacked her cheek to keep her awake, he said, "It's too soon for you to pass out, Lila, we haven't even begun to have any fun yet. Now Lila, if I take this duct tape off your mouth so you can breathe easier, do you promise to be good girl and not scream?"

Lila nodded emphatically as she felt like she was going to pass out any second.

"If you're lying to me, there will be severe consequences. You know that, right?"

She nodded again, with less enthusiasm as she was starting to get lightheaded, and closed her eyes.

Robert ripped the tape off in one painful tear, and Lila took a much-needed gulp of air as she tried to make sense of what was happening to her again.

"Why are you doing this to me, Mr. Johnson?" she pleaded, the tears flowing freely down her cheeks and over the faint scars that appeared white and more prominent against her flushed cheeks when she got upset or overheated.

"Now Lila, you know we have unfinished business. I told you, you were always one of my favorite students, always teasing me with your tight jeans and lowcut tops. And then you go and disrespect me by fucking the principal? That wasn't nice, now was it, Lila?" he said, as he quickly and effortlessly secured Lila's right ankle to the leg of the family's heavy wooden dining room table.

Lila knew she had to fight back at some point but she knew he would kill her if she tried and failed. She had to figure out a way to outsmart him, maybe get to her phone, just as her cell phone started ringing and vibrating on top of the coffee table nearby where she had left it.

They both stared at each other, as they waited for her cell to stop ringing.

"I'm sorry, I can't come to the phone right now, I'm a little tied up," Robert said in a high pitched voice pretending to be Lila's voicemail, followed by a maniacal laughter at his own joke.

"Please, don't do this to me," Lila begged.

He took the same silver hunting knife he had with him the night in Ybor out of a sheath strapped to his calf and cut open the front of her t-shirt followed by the sports bra she was wearing underneath to expose her ample breasts. Lila tried to wiggle away from him but with her hands zip tied overhead and one leg tied to the table, she was at a significant disadvantage. He held the sharp knife to her neck, tracing the scar from when he cut her in Ybor City.

"Hmmm, maybe we should just open this back up," he said, as he cut her neck enough to draw blood but not enough to hit anything important. The sight of her blood aroused him instantly, just as her cell phone started to ring and vibrate again.

"Jesus Christ, who the fuck keeps calling you?" Robert asked, enraged by the constant interruptions. "I'm going to turn that fucking thing off," he said as he got up and stepped over Lila to get to the coffee table.

* * *

Marcelo and Catherine were on their way to Lila's apartment to show her the headshots to see if she recognized Judge Stephens when Marcelo got the call from Hallie. She told him about Paige's paralegal, Heather McLean, who explained that Robert Johnson was her estranged husband, Bobby Jackson, who she had escaped from eleven years ago when he tried to kill her. The injuries that Heather described sounded very similar to the current victim's injuries Hallie had heard about. She also explained that Robert Johnson was a teacher at the high school where her husband was principal and where the Ybor victim, Lila Martinez, was a student a few years back. She finished her call warning the detective that Robert Johnson was not in school that day.

When Marcelo and Catherine arrived at Lila's duplex, they scanned the cobblestone street to see what cars were present. There was a beat-up, red GMC truck, a blue Volkswagen, Lila's white, used Toyota in front of her house, and a black Honda Civic on the opposite side of the street a few doors down.

"You know, Chrissy Wright thought that the car that she got into the night she was attacked was black," Catherine said, pointing to the black Honda. They pulled up behind it and Marcelo pulled up one of his contacts and hit send. After two rings, a woman answered.

"Hey, McCrink, Garcia here. Can you run a plate, stat, for me? It's important and I'm out in the field."

"For you, Garcia? Of course," the female officer replied, as Catherine rolled her eyes.

Garcia recited the plate number and they waited while Officer Tracy McCrink ran the plate.

"Ok, here we go, the car is registered to one Alma P. Johnson, age 82."

"Hmmm, okay, thanks. Sorry, one more favor, can you run Alma P. Johnson through the system and see what you come up with?"

After a few minutes, Officer McCrink came back on the line, "Well, unfortunately for Mrs. Alma P. Johnson, she died about ten years ago. But according to the Hillsborough County Property Appraiser's website, her house went to someone named Robert Jackson Johnson. I assume he never bothered to update the title on her car or to register it in his name. Does that help?"

"More than you know. Please send back up immediately to 2337 W. Spruce Street. Tell them officers need assistance and the suspect is likely armed and dangerous with a possible hostage."

Marcelo and Catherine got out of the car and snuck up to the front of the duplex. Catherine peaked in the window as Marcelo took his gun out and aimed it towards the front door in case Robert came out. Catherine quickly retreated out of sight and nodded to Marcelo, indicating Robert Johnson was in the home with Lila. She took her gun out and took her position behind Marcelo. He motioned to her that on the count of three, he would kick in the door.

* * *

Robert was fiddling with Lila's phone, trying to figure out how to turn it off, when the front door busted open and there stood Detective Garcia and Officer Catherine West, guns drawn on Bobby Jackson, a/k/a Robert Johnson. Lila screamed and Robert reached for his knife.

"Freeze mother fucker. Take one step to give me an excuse to blow your fucking head off," Marcelo said, never taking his eyes off of Robert.

Lila let out a sob, as Catherine bent down to cut her free from the table and bring her outside. Within five minutes back up was there and Robert Johnson was under arrest for the attempted rape and kidnapping of Lila Martinez, for starters.

CHAPTER THIRTY-NINE

Robert Johnson sat shackled to the metal chair and handcuffed to the table in the interrogation room, the irony of his predicament not lost on him. Marcelo had read him his Miranda rights when he arrested him and then reminded of him of his rights when he brought him into the interrogation room before quickly leaving to purposely leave him sitting there alone. He and Catherine watched him through the observation window, discussing how they were going to approach him. At this point, they had Lila's statement that, in addition to attacking her today, he was the same man who attacked her that night in Ybor. The police found Lila's original keys in his pants pocket and her phone she had with her the night in Ybor in the glove box of his car, which corroborated her identification of him as her attacker. The crime scene technicians were going through his car now searching for other evidence to place him in Ybor that night or connect him to any other victims. About thirty minutes before, they learned the district attorney had obtained a search warrant to search his home signed by Judge Amy Gratzick who had recently returned to the bench. There was no question that they had him for the attempted rapes and assaults on Lila, but they had to determine if he was connected to any of the other recent murders or the attack on Chrissy.

Catherine walked in first, followed by Marcelo behind her. Marcelo didn't make eye contact with him and pretended to be reading the thick file in his hand, which contained the reports from all of the recent murders and attacks. Marcelo didn't need to study the file – he had memorized every report and knew every detail surrounding the attacks and about each victim. Catherine took the lead because they wanted to see how he responded to a female detective. His reaction to Catherine would tell them a lot about their suspect.

"Mr. Johnson, I'm Detective Catherine West. Can we get you a bottle of water?"

"Nah, but a cigarette would be peachy," he responded flippantly without the slightest accent of any kind.

"Sorry, no smoking inside the building, Mr. Johnson. Or should I call you Robert? Or is it Bobby? What is it this week?" Catherine asked, intentionally trying to agitate him.

"Darlin' you can call me anything you want just as long as you call me," he answered, full southern drawl dripping from every word, smiling and never taking his eyes off of Catherine, as if this was all a fun game.

Marcelo looked up from his file, interested to see how Catherine would react to the sudden change in his accent and creepy come-on.

"Is that what happened, Bobby? You got pissed off when all those pretty, young women blew you off and wouldn't pay any attention to you?" Catherine retorted, without any hesitation. Marcelo was impressed.

"Fuck you, bitch," Robert spat at her, losing his cool quicker than either of them expected.

"Why don't we make this easy on you. I'm going to share with you what we have so far," Catherine started, "let's start with Lila Martinez. Beyond her statement identifying you as the man who her attacked today as well as in Ybor City, you had her keys that were stolen from her that night in your pocket; her cell phone was in your glovebox; and we were just informed that her purse was found in a box in the back of your closet at your home."

Catherine continued, "and then there's Lauren White. Let's see, what do we know about her? Well, we know she called an Uber and never connected with her Uber driver. Interestingly, that's the same thing that happened to Chrissy Wright, but she was lucky enough to get away, now, wasn't she? Didn't count on that, did you, Bobby?"

"It's Robert."

"Oh, I'm sorry, Bobby, does that name bother you? Your estranged wife, Heather, used to call you Bobby, didn't she? Was that before or after you beat and stabbed her within an inch of her life?"

Robert shifted awkwardly in his seat, unable to move more than an inch because of his wrists handcuffed to the table and his legs shackled at the ankles underneath the bolted down, steel table. He was confused how they knew about Heather and why they were bringing her up now.

"Are you uncomfortable, Bobby? How does it feel being handcuffed to a table? Unable to get up, get away? Does it make you feel anxious? Nervous? I'm sure Chrissy Wright felt that way too, but she outsmarted you, didn't she? Well guess what, five minutes before we came in here, she identified you as the Uber driver who picked her up, attacked her, and handcuffed her to a table in your home. The same table our forensic team is picking up as we speak as they tear apart every inch of your house."

"I want to call someone."

"I bet you do," Catherine mocked, barely able to contain her anger and disgust at the man in front of her. Marcelo knew it was time to take over.

"Robert, before you call anyone, let me ask you something," Marcelo said, trying to signal to Catherine with his eyes to back down. "Is there anything else our technicians are going to find at your home linking you to Lauren White, Chrissy Wright, Naomi Banks, or anyone else? Because if there is, this might be your only opportunity to come clean to avoid the needle, if you know what I'm saying, man."

A few minutes passed, the deafening silence filling the room, before Robert finally spoke, "I'll tell you anything you want to know on one condition."

"What is that?" Marcelo asked.

"I want to speak to my wife."

"I don't think she wants to speak to you, Robert, and we certainly can't make her," Marcelo responded, shaking his head.

"If you want me to tell you anything, you have to bring me Heather. That's my condition. I have nothing else to say until I get to speak to her," Robert said calmly.

Catherine and Marcelo left the interrogation room and reconvened with their captain who had been watching and listening the entire time through the one-way glass that allowed her to see into the interrogation room.

"So, what do you think?" Captain Mastandrea asked, looking at the two detectives.

"I interviewed Heather McLean, Captain, and that's going to be tough. She's absolutely terrified of this guy. She has a three inch scar on her neck from the last time he almost killed her, and I'm not sure she's going to be too excited to get reacquainted with this piece of shit," Catherine said.

"I get that, but what if she knew that he might confess if she talks to him, which guarantees he'll spend the rest of his life in prison, far away from her, and she can stop running from him?" the Captain asked.

"True, that might work. She's been looking over her shoulder for the past eleven years, from what I understand. She might finally get to stop doing that if she knows he's in prison," Catherine said.

Marcelo spoke up next, "I think I should go with you when you talk to her. You've already developed a good rapport with her, which we want to keep, but if she's reluctant, I can suggest that anything can happen if he doesn't confess and this goes to trial; you know, plant the seed that without a confession, maybe he ends up free again."

"But there's no guarantee that he will confess. We might subject this poor woman, who has suffered enough abuse from this guy, to additional trauma. What if he just threatens her and terrifies her further without confessing. She may not even testify against him and may run again," Catherine countered.

"Well, that's true," the Captain said, pausing to think, "but she's our best shot at getting a confession. We need to at least try, and we can assure her that we'll be watching and listening and can intervene the minute he threatens her."

"Okay, well, I agree, we have to at least ask her," Catherine said while Marcelo nodded in agreement.

"I'll take care of transporting Mr. Johnson to one of our luxury suites in holding while you guys go speak to Heather," the Captain said.

"Looks like we have a plan. You drive, Marcelo," Catherine said, leaving the Captain as they headed for the exit that would lead them to the parking lot behind the precinct.

Across town, Heather McLean was busy packing her essential, must-have belongings into suitcases and bags, only stopping from time to time to peer out her window to make sure Bobby hadn't found her yet.

CHAPTER FORTY

Heather's hands trembled as she continued packing the contents of her closet into her two suitcases and other totes and bags she had collected over the years. She grabbed some garbage bags from underneath her kitchen sink for her linens, looking out the front window once again as she walked by. Oscar had picked up on her fear and was following her from room to room, unsure of what was going on but not wanting to leave her side.

"Don't worry, Oscie, it's going to be okay; we're going to find a new place, far away from here, where we're safe," she said, stopping for a moment to scratch her orange life mate behind the ears to reassure him, or more likely herself.

She returned to the tasks at hand, emptying a file box with work files she had brought home recently for a project she was working on for one of the partners, and filling it with her personal things she couldn't leave behind: her childhood photo album that contained her only pictures of her parents, her file of important documents, including her birth certificate, social security card, and her father's death certificate, all of which reflected her real name: Heather H'ebert. She legally changed her name to McLean, her mother's maiden name, when she ran away from Bobby. She had never talked much about her mother with Bobby since she had died when she was young, nor did she talk much about her father with him. She preferred to keep her parents and whatever memories she had of them to herself and wasn't willing to share that part of her with anyone, including Bobby. And he never asked.

She filled the box with the rest of her personal belongings that she wanted to keep and that would fit in the box and placed it by the door next to the rest of her belongings. She paused to look out the window again, relieved to see the quiet street empty of any unusual cars or inhabitants and headed into her bathroom to gather her toiletries and make-up, the final room she had to pack up before putting Oscar in his carrier and leaving her cottage that had been her haven for the past eleven years. Her relief was interrupted by the sound of an approaching car, which sounded like it stopped just in front of her house. She froze, except for her trembling hands, and held her breath, praying the car was actually at one of her neighbor's homes, praying it wasn't Bobby, and praying she could still get away. When she heard the car door shut, she knew it was too close and it had to be in front of her cottage. She locked herself in the small windowless bathroom, instinctively clutching her neck, knowing that he would finally finish what he promised all those years before.

She caught a glimpse of herself in the mirror, holding her hand over her scar, seeing the terror in her eyes, and she didn't recognize herself. Who was this woman? This was not her. This woman had dark circles under her dull hazel eyes that used to sparkle when the light hit them just right; she was thin, too thin, with her cheek bones highlighting her sunken cheeks and her t-shirt hanging off of her gaunt frame; and her hair that once elicited compliments from strangers was as uninteresting and lackluster as the rest of her. When had she become this woman, she asked herself? And in that moment, she realized he had succeeded on that beach eleven years ago. She was no longer alive and hadn't been in a long time. Maybe he hadn't killed her physical body, but he had certainly killed her spirit and turned her into someone she was not – someone who was always afraid, always hiding, always running. She sat on the floor and started to cry. For the last time.

And then she heard the knock at the door.

* * *

Marcelo and Catherine stood outside of the small cottage, waiting for Heather to come to the door. Catherine knocked again.

"Do you think she already ran?" Marcelo asked.

"Her car is here. Even if she is going to dump her car, why wouldn't she leave it at the airport or train station? No, she's here. She's just scared, I'm sure. Let me text her to let her know it's us."

Catherine typed out a quick text message to Heather, explaining that she and Detective Garcia were at her door and it was important that they talk to her. Five minutes later, Heather came to the door, looking first out her front window, and then opening the front door to let the two detectives in.

"Heather, this is Detective Garcia. He's been investigating some recent attacks on young women in the Tampa area, including a young woman who was attacked today. Your husband, Bobby, who goes by the name Robert Johnson now, was apprehended at the victim's home while he was attacking her for the second time."

"Oh my God, is she okay?" Heather asked.

"Yes, luckily we got there just in time. We were actually the detectives who arrested him."

"So where is he now?"

"He's in jail, in Tampa, awaiting arraignment on charges of attempted rape and kidnapping. But we think he's responsible for hurting other women, Heather. If we can connect him to those other cases or get him to confess, he'll go to prison for the rest of his life and you won't ever have to worry about him again."

"He'll never confess," Heather stated matter-of-factly, without any hesitation, shaking her head.

"Well, we think he might," Catherine said softly, "if you help us."

"What do you mean? What can I do?"

"He's asked to see you, to speak to you."

Heather jumped up, starting pacing, "holy fuck, are you kidding me? So, he knows I'm here? Oh my God, who told him I'm here? I have to go. I have to get out of here. Now."

"Heather, I know you're scared, but he can't hurt you. He's in jail right now and, if we have anything to do with it, will not get out. The district attorney is going to request that he be held without bail due to the seriousness of the crimes, but that's only if we can connect him to the other attack and the murder of a young co-ed."

"Oh my God, I knew that was him, I knew it when I saw it on the news. Shit, I have to get out of here."

Marcelo spoke for the first time, "Heather, do you understand that if he confesses to the murder and the other attacks, there won't be a trial, just a sentencing, and he'll get life in prison, and be sent to Florida State Prison in Raiford, Florida, just outside of Starke, one of the most dangerous prisons in the country."

"But he won't confess, I promise you."

"But he might. He's asked to see you. We have a lot of overwhelming evidence on him. He has suggested, although it is not guaranteed, that if you agree to see him and speak to him, he'll confess."

"Fuck that, no way. I can't," Heather said, continuing to pace and wring her hands.

Catherine spoke next, "Heather, aren't you tired of running and looking over your shoulder? This is your best chance to have a life again. We would be there with you. He can't hurt you anymore. He'll be handcuffed and shackled and won't be able to get to you. And the minute he starts saying anything that sounds threatening, we'll pull you out of there. You can do this, Heather."

Heather stopped pacing, sat down on her couch and put her face in her hands, rubbing her temples. She thought about earlier when she was in the bathroom, barely recognizing her reflection in the mirror. She did want to stop running. She loved her cottage in Indian Rocks Beach, she loved her job, and she didn't want to give him one more piece of her.

"Okay, what do I need to do?" she asked, frightened that she had said the words out loud.

* * *

After spending a sleepless night in his holding cell, Robert was brought a breakfast of runny, gray scrambled eggs, a piece of dry toast, and a juice. Shortly after skipping the inedible breakfast, he was brought back to the interrogation room where he had spent most of the previous day. He was handcuffed to the table once again but this time his shackled legs were connected to a bolt on the concrete floor. Well, this was special, he thought. An added precaution that they hadn't bothered with yesterday. Did this mean he was going to see his precious Heather? The thought aroused him, although he did wish their first reunion wouldn't have happened this way, with him unable to hug her, hold her, choke her. How ironic, he thought, that she was living in the same city as him all this time and he never knew it. That was unfortunate.

The door to the interrogation room opened and Detective Garcia walked in.

"Is she here? Is Heather here?" Robert asked.

Without answering his question, Marcelo began, "Robert, there are going to be some ground rules. Detective West is going to be in the room with you the entire time. If you threaten Heather in any way, at all, we will shut this down and pull her out of here. I'm serious, man, if you so much as blink aggressively, we will stop this instantly and you're done. The minute she's uncomfortable, we're pulling her out. You got it?"

"I want to meet with her alone. I don't care if you're listening in through your little mirror thing but I want to meet with her without Detective West in the room," Robert responded.

"No, absolutely not."

"Well then I guess we have nothing left to discuss. Please take me back to my cell. I believe my arraignment will be tomorrow morning and I need to practice saying "not guilty, your honor.""

Before Marcelo could respond, Captain Mastandrea came into the room. She stood across from Robert Johnson, looking down on him in a way that only she could. She intimidated most people and had not lost her edge from when she was a detective interrogating witnesses. She held up her hand to Marcelo, politely, effortlessly, as if motioning to a friend, and smiled. The smile was disarming to say the least.

"Mr. Johnson," she began, "I understand you would like to have a conversation with your estranged wife, Heather, who is right on the other side of that door, before the State of Florida possibly injects your veins with poisons that put you to sleep forever. Is that right?" she asked, the smile never fading, as if she had just asked him if he enjoyed sweet tea in the summer.

"Alternatively, Mr. Johnson," she continued, calmly, without an ounce of aggression, "we can all just call it a day, Heather will go on about her life without having to interact with you, and I guarantee you, whether you are on death row or spending the rest of your life in our beautiful facilities up in Raiford, which make our little humble abode here look like Disney World, she will never visit you and you will never have the pleasure of communicating with her, in any forum, again in your life. So, Mr. Johnson, let me ask you, and I'm only going to ask you once, would you like to see your wife, Heather, under the conditions Detective Garcia described to you a moment ago?"

"Yes. I want to see her."

"Excellent. Detective West will bring her in shortly and will be accompanying her the entire time. After you meet with her, we would like to discuss with you additional evidence that the forensic team uncovered at your home. Would that be okay?"

He nodded and they left the room. Captain Mastandrea met with the detectives and Heather and assured Heather that they would intervene the minute he made any threats. Heather nodded, relieved that Catherine was going in with her, but still filled with trepidation at seeing him again after all of these years. She had on very little make-up and had her hair pulled up into a bun. When they were together, he always insisted that she wore heavy make-up, bordering on slutty, and kept her hair long. She purposely wanted to look very different today, showing him that he no longer controlled her.

She walked into the interrogation room and saw an aged man sitting in front of her. He didn't look anything like he used to. He was smaller, balding, and pathetic looking. If she didn't hate him so much, she might have felt sorry for him.

"Heather, baby," he said, longing in his eyes.

"Fuck you," Heather replied, surprised at her bold response.

"Oh look at you, so brave. When I'm not in these handcuffs and shackles, will you say that to me then?"

Detective West started to intervene when Heather motioned to her that she was okay

"Fuck you, Bobby. Fuck you forever and for what you did to me. You will never hurt me again. And you will never get out of those shackles because you're a bad person and you've done bad things and now you're going to pay for it, finally, and I'm going to do whatever I can to help them put you away forever," Heather said, feeling more empowered with every word she spoke.

"You should have never left me. Even if I'm stuck in prison for the rest of my life, you know I'm going to find you, watch you, always be with you. Prison walls will not separate us or kill our love."

"You're fucking out of your mind. I know that now. And you can't hurt me anymore. I'm done," Heather said, motioning to Catherine to take her out of there.

"Wait, don't go yet," Robert pleaded, appearing vulnerable for the first time ever that Heather had ever seen.

"I love you, baby," he said, "I need you to know that. No matter what I did to you, it was out of love, because I didn't, no I couldn't lose you. You know that don't you?"

"Oh my God, you're insane," Heather yelled, "you fucking lunatic, psychopath, no, that's not love! What you did to me was not love! It was sadistic and controlling and abusive and horrible. And I'm glad you're never going to get out of prison to do it to me or anyone else ever again.

Please, just do everyone a favor and fucking confess," Heather said, exasperated.

"Okay, I will. That is my final gift to you. I will confess. I love you, Heather. You're the only woman I've ever truly loved. But if I had the chance right now, I would also choke you until the life drained out of your body because that way, in death, we would always be one and together. That is love."

"Get me the fuck out of here. I can't listen to any more of this," Heather said as she walked towards the door, and never looked back.

CHAPTER FORTY-ONE

Hallie planned to arrive at the courthouse promptly at 4:30 that Friday afternoon. The courthouse closed at 5:00 p.m., but on Friday's, it was practically a ghost town. Hallie wanted to confront Judge Stephens in person, for her own satisfaction and closure, and to see if she could get him to confess to any of the crimes he committed. Hallie knew recording him was illegal, and definitely not admissible in any court proceeding, but she wanted his admissions as leverage to keep him away from Katie in the future, if Katie ever learned of his identity.

On the way to the courthouse, Detective Garcia called Hallie to tell her that Robert Johnson had confessed to Lauren White's abduction and murder, and the attacks on Lila Martinez and Chrissy Wright, in exchange for the State not seeking the death penalty. Lila and Chrissy both positively identified him as their attackers. He also professed his undying love for his estranged wife, Heather, while promising he would kill her if given the chance.

"What about Naomi Banks? Did he kill her too?" Hallie asked.

"No, he didn't confess to killing her, although at first he didn't deny it. But then it was obvious he didn't know anything about her murder so we still think Judge Stephens killed her. But we're still gathering evidence to connect the judge to her abduction and murder beyond just the DNA found under her fingernails and the possible connections through the genealogy site. A good defense attorney will say that they had some type of consensual relationship and the judge didn't see her after she left his house that night. We're working on subpoenas to search his car and home so we can get other corroborating evidence before we arrest and charge someone of his caliber and standing in the community or he could potentially walk," the detective explained.

"That makes sense but I hope you get it soon before he hurts someone else," Hallie said, feeling more uneasy about her decision to meet with Judge Stephens alone.

"Hallie, there's something else that I think you should know."

"What is it?" Hallie asked.

"It's about your husband, David," he paused, and then continued, trying to choose his words carefully, "he had a connection to Lila Martinez too."

"Yes, she was a student at the school where he is the principal. He just learned that," Hallie replied.

"No, it's more than that. According to Ms. Martinez, your husband is the father of her four-year-old daughter."

"No. No. Absolutely not," Hallie said, trying to process what she just heard, as she pulled into the garage next to the courthouse.

"Hallie, I'm not telling you this to cause you any grief but because Ms. Martinez was a minor, there are other implications here that we have to pursue. I wanted to be the one to tell you so you aren't blindsided. There could be charges," he said gently.

"Oh my God, this has to be a mistake," she almost whispered and wanted to believe but, in her heart, she knew it was true. So many things made sense now. But she couldn't deal with that at the moment. She had to deal with Judge Stephens first.

"Detective," she said, clearing her throat and trying to hold it together, "I appreciate you letting me know. I have to go," Hallie said and hung up the phone.

* * *

She rode up in the elevator alone until she reached the floor where Judge Stephens' chambers were, not knowing how she would feel when she saw him again. She had emailed him a few days before, asking him if he remembered her and telling him that she needed to talk to him about something important. She explained in her brief email that she had some important information that would impact his future election, if it got out. It took him less than two hours to respond to her, trying to find out what information she wanted to share with him. She involuntarily shivered thinking about the last time she had seen him. And now, knowing that he was Katie's biological father and responsible for countless other rapes and even murder, she hated him even more. She explained that it would be better for both of them if she didn't include such sensitive information in an email. He reluctantly agreed and suggested she meet him in his chambers at the courthouse at 4:30 on the following Friday. His ego and audacity were the same as they had been eighteen years ago, which she intended to use against him.

The elevator doors opened to a vacant and somewhat dark hallway as a result of one of the overhead lights being out. It was eerily quiet, with the only sounds the elevator doors closing behind her and the quiet hum from the only working overhead florescent light further down the empty hallway. The new courthouse had LED lighting that went off automatically when it didn't sense any motion for a certain period of time. But this old relic had not been updated and still relied on those damn, long fluorescent lightbulbs to light the hallways and offices.

Hallie made her way to Judge Stephens' chambers, regretting that she came alone and that she hadn't told anyone she was coming there. But they would have tried to talk her out of it, and she was determined to confront him and record him. She looked up and down the hallway to make sure she knew where the emergency exits were in case she had to get out quickly. She opened the video camera on her phone, hit record and slipped her phone into her front pocket of her black hoodie. When she tested it at home, it recorded her and David's conversation clearly from her front pocket. She hoped if he said anything incriminating, it would be just as clear. She took a deep breath and reached for the door handle of Judge Stephens' chambers, noticing the slight tremble in her hand as she did. No turning back now, she thought, and pushed the heavy, wooden door open.

"Well hello, Hallie, it's so nice to see you again," Judge Stephens said with just a hint of the southern accent that became more pronounced when he drank scotch.

"Is it?" she asked, trying to make sure she sounded confident.

"Yes, of course. How many years has it been? Fifteen?"

"No, eighteen. Don't you remember the last time we were together? It was the Law & Liberty Dinner when I was just a young associate. You remember, don't you?"

"I do remember that night, yes, it was amazing. We had such a good time, didn't we?" he winked.

"No, actually, no, we didn't. You know what you did," Hallie said, trying not to cry from her anger. Whenever she got really mad, she would cry, which only pissed her off more.

"Um, no, I don't know what you're talking about. We went to the dinner and then that's the last thing I remember. I may have had a little too much to drink that night. What do you remember, Hallie?"

Hallie was so angry and she knew she had to calm down. He was getting the better of her. She had to be smarter than him, throw him off his game.

"Well, I remember you bringing me up to your room and then raping me. Of course you remember that too, don't you, Bill?" Hallie said, more confident.

Judge Stephens paused, looked at Hallie, and responded, "I am very concerned with what you're saying, Hallie. You and I both know we shared a moment many years ago, consensually after a night of drinking, and now you're trying to rewrite history. What do you want?"

"I want you to admit what you did to me. It's just you and me, no one else here. And you know the statute of limitations has run so I am no threat to you, legally, but I can do some serious damage to your reputation and your re-election campaign."

"Is that a threat?" he asked, looking at Hallie with cold, menacing eyes.

Hallie felt very uncomfortable and knew she shouldn't have played that card so early. At this point, he had admitted nothing and everything she had on tape implicated her more than him.

"No, it's not a threat. You know I have never made trouble for you. I don't plan to start now. But I have been feeling bad about things and I'm trying to reconcile what happened that night. Please, I just need to understand what happened. Can't you at least give me that?" Hallie pleaded.

Judge Stephens paused, taking a sip of his scotch, and then said, "Hallie, I'm not sure why you came here today. I would love to give you what you are seeking but I cannot because it simply didn't happen. We were two consenting adults and you willingly went up to my room. That's all I can tell you about that night, other than I enjoyed it immensely. I am confident you did too."

That was the final straw. Hallie lost it.

"You mother fucking rapist, oh my God, I did not enjoy it! You fucking raped me. I bled from my ass for a week, you fucking sadist! I fucking hate you and I will make sure everyone knows what you did to me, and you are never re-elected to the bench, you mother fucker!" she yelled, tears welling up in her eyes and her face flushing red.

Judge Stephens came from behind his desk so quickly, Hallie didn't see it coming. He shoved her back with both hands on her shoulders with such force, she fell back onto the worn, brown leather couch that matched the brown bookcases in the office.

"You couldn't just leave it alone, could you, you stupid bitch. You fucking loved it that night, I know you did. All you fucking whores love it and then cry rape after the fact; well too fucking bad, I'm not letting that happen. We fucked, you loved it, and that's the end of it. The way I remember it, you drank too much that night," he said, as he pressed his weight against her, suffocating her with his scotch-drenched breath and pinning her arms above her head in one swift move.

"Maybe that's why you came back, huh? You want it again, don't you?" he spat while pressing his groin up against her pelvis as she tried to unsuccessfully break free.

"Get the fuck off me," Hallie growled through clenched teeth, "I will ruin you."

"Oh, is that so?" he laughed, in a sinister, overconfident way. "You know what one of the benefits of being a criminal court judge is? You get to know certain members of society who, shall we say, know how to get things done, such as making bodies disappear. Don't you threaten me, you fucking bitch, or you will simply disappear."

Seeing the hate and anger in his eyes, Hallie realized for the first time the danger she was in and that she had misjudged what Judge Stephens was capable of and willing to do. She hoped her phone was still recording, but if he killed her, he would certainly destroy her phone too. She stopped fighting him, hoping he would relax his grip on her.

"You win," Hallie said, appearing defeated, hoping she could convince him to let her go.

"You're damn right I won. I always win," he said, smiling, while looking down at Hallie's breasts for the first time.

"Please, just let me go. You're right, it's my word against yours, just like it was eighteen years ago. I didn't say anything then; I won't now. I don't know what I was thinking coming here."

Judge Stephens loosened his grip on her hands and lifted his weight off of her. As he got up, he brushed his hand against her chest, as if by accident, but obviously on purpose. He used the arm of the couch to lift his 6'4" frame off of Hallie. She fought to regain her footing so she could bolt out of the office as soon as he backed away a little further.

He towered over her, looking down at her, his dark eyes filled with rage and something else . . . was it excitement? Hallie was terrified. She knew in that moment, he wasn't going to let her go. Out of the corner of her eye, she saw the bronze Lady Justice statuette on the end table just within her reach. Without pausing to think, she grabbed the statue and smashed Judge Stephens in the head and he fell back, slamming into one of the leather chairs facing his desk, clutching his head that instantly started to bleed. He was stunned but not down and was trying to lift himself up off the chair. Hallie threw the statue at his head, not knowing whether it struck him again or bounced off his back, and ran towards the door.

"You fucking bitch," was all she heard as she ran towards the exit sign and stairwell she had identified on her way in. As a runner and driven by her fear-induced adrenaline, she knew there was no way he could catch her if she could just make it to the stairwell. She made her way down the five flights to the first floor without ever looking back, relieved when the ground floor door gave way and brought her out into the bright, Florida sunlight. She caught her breath as she looked around to get her bearings, and then ran to the adjacent garage where her car was parked.

As she drove away, she pulled her phone out of her pocket and saw that it was still recording.

"Got you, you son-of-a-bitch," she said as she drove straight to the police precinct.

CHAPTER FORTY-TWO

The murder trial would begin tomorrow. As a lawyer, she believed in the justice system, but as a woman, as a victim, she regretted that she hadn't killed him that night in his chambers. Hallie's therapist told her that her feelings of regret would pass and eventually be replaced by relief, because taking another's life, even one as deplorable as Judge Stephens, would bring about a different kind of internal pain and would not reverse the rape. Hallie wasn't ready to admit it but, deep down, she knew her therapist was right.

Hallie sat on her front porch, having a glass of wine. The cool November air blew through, rustling the trees, including the giant oak in her front yard that was starting to lose its leaves in the so-called Florida fall. Mrs. Butler briefly came out onto her front porch next door and waved at Hallie before bending down to refill the cat bowls at her slippered feet and quickly retreated back inside. She couldn't believe over a year had passed since Lauren White's body had been found in her yard. So much had happened since then. But she was okay. Actually, she was better than okay, especially since David had moved out.

Hallie confronted David after she learned that he had impregnated Lila Martinez. At first, he denied it and tried to convince Hallie that Lila was a troubled young woman who was lying about him, but when David was served with a petition to determine paternity, he confessed everything. He begged Hallie to give him another chance, said he would go to counseling, but Hallie was done. Lila was seventeen when she got pregnant but because they couldn't prove he had engaged in sexual relations with her when she was sixteen, they couldn't charge him with statutory rape. He agreed to resign and relinquish his license in exchange for no criminal charges being brought against him. Hallie kicked him out and filed for divorce immediately, hiring the best, most aggressive family lawyers in town to represent her.

Jay questioned Paige and Heather about the emails to Hallie that were sent from their office based on their connection to her. Paige didn't know anything about them, but when Heather saw copies of the emails, she knew they had to be from Natalie who worked in the accounting department. Heather told Jay about Natalie's brutal 2005 rape by Judge Stephens and why she blamed Hallie. When confronted about the emails and breaking into Hallie's house, Natalie Crawford fell apart and confessed, shortly before being Baker-acted for threatening suicide. The Baker Act was a Florida law that allowed people to be involuntarily held in a psychiatric ward for up to 48 hours if they were a threat to themselves or others. After her 48-hour stay, Natalie took a medical leave of absence from the firm to enter a residential treatment for the PTSD that she continued to suffer from being raped. Hallie agreed not to press charges against her as long as Natalie never contacted her or her family again.

With her mother's help, Katie had gotten accepted into her dream school, Bard College, which was about an hour and half north of New York City in the beautiful Hudson Valley. She missed Katie terribly, but she was happy to be completely on her own for the first time in her life. Katie eventually learned the truth about her biology but seemed to be dealing with it better than expected, thanks in large part to the support Kevin and Jodi were giving her. Kevin went out of his way to reassure her that he was her father and always would be.

Hallie bent down and scratched Juno behind the ears, thinking about everything that had happened over the last year and what would come out during Judge Stephens' trial. He had been charged with the murder of Naomi Banks and, after the coroner confirmed she had been sexually assaulted post-mortem, one count of necrophilia or "abuse of a dead body" pursuant to Florida Statutes § 872.06. The fact that Florida had to enact such a statute horrified Hallie. Unfortunately, the State could not charge him for raping Hallie or Natalie, but Hallie felt some relief and closure not having to hold onto that dark secret anymore. She promised herself that after the trial was over, she was going to take a much-needed vacation – on an island, preferably where there was no cell or internet service. Paige agreed to go with her, and Mike, to whom Paige was now engaged, agreed to watch Juno while they were away.

But first, the trial.

ACKNOWLEDGEMENTS

Thank you to everyone who made this book possible, including everyone who has ever championed my lifelong dream of writing a novel. I hope after the long wait I didn't disappoint.

First, to my mother, Pat Newman, for her unwavering and unconditional love and support. She is and always will be my greatest cheerleader. Thank you to my daughters, Lily and Kathleen, who were forced to listen to various sections of this book as I worked through them, even when it freaked them out. To my stepfather, Dan Newman, thank you for being my sounding board on trial procedures, marrying my mother and giving us Matt Newman, editor extraordinaire and master of words. Thank you, Matt, for your generous time and editorial guidance, which made this a much better book than it would have been.

Thank you to my sisters, Patti McLean, Jodi Ray, and Heather Hebert (who used her mad project management skills to help me meet my self-imposed deadlines), and all of whom graciously read early versions and offered excellent advice throughout the process – I don't know what I would do without you. To my brother, James McLean, thank you for not calling me fifty times a day when I was in the writing trenches.

Thank you to the Marotta Aunts: Eileen, Maureen, Cathy, Dorothy, and Diane. Thank you for letting my mother read the book to you on your sisters' weekend at the shore and for all of your kind emails, texts, and phone calls in response. I am so fortunate to come from such an amazing group of strong, smart, and funny women!

To my always there, ride or die, random Tuesday wine crew: Amy Stoll, Paige Greenlee, Becky Wilt, Sarah Wilt, Jenn Meister, and Monica Angel, thank you for always listening to me, always encouraging me, and always having my back. Also, thank you for being brave enough to read an early draft of this book and to tell me what you really thought of it. My favorite quote from Amy: *"I was afraid to read it; I mean, what if it sucked? I wouldn't be able to lie to you and then I would feel bad. I'm really glad it didn't suck."*

Thank you to Brigette Foresman who has been telling me for the past thirty years to write the damn book! Most importantly, thank you for the great advice along the way and all of the Mary Frayne stories over the years – your mother was a true gem!

To my lifelong friend, Jackie Campbell, thank you for your unwavering confidence in me, your uncanny ability to make me laugh (you are truly one of the funniest people I know!), and your willingness to help me whenever I ask (or don't ask).

Thank you to my early readers and dear friends: Elise Batsel, Eden Feldman, Veronica Hill, Rosemary Horvat, Courtney Koch, Dina Kuchkuda (and her book club), Michele Lowman, Tracy McCrink, Chris Mercer, Meme Mercer, Jennifer Newman, Bridget Remington, Alice Siess, and Tom Staszak. The feedback from each of you was invaluable and so much appreciated.

Thank you to Michael Connelly for inspiring me with your writing for the past thirty years and for introducing me to Heather Rizzo. And to Heather Rizzo, thank you for taking the time to read an early version of this book and for providing critical feedback to me. Your generous comments were instrumental in developing the story into its final form and validating me as a writer.

Last, but most certainly not least, I would like to thank Ed Miyagishima, my Applebee's plus-one, partner in all things networking, fellow shark-cage diver, and my own personal Julie McCoy. Your love, support, and endless patience brings me more happiness than I can express in words. You make all things better and more fun, and there is no one I would rather go to Applebee's with.

Jen Murphy is a corporate and tax attorney in Tampa Florida. She is the author of two novels, including *When She Runs . . .*, her debut novel, and *When He Watches*, her forthcoming second book in the Hallie Miller series. She lives in Tampa with her youngest daughter and her two rescue German Shepherds, Sam and Vincent.